D0558424

A History Of Zero

Martin Nakell

& Alter Fictions

Spuyten Duyvil
New York City

ACKNOWLEDGEMENTS

"Faith," *Hanging Loose,* Spring 1996
"The Liberator," *Hyper Age,* Winter 1995
"Yes" *Literal Latte,* Nov/Dec 1994
"Doubt," *The Washington Review,* Aug/Sept 1994

© 2019 Martin Nakell

ISBN 978-1-947980-68-6

Library of Congress Cataloging-in-Publication Data

Names: Nakell, Martin, author.
Title: A history of zero & alter fictions / Martin Nakell.
Other titles: History of zero and alter fictions
Description: New York City : Spuyten Duyvil, [2019]
Identifiers: LCCN 2018033355 | ISBN 9781947980686
Classification: LCC PS3564.A5314 A6 2018 | DDC 813/.54--dc23
LC record available at https://lccn.loc.gov/2018033355

Earthquakes

Now the disembodied seven-year old soul of Tomás Escéptico sat on the fallen pediment which had crumbled to the ground in the first wave of the hystrionically powerful earthquake. Tomás' soul, so young and so puzzled by death, looked on as the crew of volunteer rescue workers sweated in heat and dust passing loads of concrete to the man next in line, their backs twitching with each heave of broken cement. Small crowds of men and women, roaming the streets with no homes left to return to, gathered, watched, then drifted away back into their lost City. New volunteers came one by one to replace those whose strength had given out. These workers weren't muscle men, and they had no experience, but hour after hour they hauled and they hefted to save Tomás, whose soul had already escaped the fate of his life.

Tomás' parents and his two living grandparents, one from each side of his long lineage, never left the site. Once in a while, Tomás' paternal grandmother—Verónica—would go down towards the collapsed building, crouch near some rubble of concrete and steel rod, then yell like she never in her life had yelled before: —Tomás! Make us a sign. Groan, Tomás! Mumble! Scratch! At that very moment, Tomás—in the incarnation of his already disembodied soul—would equivocate, losing his courage to fly off. Tomás' soul would maneuver down through the rubble, enter his abandoned, crushed body already three hours dead, to moan some cry through the young lips, some high tone that would travel through the concrete to his Grandmother. The old woman's heart would stop. My God! He's alive! Dig! By that time Tomás' soul would—yielding to those natural laws of life and death, of bodies and souls—return through the maze of rubble into the stifling sunlight.

When the workers reached the body, Grandmother Verónica's suffering came in a keen of anguish that would echo through her body and the earth's atmosphere—a wail that would not stop for just a little over ninety years—when it would reach the ears of a young, already devout Priest in a church near Golden Gate Park in San Francisco. That priest, Angél Compassión, the great-great-great-grandson of Basque immigrants, via Mexico, to the United States, would drop the chalice he was in the midst of cleaning—shattering it as it hit the floor—to slap his hands up to his ears to hold off this eerie screech of a mysteriously, horrifyingly painful sound. By the following afternoon, that physical pain would subside but never quite abandon Father Angél Compassión, leaving him to wonder what it was, leaving Father Compassión edgy, testy, frightened and a bit confused for the rest of his life. Also, it would make him an exceptionally devout, powerful worshipper, a Priest whose calling had doubled down on its original commitment, a Priest who must, by his devotion alone, come closer to knowing God and come equally closer to knowing, and helping with his compassion stemming from his own suffering, mankind. Some would call Father Compassión a Saint. Some would say that—if this compressed intensity of living were Sainthood—then Father Compassión could surely have it all for his own. Father Compassión, who had written the secreted-away text he titled his Song of Pain Song of Communion, in which he argued that he who can totally absorb the total pain of living looks into the very eye of God embraces the unembraceable accepts the unacceptable believes the unbelievable creates the universe giving birth to the word shaped in the newborn wail of each holy infant recapitulated in the birth pangs of each sacred mother, for which text the Church excommunicated Father Compassión, posthumously. Pain is love, he had written, his last words before dying, death is birth.

The soul of young Tomás saw the progress of his Grandmother's scream as it led a trail 167-years backwards in time, and then 99-years forward through history. It rose in a gravity-bound parabolic curve. The last thing Tomás Escéptico would hear on earth was his Grandmother wailing, the last thing he would see was that wailing trailing backward and forward.

This wail, which had begun long before it found Tomás' Grandmother, had stopped several places along the way of a twisted history. One stop was in the hands of Tomás' paternal great-great-great grandfather, Lobo.

Five generations before Tomás was born, Lobo, a Basque peasant, earned his living as a tinner, making and selling pots and pans. Twice a week, Lobo took his products on a horse-drawn cart into the village where he sold them at the town market. He made nearly a sufficient living. Unable, as a peasant, to own land, Lobo could own two things which made up for the lack of that unfulfilled urgency for a secure piece of the earth: he owned his own heart and his own mind, dark and bright as they were, and he owned his craftsman's hands.

One market dawn, Lobo traveled the road into the village, walking his horse-drawn cart filled with carefully packed pots, pans, his four-year-old son Jesús, and lunch for two. At the village, Lobo pulled up to his usual stall to find it occupied by two strange things: another vendor in his place, and, a large sign bearing the declaration: NO FILTHY BASQUE TO TRADE IN THIS MARKET. Fear, passion as fear in the form of a solid, dull, enduring pain, traveling some distance from its previous ancestors, entered Lobo's labor trained hands.

When he escaped Europe for Mexico, in the Americas, Lobo found his way to Mexico City. For the rest of his life the pain that had settled in Lobo's hands when he was expelled from the marketplace so agonized him that it made every day's labor go slowly. To keep from transmitting the pain to his son, Jesús, Jesús's father touched him never again.

Jesús grew used to not being touched. He cringed when people touched one another, especially fathers and sons. Late in

Jesús's life, the need to touch and to be touched broke through the surface of his physical solitude, his emotional isolation. Jesús obsessively touched people and things. He would take men friends by the arm, women friends by the hand. He would touch statues on the street as he passed them. In a clothing store, he would finger all the fabrics. He would go into music stores to caress the instruments. He would rub his palm along the rough texture of a tree trunk. At Lake Texcoco, he ran sand through his hands. Even if he didn't swim, he had to walk to the shore to feel the water. By touching, he knew he was alive and real. He became known as The Toucher, or Jesús-the-Toucher.

Moving backwards a short way in the airborne trajectory of this painwail that had settled in Lobo's hands as a physical pain, we come to Ramòn. Ramòn precedes Lobo by two generations. Yet it wasn't Ramòn himself who inherited the wail, he transferred it to his fiancé.

In the village of Oviedo, in the Basque region of Spain, Ramòn, son of Reuven and Elena, was an extraordinarily brilliant student, that rare young man —interested in ideas for their own sake, as his teacher, Father Conocimiento, said. Father Conocimiento was himself a widely renowned and beloved scholar of texts and mythologies, including, of course, the 200-year old Spanish masterpiece, *Don Quixote*. A man of exceptional sweetness, he took young Ramòn under his wing, even to the extent of hiding Ramòn during the uprisings, saving Ramòn's life at the risk of his own.

Ramòn was engaged to Enduré. Ramòn had known, loved, and fantasized of her all his young life. He was mad for her, a village girl with a flair for a quiet honesty. Enduré carried a flame for Ramòn. She too dreamt of him; she slept only to have those dreams of a young man with a penetrating genius and a powerful pain in his life.

When he came of age, Ramón asked for her hand. Enduré begged her wealthy, family-crested, landholding father, hound-ed the family, until the marriage was arranged. To avoid the fate of his daughter marrying into poverty as well as the shame on the crest of a landed family, they sent the brilliant Ramòn to study in France, at the Sorbonne. He could come home a man of honor. After a two years of studying, monk-like, alone, a foreigner in the city, Ramòn met and fell in love with an Englishwoman, Cecilia, whom he married.

Cecilia had been traveling with a tutor. Her family disdaining her marriage to any peasant Basque. Ramòn and Cecilia married secretly in a ceremony presided over by an all-but-defrocked Priest, a Catholic Priest marrying a Protestant woman to a Catholic man, condemning himself to Hell for a few sorely needed Francs. Its thin legality cemented its prodigious commitment. Cecilia was a romantic; her family sent her on this Grand Tour to cure her by way of exposure and experience. She saw in Ramòn a dark complex maze. She traded ideal romanticism for a share of earthly indulgence. As her family didn't understand either idea, Cecilia remained an exile in Paris with her husband.

Learning of Ramòn's marriage, Enduré kept up Ramòn's support. Why not? She hadn't sent him to Paris only to become educated enough to marry her. She'd sent him because she understood the gravitas of his powers. He knew everything there was to know about language. He'd mastered his native Basquen, Polish, English, French, Spanish, Latin, Italian, and ancient Aramaic. He invented words and phrases of his own. He discovered deep structures of grammar hidden in every language. He had an uncanny sense of perception which would wither if it weren't challenged. Ramòn could see life, requiring training to bring it to maturity. Enduré continued to send money, and with each envelope entrusted to the courier, her pain dug deeper, came closer to fatally invading her bloodstream. Enduré, living daily with this pain, risking her life, hadn't chosen the gamble—life had chosen it for her.

In a Paris winter, Cecelia died of pneumonia. Day after day, Ramòn left their sparse apartment to walk the streets. After exhausting his memories of Cecilia, who had transformed his life from its pursuit of intellectual abstractions into the daily fact of sensual, sexual and intellectual realities, Enduré pursued him in delirious visions. He didn't know, but he sensed, the pain that Enduré must have felt in the two years of his marriage to Cecilia. As he wandered along the river, crossing its bridges in random patterns, he finally saw that his marriage had been a betrayal that might have dangerously pained Enduré, perhaps even killed Cecilia. Cecilia, who, in the her exuberant youth, had married naïvely. And yet, she'd looked patiently into the crevices of his personality to search out whatever twists she might find. He loved to lay with her late at night as their lives unfolded far from either's homeland. He couldn't regret any of it. Even if it carried a burden that had—without either one of them realizing it—weakened her, made her more vulnerable to the threats of the winter. He had given Cecilia what she had come to him for albeit neither one of them had realized the cost.

When Ramòn met Jenny, the pain came infinitesimally closer to Enduré's life flow. It awakened Enduré in the middle of the night. Jenny sang on a small stage at a cabaret. There were only 10 people in the audience. Hardly noticeable, this small singer, five foot two inches tall, dark, filled with a mixture of bloods, had the natural voice of wandering. Her origins were as complicated as Ramòn's intellect. Alone against a fate that had sharpened her senses but drained her strength. Her loneliness had made her as vividly qualified to live on the edge of tenderness as the death of Cecilia had made Ramòn intimate with the enormous and empty sorrow of his own tenderness. When Ramòn touched her, he would touch the nerve of a self-contained power. He heard the sound of it. And without knowing what the sensation was, he also felt the pain that dropped one level deeper into Enduré as he sat down in the cabaret.

Enduré was as determined as Cecilia, as dedicated as Jenny. She didn't become morose. She didn't listen to those who told her to stop paying for Ramòn's life. Every morning, Enduré braided her hair carefully; every night she set it loose before bed, brushing it one hundred strokes. Every day, she studied a little on her own, reading the most interesting, or most poetic, or most challenging parts of the literature. Every day she bore pain, but she just watched it, careful not to indulge in it or let it turn her toward self-pity or bitterness. By the time Jenny died in a carriage accident, run over on a Paris Boulevard, the pain had become an integral part of Enduré, such that, when Ramòn, returning home to Oviedo, laid eyes on her for the first time in five years, that pain rose from within her to emanate from her skin as a vibrancy. Then the wail of that pain escaped her, leaving room, finally, for Ramòn himself, matured enough now to displace it.

That wail came then to Mexico, following the family line, just when Tomás Escéptico's Grandmother Verónica—a Great-Great-Grandaughter of Ramòn and Enduré—screamed. As she howled, she expelled that wail which had saturated her. Her prodigious vitality sent it on a new course out of the family for the first time in two hundred and fifty-two years.

Tomás tried to take his Grandmother's howl with him into death. Rising up off the pediment, Tomás flew towards the howl already in rapid ascent, rolling arc-wise into the air. He grabbed at it; it ripped his hands. He wrapped his arms around it. It exploded against his body, sent him flying. He retreated, then attacked again. By this time, the howl had gained such momentum that, as Tomás got near to it, it threw him back, shaving off an ear.

When it came time to journey into death, Tomás had to set off not only alone, but missing an ear. As the howl had come from his Grandmother such that his Grandmother became at once a bearer and a disseminator of the pain, that howl made its bearer very special, uniquely important. Tomás wanted his Grandmother's howl. When he couldn't wrestle that howl into his domain, Tomás fell away from the struggle, defeated. In a rage, Tomás, fallen back momentarily, spit into the face of one of his would-be-rescuers. Because the saliva of the second-born child has certain properties, the acid blinded the worker in both eyes. For that one act of stupid destructive pride at a critical moment, Tomás' soul came to a region of death totally absent of compassion, and worse, without language. His fear of abject loneliness in death came true, lasting for three hundred and eighteen years, until Angél Compassión died.

Father Compassión, who had learned a great deal over many years about the pride of passion and the pride of pain, the passion of pride and the pain of pride, stopped on the way of his own death to take the repentant Tomás with him into that place where the dead can express, in whatever art, their displeasure and/or their pleasure with death and/or with life.

Protodaddy's Will

Proto

Daddy died in the way he would have most wanted not to die. At his time of power.

As on all workday mornings, a little after 10 o'clock, at 10:06 a.m., ProtoDaddy took the *Wall Street Journal*, the *New York Times*, the *London Times*, and the Minneppossett, Michigan *Sentinel* into the bathroom along with a half finished cup of coffee and the morning's reserve of excrement rumbling through his caffeine-awakened bowels, whose natural progress through his intestines was aided by the astringent smoke of English Oval cigarettes, one of which he held at this last moment of his power on earth. He held the cigarette British style, between thumb and forefinger, a touch he would have admired in his death swoon had he known it was coming, had the cigarette not fallen from his grip.

Although ProtoDaddy had gained power and fortune by foreseeing what was coming, and by seeing his own ruthlessness as a gift from the gods, he hadn't one thought of death when he went into the bathroom at the office that Thursday morning. Had he known this was coming, ProtoDaddy might have feared, he might have talked to those whom he'd always overpowered, including his sister, Lena. Had he known it was coming, he might have forgiven his son and daughter for not fulfilling his dreams. Or curse them for it.

ProtoDaddy was born to do things his way, pushing his sister Lena and her husband Freddy into obscure corners where they'd stay out of the way, pushing events, pushing himself. He had re-made a world in his image, re-made himself into just what he'd wanted to become: he spoke with a slight touch of an English accent and with the exact measure of articulation and reticence he'd aimed for. His bearing was relaxed with dignity, his eyes calmly sophisticated, alert.

But others around him didn't always come out right. The

children, for example. All wrong. ProtoDaddy's son, Thomas, his first-born, was to inherit the high culture, power, respect and position—to say nothing of the money—that ProtoDaddy had acquired. But so far as ProtoDaddy could see, Thomas was born with little imagination, ambition, curiosity, or intellect. What grace Thomas did have was a body so strong and agile and feet so big that he could cross a basketball court faster than anyone else, if more noisily. ProtoDaddy's daughter, Maria, was born nearly pretty, so close to—but not—beautiful it pained ProtoDaddy and it came to distract Maria's image of life. Angela, ProtoDaddy's wife, could have cared less. Angela just wished her nearly pretty daughter would stop spending all her afternoons dancing in front of the mirrors ProtoDaddy had installed into the walls of the dance room he had built in the basement of the house they called ProtoDaddy's Testament, although most people referred to it just as Testament, or 'Ment, even.

ProtoDaddy's family had originated in an Egyptian village on the Nile. They left Egypt, migrating from there through several European countries, settled for a few generations in Romania, spent a generation in Italy, a few years in Liverpool, then came to America where they joined cousins settled in Detroit.

ProtoDaddy, first-born in America, having never seen Egypt, Romania, Rome, Liverpool, nor any other part of Europe, knew only Detroit.

When he got out of jail, he drove for several days alone until he found Minneppossett. Here, no one knew him. No one knew he'd been in prison. No one knew anything about Gypsies outside the quaint view of them singing by wagons at firesides.

By the time he left prison, at 20, ProtoDaddy had put everything nefariously Gypsy behind him, from begging in costume-rags to petty thievery to small-time con-jobs on little people to stealing jewelry from gullible widows to gun-point hold-ups at night in rich neighborhoods to a deeply buried vision of himself as an eternal foreigner. He had never killed a man. ProtoDaddy took many lessons with him from prison, including the understanding that in America—unlike Egypt or Romania or Italy or even England—everyone could wear the same mask, anyone could wear any mask.

ProtoDaddy drank refined culture through a very long straw. On the merits of his family's brief stay in England, he determined to build himself an empire in the New World based on grace, knowledge, and the exercise of an outwardly invisible power whose superiority as a way of life he had imagined as something very British.

ProtoDaddy's son, Thomas, instead of rising gently into the dominion he would inherit, that empire whose raw beginnings he would never have to know, played basketball day and night, dribbled, passed, threw, shot, ran, while avoiding pivoting, a talent he left to others with less cumbersome feet. ProtoDaddy's daughter, unbeautiful, rather than imbibing his power to transform it into a female attribute exercised with wit, instead danced all too clumsily in unfortunate, disappointing, frustrating, yet desperate self-admiration before mirrors which, for her, *were* her father, ProtoDaddy himself.

Had ProtoDaddy thought his death was imminent, he might have taken the other option he'd considered too often enough: writing his son and daughter out of his will altogether. Why pass this empire on to a brute? to a nearly beautiful, mildly talented daughter who gazed into mirrors seeking reflections that would lie to her.

ProtoDaddy could find some sharp young man to cultivate as the heir to his creation if neither his son nor daughter would fit. Lena and Freddy were older. He had planned for their deaths.

As it was, ProtoDaddy died with his pants down, with the eternal effort of excretion just about to give way to the pleasure of release in the tissue of his deep system, and with one unspoken name on his lips: BIG. Even though ProtoDaddy never had a chance to call out, Big must have heard ProtoDadddy call him. Moments later, others in the office, hearing the crash against the bathroom door, yelled simultaneously: —BIG! Big, already on the run, had dropped his wrench at the gas station next door. That gas station that was the cornerstone in what had become ProtoDaddy's Kingdom—a kingdom begun by his sister, stolen by ProtoDaddy. Yet she, Lena, ProtoDaddy's older sister, confided to her husband, Freddy, the night after Proto-Daddy's funeral, that —perhaps it was true, Lena told Freddy, —perhaps ProtoDaddy had made more of that empire than I— or you—ever would have had the gall to do.

Big had been Big William in the Michigan lumber woods until ProtoDaddy found him, took his saw, put auto mechanic tools in his hands nearly too large for anything smaller than a chainsaw, then taught him about everything from fuels pumps to the finest points of the internal combustion engines from Fords and Chevys to Cadillacs to Merceds Benz. He renamed Big William just plain Big. It was more efficient in those days when time was of the essence and when everything was Proto-Daddy's to rename.

Between the time the white English Oval fell from Proto-Daddy's fingers and the time it hit the ground, ProtoDaddy saw a hundred scenes from his life, images he always saw, but with life about to be stripped away they flared up: Laurel Ann Nunn naked in bed waiting for him, the sheet and blanket pulled up to her neck.

ProtoDaddy wore light grey summer suit trousers on the day of his death. He hadn't worn them in a long time. They were the same trousers he'd worn on the day he triumphed over Michigan's Governor Knott, cuffed grey trousers that fit him then and now on the day of his death so well they were neither demure nor ostentatious of his body, which was not overly muscular, but handsome and trim. Those trousers, that suit, had cost Pro-toDaddy more than he could afford in those early days, but had been necessary. Where he got the money for such a suit, no one knew, but several, including Lena, wondered.

Wearing those trousers, that suit, ProtoDaddy had seen Laurel Ann Nunn for the first time at a conference. She wore a press badge. He knew he was the only one who understood what Laurel Ann's presence meant, and he knew it just in time, when his business was waging battle over a piece of land surrounded by rising housing tracts way up near the new electrical plant at Ranford. The State of Michigan wanted that land for a highway; ProtoDaddy wanted it for gas station number 6 of the burgeoning *Esquire Empire Oil Co., Inc.*, Michigan.

ProtoDaddy's brother-in-law, Freddy, with his excellent eye for locations, had found the land site near Ranford on one of his solitary wanderings up down and around the State of Michigan in the Cadillac ProtoDaddy had given him. ProtoDaddy slid money out of the company into his own individual bank account, then bought the white car for Freddy, calling it a personal gift from him, ProtoDaddy, to his dear brother-in-law, Freddy. In warm weather, Freddy would open the windows to let the wind cleanse him of every thought pure and otherwise. In cold times he'd close up the car to revel in the heat that the gasoline burning and exploding in the engine churned out and over him. Freddy could drive more than anyone. He could drive all day and most of a night. He could sleep in small rooms in cheap motels with peeling plaster, thin sheets, and lousy beds, or he could charge a room in a Five-Star Hotel. He could sleep with a lonely woman he'd met in some little town or with a hooker paid for by him or by someone who wanted favors from him, or he could sleep alone, and in any case he'd have a good time. Freddy could eat burgers or rack of lamb done medium rare. As long as he could ride that Cadillac with which ProtoDaddy had bought Freddy's self respect and glory, was a man clean and ready for work, which work originally was to scout gas station locations, and then over the years to ride from station to station making sure things ran right. He'd drive along in the middle of

January, the roads frozen, the fields dead with wheat and corn stubble and snow, the Michigan sky dark, descending. Then, in a vision, he'd see a sign at a desolate crossroads as if it were really there: *Stallion Gas*, he would see. And in small letters: *A wholly owned subsidiary of Empire Oil Co., Michigan.* By the time ProtoDaddy died, Freddy had seen 378 of those blue and red signs where nothing had been before, and ProtoDaddy had bought 375 of those sites to build stations on them, all the time while Big was busy back at the first station pumping gas and fixing cars and giving away trinkets and cashing factory workers' checks and selling sodas and selling oil, while ProtoDaddy was busy pushing aside his sister, Lena. Lena had conceived of the idea for these gas stations, had bought the first one with money she'd saved from over twelve years running her coffee shop on the lake. Every month in those tight-money coffee shop days, Lena went to visit her little brother in jail. He wasn't yet called ProtoDaddy by anybody. At first he heard a name whispered about, Little Gypsy Boy. Then he heard it out loud. Then he heard it to his face. Then he heard it from the low-life prison guards. In prison, ProtoDaddy took tutoring in accounting from a fellow inmate, a British con-man named Steve Cooley.

They'd met one evening when Cooley approached him sitting at a table in the yard. —Where you been? Cooley asked him. —Nobody's seen you all day. We all keep tabs here. It matters. Turns out, Steve Cooley had killed a man.

—They came to get me about 3:00 this morning, Little Gypsy Boy told him. —They took me in shackles handcuffed to a sheriff. We went over to her apartment. I was the only one there, except for her nurse. We were too late. She was in her death throes. Violent death throes. Her whole body shaking jumping around and I said this to her, I swear this is what I said to her: I said to her, 'A curse on you, I curse you and I send you to Hell.'

—Jesús! Pretty damn heavy, Gyp. Because of the way she

betrayed your father? Steve Cooley asked him.

—Because of the way she betrayed me.

—What…???

—She swallowed my name, Steve.

—Don't go upside-down on me now, Little Gyp.

—I'm not crazy and I never will be. I cursed my mother on her deathbed and I meant it. Do you know…

——That'll remain between you and her, so far as I'm concerned. I don't want to even know.

—You don't need to even know.

—Let it go, Steve Cooley said.

—You don't let that kind of thing go, Little Gypsy Boy said. —You make them pay for it.

—She was your mother! Steve Cooley said.

—She wasn't nobody's mother, Little Gypsy Boy said.

—Get over it, Steve Cooley said, —or it'll screw you up forever.

—I'm screwed up, Little Gypsy Boy said, —look at me, already plenty screwed up.

—You're smart, Steve Cooley said. —Too smart to stay this way.

—We'll see, Little Gypsy Boy said. —Now she's gone and we'll see.

Little Gypsy Boy studied hard with Steve Cooley. When Little Gypsy Boy came out of prison as ProtoDaddy, ProtoDaddy knew things about keeping books that Lena hadn't ever dreamt of, things that would spin her head in confusions of columns and numbers hidden inside other numbers.

Lena knew only one thing about bookkeeping: debits left; credits right. You take money in, you write it down; you pay money out, you write it down. You add up the two columns. Boom. That's it.

When he left prison, ProtoDaddy—now called ProtoDaddy by his fellow inmates in honor of the way he'd played football in the prison yard, of the way he'd established and run the Inmate Protection Society, of the way he'd organized the distribution of contraband, of the way he had negotiated with the prison authorities for a host of new privileges: one more conjugal visit per month, second helpings at dinner, two hours more per week in the yard, and in admiration of the way he'd made money off of each of them—ProtoDaddy came home. He climbed a ladder himself, took down the two signs that read *Lena's Gas and Oil*, then raised two others, blue and red, with the picture of a horse reared up on two hind legs: *Stallion Gas.*

He found Big William.

He sent Lena's husband, Freddy, on the road, out of the way.

He moved the business from the outskirts of Detroit to Minneppossett.

He taught Lena to never reveal their Gypsy heritage, and told Freddy that if he ever revealed it to anyone that he, ProtoDaddy himself, would strip him of everything he had, including Lena, including his underwear.

Then, because he knew more about business and books than debit-left credit-right, ProtoDaddy convinced Freddy, then, when her vote didn't matter anymore insofar as it was already 2-0, ProtoDaddy convinced Lena that they needed a new company. Then, it was 3-0. ProtoDaddy formed the *Esquire Empire Oil Co., Michigan, Inc*, with all three of them as equal partners, ProtoDaddy, Lena, and Freddy. Lena: President. Freddy: Vice President. ProtoDaddy: Treasurer.

In those days, *Esquire Empire Oil Co., Michigan, Inc.* didn't have the capital to fight for a piece of land they wanted. So Laurel Ann Nunn was necessary for the cheap acquisition of land whose price was rapidly rising amid speculation. She was as beautiful as ProtoDaddy's not-yet-born daughter wouldn't quite be. Laurel Ann Nunn, white skinned, beautiful, inaccessible not in the rounded British which ProtoDaddy had adopted, but in a small-mouthed, quick American speech. ProtoDaddy could succeed with Laurel Ann Nunn only because he had no choice and because he wouldn't do it for lust or love. Had he done it for the real passions he felt for Laurel Ann Nunn, he would have failed. First, ProtoDaddy had to conquer his desire to be recognized by Laurel Ann Nunn. Then, he had to conquer his desire to be known by her. Then, he had to conquer his desire to explore the world with her, to be honest with her, to discuss perceptions, needs, differences. He had to conquer the desire to create and to enter with her that other world that two people can enter only with each other, and in which they can reside more aware yet more content with the mysteries of living. Having conquered those things within seconds of first seeing Laurel Ann Nunn, ProtoDaddy found someone to introduce them.

At the moment of ProtoDaddy's death, at the instant in which the English Oval rolled from his thumb, rolling his forefinger with it, but not yet falling across the edge of his thumb into the air, Laurel Ann Nunn, whom ProtoDaddy hadn't seen for three years four and a half months, spoke ProtoDaddy's name with nostalgic unease. At the moment of ProtoDaddy's death, Laurel Ann sat at a café in Mexico City with Roger Alles, a fellow Michiganian, now an officer in the United States Diplomatic Corps, posted to the Embassy in Mexico City.

—How, Alles asked Laurel Ann Nunn, —could a man like ProtoDaddy ever have gotten to the impenetrable Governor *Knott?*

—What do you mean? Laurel asked, —by *a man like ProtoDaddy?* By the wavering in her voice, Alles knew that Laurel Ann had been ProtoDaddy's willing conduit to Governor Knott. He knew that she had been intimate with Governor Knott. He knew that Laurel Ann Nunn wouldn't last much longer in the Service. She would go back to journalism. She, on the other hand, at that moment tasted dry white paper on her tongue. She drank from her water glass. At that very instant, when the English Oval rolled out of control to slide up and over the crest of the inside of ProtoDaddy's thumb, his life flashing before him, ProtoDaddy saw an image, as he'd often seen before, of Laurel Ann Nunn in bed, naked, with the sheets drawn up to her chin, waiting for him as he approached in the daylight. Beautiful as she was, his triumph was not over her.

Laurel Ann didn't understand that ProtoDaddy desired the control of his own desires more than he desired her, even more than he desired the land. Laurel Ann couldn't understand that a Gypsy, even one born and raised in Michigan, knew that that control of the outside world depended on control of the inner world. She introduced ProtoDaddy to Governor Knott at the Governor's mansion. Governor Knott, really, was a rather thick man. So many politicians were, Laurel Ann Nunn was then beginning to learn, thick men. And selfish. And she didn't want thick, selfish men. She wanted men of dignified intelligence with whom she could talk.

As ProtoDaddy first bent forward, following the arc of the English Oval cigarette toward the bathroom's white and green tile floor, Big was fine-tuning the ProtoDaddy's Rolls Royce's engine, and Thomas, ProtoDaddy's teen-aged big-footed son, was telling his friend and neighbor, Eliot, about the new car. Thomas had a red Corvette in the car barn his father had built to house Thomas's fifteenth birthday present, but Thomas wanted more than life to press his foot ever so easily onto the gas pedal of the Rolls Royce. He told Eliot that some night they should get together late, two o'clock in the morning, and push the Rolls down the long driveway from the house, hearing only the sound in the night of those Rolls Royce tires crunching the driveway's white stone. They could push it onto Route 24 that passed in front of the house, then start it up to drive on the highway through the corn and the hay and the bean fields of central Michigan like grand rich men in a Rolls Royce. —I, said Thomas, —can do it. Can you?

—No, said Eliot. —To tell you the truth, your father scares

me to death. If he caught us he'd have the Governor put us in jail for a hundred years.

—He doesn't scare me, Thomas said. —I'm already bigger than him. And look at him. He slouches. He's weak.

—He slouches, Eliot said, —but just a tiny bit, and he does it on purpose because he wants everyone to know that he doesn't have to stand absolutely straight up. He doesn't have to prove a thing. You don't know your own father very well. That man scares me to death and he ought to scare you, Thomas.

—To hell with you, Thomas said. —I'll go alone. You keep your mouth shut.

—My mouth doesn't care to talk about things like that. Believe me.

Thomas went to the car barn and there started up the new red Corvette. But he couldn't even drive that off the property until he turned sixteen. His father had warned him the State Police would not disregard the law for him.

Thomas backed out of the car barn, sped down the driveway, stopped at the highway, and sped out onto it in the most conspicuous vehicle he might have chosen to break the law.

By the time Big was lifting the bathroom door at the office off its hinges - with the dead weight of ProtoDaddy's dead body pressing against the door - Thomas had pulled into the parking lot of his high school, run to the gym, shot two baskets, missing one, hitting the other, while Eliot rode his bicycle to join Thomas. When Eliot entered the gym, Thomas heaved the basketball straight as his gut. Eliot caught it.

Thomas said, —Never fear my father. Never. Never fear that false face of his! Worship the real! If you can ever find it. Worship life and truth but not that phony bluff of a human being.

Thomas never knew Laurel Ann Nunn, but Laurel Ann Nunn knew Thomas. Laurel Ann Nunn knew that at the moment Thomas was born, ProtoDaddy was with another woman, not his wife and not herself. Laurel Ann liked ProtoDaddy's wife, Angela, more than she liked ProtoDaddy. When Thomas was born, Laurel Ann had gone to a gift store in Detroit where she bought a gold cross because it was an endurable gift the child could have all his life to protect him from harm. Jimmy Dean, a runner for the Minneppossett *Courier* for twenty years, delivered the cross. Jimmy Dean told the family the cross came as a collective tribute from the local reporting staff. Thomas was born 6 days early at 10:58 a.m. in July. ProtoDaddy arrived at the hospital that afternoon at about 4:35 p.m. At the post-natal viewing room the nurse held up his son. ProtoDaddy urged the nurse to hold the child right up to the glass, and then ProtoDaddy kissed the glass fully where the baby's face was, and said, —Thomas, after my brother.

—But your crazy brother could still be alive somewhere in France or England or maybe he went back to Egypt or who knows, what if he's in Cairo? Tehran? Anywhere.

—My crazy brother is dead, ProtoDaddy said. —His memory will be honored.

—How do you know that he's dead?

—Are you going to argue with me about the naming of my son?

—Just tell me how you know.

—I've seen it often. I've seen how he died. I've dreamt of it. He's come and talked to me.

—And you believe all that?

—I believe whatever I see with my own two eyes and hear with my own two ears. Rest, Angela.

—What about my father?

—We'll name the next one after your father. Rest.

—And if it's a girl?

—Then we'll name her Frieda. Or Frannie. Or Francesca.

—We're not Italians, darling.

—No. We're not. We're Americans, aren't we? So not Francesca. But I do like Francesca. And she'll be a dancer like that

Francesca Ritto we saw in New York. Do you remember her? She was fantastic. That long jet black hair. Now rest.

—Where have you been all day?

—Here. I'm right here.

When the gold cross arrived in a small black jewelry box wrapped with dark blue gift wrap, ProtoDaddy sent Jimmy Dean back to the newspaper with a note in a sealed envelope addressed to Laurel Ann Nunn. Jimmy Dean drove along Route 24, past the golf course, past the new housing development, then turned right onto State Highway 6. He didn't open the envelope. He took a flashlight from the glove compartment, but then put it back. He pulled into an alley by trashcans but he didn't tear up the note. He parked, then walking by another trashcan, he didn't tear up the note, again. Going in the front door, up the narrow stairs, he gave the note to Laurel Ann Nunn in her office. He watched her embarrassment for a moment, but he didn't say anything. She said, —Thanks, Jimmy.

As the English Oval touched the tip of his forefinger, he had left contact with the toilet seat, his bowels had moved in an arc of progress of their own, ProtoDaddy's legs burnt, the pain tightened his chest, his head losing ground. His stomach tightened, gripped as if to hold on to something. His feet loosened their footing. His hands went numb. His eyes rolled toward his skull. His skull turned hot, parched, cracking as the four sections of his skull separated, releasing heat. At the moment when the English Oval first entered the air, free altogether of any contact with ProtoDaddy's fingers, ProtoDaddy knew the dark green door of the small bathroom came toward him, or that he lurched toward it. His larynx useless, his tongue swelled and thickened, his teeth cold.

At that moment, Angela and Lena spoke on the telephone.

—I walked into the office, Lena told Angela, —the office that was built from the sweat of the money I gathered every day in a little bank account. The sweat of the money I invested with clarity and good business sense in that first gas station. While I nurtured my brother, your husband, Proto-god-damn-and-cursed-Daddy through his prison years. Then with foresight enough, bought another gas station. I don't give a damn about his charm, Angela. His wit. His suits from London. I don't give a good god damn. My brother! My money!

—What happened? I'm sure...we...can...

—What happened is I walked into that office this morning at 8:00 a.m. to make a long distance phone call to my cousin in Florida. My cousin. And Mister Proto God Damned Fucking Mister Proto Daddy tells the secretary, Denice, to tell me, who built this business one brick at a time, that I can't use the office phone for personal long distance calls. In fact, I was not to use the office phones for personal calls at all. 'Your brother,' Denice tells me '...I mean Mr. ProtoDaddy says you better not use the phones,' she says. That brother of mine threw me out! I gave him everything, Angela. I even signed his unholy contract just last Thursday. Do you hear? I signed his death warrant on me because he's got Freddy wrapped around his sophisticated little finger and Freddy'd already signed so I gave in and I signed. This world is a cruel world, Angela, and you're an innocent in it, but I'm telling you....and I don't know why I'm telling you. I won't have that monster throw me out of my own office. I gave him everything. The house you live in is mine. ProtoDaddy's Testament is a testament to Lena's hard work. All he ever did was work the books. You want to hear one, Angel-little Angela? You want to hear? He told me once, his own older sister who took him in to everything he told me very condescendingly, he said, 'Lena, all you know about books is credit-left-debit-right. I told him he was damn right that was all I knew and it was all I needed to know I'd come a long day knowing that much and you know what he said? He said, —Lena, books are a fiction. You can write anything you want in them. You can make your-self a millionaire. And if you do, everyone will believe you are a millionaire. Everyone will give you everything. What a sham! Everything we have began with my hard work and grew on his slick tongue. I'm going back down there and I'm ripping every phone out of the wall. He's broken my heart, Angela. My heart. If my mother were alive......my mother didn't bring us from the sewers of Liverpool for betrayal. I don't betray my kind.

—What contract?

—Oh. Oooooh. You don't even know. The innocent are spared the knowledge of the knife.

—What contract, Lena?

—The contract on my death. On Freddy's death.

—Lena! My husband does not deal with mafia...

—Your husband deals with power. Everywhere with power. With judges. With senators. With governors. With mafia. And he powered over my simple-minded Freddy his own brother-in-law to sign a new partnership agreement whereby, my dear sister-in-law, if one member of the partnership dies, that partner's family gets nothing. The whole share of their wealth goes right back into the business. Now you're clever enough to understand, aren't you? If Freddy dies, I don't get all of Freddy's share. If I die, Freddy doesn't get all of my share. The dead partner's share goes back into the business to be divided by the remaining two partners. Now where did my brother learn to write contracts like that? Where did he learn to steal like that from his own? In some fancy business school? I don't think so.

—Oh my God. He's betting that you'll die before he does.

—Yes, oh your God. If I die, dear heart, half of what's mine goes to you. No. Nothing has ever gone to you, has it? It goes to him. To ProtoDaddy. My younger brother is betting on my death. On Freddy's death. Who made this monster, ProtoDaddy? I didn't. I gave to him from what I had. Lena's voice trailed off, almost inaudible. Lena's voice became plaintive. —Why did I do it? Why did I give everything to him. Why did we all? Then her voice, humbled and small. —He was my brother, she said.

Angela hung up the phone without saying good-bye.

She climbed each one of the sixteen carpeted stairs that took her to the upper level of the house. In the bedroom, she stared at the photo of her husband on the bureau. He was handsome. He smiled with confidence. One shoulder hung just a bit lower than the other in a comfortable slouch. He wore a white shirt, a dark blue striped tie, a blue, gold-buttoned suit. His hair had a natural wave to it. He was not a stitch less debonair than the day she met him, the day he captured her weak heart and soul, her lonely body, her hyper-imagination. Looking at his eyes in the photograph, she looked for cruelty there, or coldness, but saw only joy. Yes, he could be a bastard. He was a man. All men are bastards. But a monster? Angela looked into the mirror. In the bathroom, she looked again into the mirror there. In the mirror in the hallway, also. Angela felt her face, felt the cheekbones, the nose, the hair of her eyebrows, the inward arc of her eyesocket. She ran her forefinger over that arc in each eye several times. Taking an English Oval cigarette from the pack on the dressing table in the bedroom, she lit it. She took a drag, coughed, put it out. How he had carried amusement and grandeur together. How we all have given to him. Angela looked once more into the mirror in the hallway. Then she went to the phone to call ProtoDaddy.

The English Oval cigarette hit the floor just before Proto-Daddy's head hit the door. The coroner estimated that Proto-Daddy had been dead before his head hit the door, but in any case the blow to the head was not the cause of death. Big William thought it might have been the cause of death; it was so loud he'd heard it in the gas station next door. That morning, when Big heard Denice tell ProtoDaddy's sister, Lena, that, under ProtoDaddy's orders, Lena was not to use the office phone for personal calls, and Lena said she'd go talk to ProtoDaddy about it, Denice said that ProtoDaddy was in a meeting, and Lena asked, —well, a meeting with who? and the secretary

said, —with the Governor, and Lena left, Big looked in on ProtoDaddy in his office. Only ProtoDaddy at his desk, alone.

—Without ProtoDaddy, Big said to Denice, —what am I?
What is any of us without ProtoDaddy? We're nothing again.

—I've been with him since I was seventeen years old, the
secretary said. —Can you imagine? I have a son named after him. He chose my husband for me he said to me one day,
Denice, I've met the man you'll marry. He said that to me. He
knew. He was an amazing man. We won't see the likes of him
again.

—In 1912, Roger Alles told Laurel Ann Nunn, —President
Woodrow Wilson sent the Marines into Mexico, into Veracruz.
Wilson changed the course of the Mexican revolution. Of his-
tory. Did you know that?

—Yes. I knew it quite well my young intellectual darling.

—Do you know what it means? It means the Communists
of Latin America will never succeed in Mexico, wherever else
they might succeed. No American President will ever let that
happen. That's power, Laurel Ann. And that's my job here, in
Mexico City. To make one phone call to let Washington know
when the time has come to send the Marines again. That's my
call to make.

—Did you know I had an affair with ProtoDaddy?

—I figured.

—Do you know what I like most about him?

—Do we have to talk about other men right now?

—Do you know?

—Tell me.

—He isn't naive. About anything. He has great faith in his
own power, his own will, you might say. He gives purpose to
life, to everyone's life. Do you know what it means to come into
contact with that? Do you know how rare that is to do? Do you

know what they call that big country house of his?

—Yes. Testament. Some religious thing or something.

—No. He told me why, once. In bed. Just like we're lying here now, me and you, in bed. He calls it Testament because it testifies to his will, he said. He loves culture. He loves knowledge. He loves great things.

—Why are we talking about ProtoDaddy just now?

—Because just now I've realized how I don't want to be here with you, how much I yearn for him and never admit it and it feels good to admit it.

—An hour ago you wanted rather desperately to be here with me.

—He isn't naive about anything.

—If you print what I said about the phone call to Washington I'll deny that I spoke to you. I'll discredit you.

—You're safe. I'm very discreet. I'm sorry, I shouldn't have wasted your evening last night. Your morning. My mind is obviously somewhere else now.

—ProtoDaddy telephoned me here.

—Here?

—About a month ago. He wanted me to introduce him to some Mexican officials. People from Pemex.

—Have you called them?

—Of course. I met with them. I have an appointment to call ProtoDaddy. Tomorrow at noon. Alles sat up. —Oh my God, he said. —He sent you, didn't he, Laurel Ann? ProtoDaddy sent you here to check me out. What a....

—No, my handsome young Turk. Fear not. He used me once only. I let him use me. I begged him to use me. I knew he would never use me again, and he never has. You see? That's the kind of man he is. Do you understand?

—No.

—Of course not. You'd like to make love again, wouldn't you?

—Yes. Yes I would.

—No no. I'm sorry. It wasn't an invitation. It was a.....well, an unfair question. I'm very sorry. I have to be up early. It's after 3 already.

—Mother told me that she has an awful cigarette taste in her mouth that won't leave her, Maria told Thomas before the funeral.

—The car is mine, you know, Thomas told his sister.

—What car? The Rolls Royce?

—Of course. The Rolls.

—We'll see, Maria said.

—It's a symbol of his manhood, Thomas said. —It will go to his son.

—What if I say it is a symbol of his love, it should go to his daughter?

—You're so goddamn self-centered, Thomas shot back at her. —He would take you to task for that. He hated selfishness. He was generous. He gave tons of money to charities, do you know that? Do you know anything about him? Look at all the people here. Have you ever seen a line of cars like this at a funeral in this town? The Governor of Michigan is here. Do you know who that is over there? Of course not. He's the Chairman of the Board of General Motors. Do you understand who your father was? I don't think you really do. I don't think you know what that car means.

—Then you take the car. I'm afraid anyway.

—Afraid? What of, Maria? Don't be afraid.

—Leave me alone, Thomas. I'm going to go away. There's something wrong here. There's something wrong with me.

There's nothing wrong. Here. Take this. Daddy gave it to me when I was born. You take it now. When you get afraid, hold it. There. It looks nice. If mother asks you, tell her I gave it to you.

At the graveside, Laurel Ann Nunn heard the Priest, but she wasn't moved. His prayers seemed to weep, yet by the time it was over the weeping was done. She would write the obituary for him, adhering to ordinary journalistic objectivity: —..... funeral procession as if for a great statesman....ProtoDaddy, as many affectionately called him, meant a great deal to many lives. Many local people say that without him they wouldn't be where they are.

Next to Laurel Ann, Governor McCall and Senator Francis Bradddock stood together. —I think, Governor McCall said to Senator Bradddock, —ProtoDaddy thought he would live forever.

—Christ, Senator Braddock answered, —I believed he would live forever. He was that kind of man.

—He never gave one thought in his whole life to death, Laurel Ann said. —He was that kind of man.

As they left the gravesite, Laurel Ann asked Governor McCall, —Are you relieved?

—Relieved? Gov. McCall asked.

—I know how it is, Lauren Ann said. —You won't have to look over your shoulder to make sure he isn't unhappy with you in some way.

—Well, the Governor said, —yes and no, he said. —Both. Relieved, yes, perhaps, yet a little lost, I suppose.

—I'm not, she said. —I'm not lost at all.

—I think you knew him quite well, said the Governor. —No?

—Not at all. And I'm not lost at all in this loss.

On her way to her car, walking over a great lawn, Laurel Ann crossed paths with Thomas. —What will you do, Thomas, now? she asked him.

—I gave my sister the cross you gave me at my birth, Thomas said.

—No, Laurel Ann said. —Not me. The whole staff at the

newspaper gave that to you.

—I'm not naïve, Thomas said. —You gave it to me. You want to know what I'm going to do now that he's gone? I'm going to worship life and truth, real life and real truth, that's what I'm going to do.

—You're very mature, Laurel Ann said to him. —You're right, don't ever be naïve.

Left alone on that expanse of lawn for a moment, Thomas looked around. Crowds drifted away from the cemetery, leaving the trees and the graves and the well-tended grounds and beyond the trees and the grounds, the expanse of wheat and dairy and soy and corn farmland to the horizon. —I will, Thomas muttered, —I will worship life and truth. I will become them. You'll see.

A Buick Lesabre, Midnight Blue

Later,

when the one named Arthur insisted that his name wasn't Art, at that moment, when it was the most irrelevant thing he could do, Thomas remembered the way Mary had put the food down in front of him, and he thought, —That's art: the way she put that food down in front of me, awkwardly, with a delicate grace, and even so, letting me know just what she thought of me by the way she did it. That's art.

When Mary came her uncle had been talking about Dr. King and the clergy's duties and responsibilities. He was recalling the great Marcus Garvey's parades through Harlem, he was telling the young boys to above all be careful.

At the moment Mary pushed open the door from the kitchen to the dining room, Thomas had been arguing with Mary's uncle that Dr. King, as a minister, had every right to interfere in politics. Politics was religion, religion was politics.

—What's religion, Thomas argued, —but politics, the way we treat each other, that's what politics is.

Reverend Hooper disagreed. —Politics in America is definitively not religion. That's what makes this country unique. Politics is economics, jobs, foreign policy. War and peace and diplomacy. Religion is God.

—That's just capitalism, Thomas argued. —Politics is more than capitalism, it's the way we live with each other. Thomas sensed Mary come from the kitchen door behind him, but when he looked over his shoulder he saw just the white door as it stood unswung on its hinges. Thomas did not speak about the negation in her absence. —We shall overcome, Thomas said, —that's politics and it's religion and it's the... Mary, appearing as from nowhere now, stood behind Thomas to slip a heavy silver platter of sliced New York strip steak on the table. Just before it touched the table, the platter teetered, almost spilled. Everyone almost said something or began to reach out to save the dish, but before anyone spoke or moved, Mary, with a strong right arm, had made the save herself. That left everyone, Thomas included, with something they had just meant to say, or do, so that later Thomas would feel there was just something he wanted to say to Mary, or do for her.

—It's the what? Reverend Hooper said.

—It's the....what? Thomas asked.

—You'd just said it's the....something or other, your 'We shall overcome,' you said it's politics and it's religion and it's...

Thomas said, —It's the truth. Mary had disappeared. Just her hand and arm had slid past Thomas, the bilious sleeve of her white cotton blouse brushing his ear.

—It may be the truth. Reverend Hooper leaned forward, took the plate of meat, served himself two pieces of steak on which he lavished a ladleful of heavy gravy. —Spiritually, I'm on your side. The Protestants and the Catholics and the Jews and the Whites and the Negroes should be allies. We share a fate. We share oppression. Oh, you may think that strange, but don't forget our Protestant ancestors fled England to escape religious oppression. We were the Negroes — and worse — of Europe, you know. I'm on your boys' side a hundred percent. It's the idea of the clergy that worries me. When you have the clergy running marches down streets in Washington, next you'll have them running for President and that's not right, you see. We've got to protect that separation of church and state. That's what makes us all free, Jew and Protestant and Catholic and Negro and White and...and Jew. Reverend Hooper leaned back in his seat, surveyed the faces of his audience, then sat forward, cut a piece off his steak, raised the forked meat to his mouth.

Thomas had taken meat, John, Big John, heaped his plate with six or eight slices.

Mary, appearing again as if from some white hole in space, took the meat platter from her brother to carry it down to the far end of the table, whisking her sleeve once more past Thomas. So when the skinny guy brushed that knife across Thomas's ear so close Thomas felt how sharp the blade was without feeling the blade itself, Thomas remembered Mary's sleeve that way, that it too had cut him.

He came from the bathroom wearing the thick Turkish robe he'd gotten from his parents for his 17th birthday. When he walked past Mary's bedroom she called him: Thomas. Was it possible a whisper like that could travel through the closed walls yet be so distinctly heard? He cracked the door on the darkened room. Mary breathed evenly. Thomas sat on her bed. Mary slept.

Each breath Thomas took was water rushing in his brain. Mary lay on her back, her eyes closed, her chest moving in light expansions and contractions, out and up, in and down. Thomas got up to leave. —I was waiting for you, Mary said.

—Did you call me?

—Not out loud.

—No?

—I want you to do me a favor, Thomas, because I think you're in danger and I don't know what's going to happen.

—I'm in....?

—There's nothing we can do about it. Before you go, touch my breasts. Hold me there for a minute.

His arm crossed her body. Her breast filled his palm. He caressed it. Abandon held itself just behind his eyes.

—Your eyes are closed, aren't they?

—How can you see me in this dark?

—I don't know, Mary said.

—Have you ever felt confused? Thomas asked.

—Confused?

—Disoriented.

—I don't know....

—I always feel confused, Thomas said, —disoriented. And

now more so. As though confusion and disorientation resovled themselves in confusion and disorientation.

—Just keep doing it, Mary said. —No one's ever done this. I wanted you to do it just in case. Her breath came from below her diaphragm.

—In case what? I....

—In case you don't come back. I'll have this for the rest of my life, you touching me. My God, Thomas, that's such a breath-sucking feeling. Are you frightened? No wonder they all talk about love all the time. It feels like your hand has all of me in it like all of me rises up into your hand your hand is all over me is all of me.

—Mary...your uncle, I...

—Thomas, Mary said, —put your head on my breast. Rest here for a minute.

—Do you want me not to go, then, if there's so much danger?

—No. You go.

The rest of the house slept, Reverend Hooper, Mrs. Cummings, John.

—I have John to protect me, Thomas said. —Who would mess with Big John?

—Don't talk like that. It's not smart.

—But it's true. Who would touch Big John?

Thomas flipped, turned. He woke up and stared. Had that happened with Mary? His face against her bare nipple. My God! What I've done on a night when above all I should stay clean, pure, and be surrounded by goodness as protection. I've violated the Reverend Hooper's trust. Mrs. Cumming's. She fed me, gave me a clean bed, a room, and what have I done? Nearly molested her daughter. Preceded by an instantaneous flash of joy a nearly unbearable weight of remorse pressed Thomas against the bed. —My God, I'm hopeless.

They had talked about it on the way, walking in the still dark. It was Thomas's idea, not John's, but Thomas made John promise to stick by him. —You'll stick with me?

—Yes.

—It might get hairy.

—It's OK.

—Have I ever betrayed you, John?

—No.

—Then don't betray me, Thomas said.

—Look at me. John said. —What should I run from? You know anyone bigger? Stronger?

—What if they have clubs or knives or guns?

—Who?

—I don't know who. The KKK.

—You lied to my uncle. John said. —You lied to a priest of the cloth.

—We can't take a cab. Thomas said. —There are no cabs. Look. The city is just blue and quiet. No one but us.

—Through Harlem, Thomas!

—I know it's Harlem.

—You're crazy.

—I won't go to march for people whose neighborhood I refuse to walk through in the dark. I hate hypocrisy and I won't ever be a hypocrite. If we're ever going to do anything with ourselves we've got to be pure. OK? Straight. Honest. That's the way in Washington. When we get to Washington. Stick with me.

—I'd never abandon you. John promised.

They had reached 110th Street, had turned right to cross over to Fifth. The Body of Christ Church. The Body and Blood of. How well Thomas knew that phrase, the language of the language that he thought in. He pulled John in close to him.

—I believe you, John, I do. I need that.

—I know. It's because you're lost somewhere, John said.

—Lost?

—I don't know. Like you need taking care of. Like you already need me to help you out of a jam you're in. Or think you're in. I don't know. I'm here, though. Don't worry.

Thomas walked on top of the world. Exhilarated. Safe. He was going to Washington, District of Columbia, to march with Dr. Martin Luther King for the freedom of all people. He was walking right up through Harlem. He wasn't scared. He too would be free some day. He too would overcome. Even his confusions. For now, John. Thomas had both protection and freedom on his mind, in his heart, as if somehow those two contradictory things were one and the same. Maybe he wouldn't even go home after this was over. He'd stay in New York. What a thought. Near Mary. His young life was awakening brilliantly in his nostrils, in the fresh succulence of its truth as he took in the deliciously foul air smelling of garbage and concrete and excitement. Smelling the green of the bushes beside them, across the street, in the park.

All three of them sauntered out from those bushes. They appeared to Thomas first in the very corner of his eye without looking. Three. John's body so quietly disappeared without turning or running or walking away. It dissolved. He said quietly, trying to insist: —John. His heart stopped pumping any more blood his lungs gave up their oxygen his crotch crawled up. That foul air was now jets of fire up his nostrils, burning in his eyes. The three danced around him. When he ran forward yelling —John! he ran into the one named Arthur the one they called Skinny Man and they also called him Mr. Bones. Arthur, Skinny Man, Mr. Bones pushed Thomas back hard against his chest. When Thomas turned on the pivot of his shoes to run the other way he ran into the skinny one yelling nearly weeping *John you have abandoned me!*

Could John have just dissolved? But then the one named Arthur was there again and they kept circling and then he ran into the other one the one with the thick arms.

He fell back again. He couldn't breath at all now because

John was breath and he couldn't find breath. His eyes were enflamed. Breath would not cool them. No. Breath would feed the fires. Where was John? He could survive alone. No. He'll die. Now he'll die for some sin or some sin against him or some stupidity. As his hand clamped shut something soft fell out so his hand closed hard on itself.

They were poking him. One of them slapped him. Which one? If he could remember which one he'd avoid him. Not the one with the knife. That was the other one.

For one second John appeared behind the one with the knife, but when he looked carefully John wasn't there. Had he been there and disappeared again? The strong one the one with the thick arms carrying the knife? Why not the skinny one like before? How stupid. The strong one gave the skinny one back the knife. Must've been.

The bushes that surrounded him damp. Bushsweat. Beads of bushsweat. Why did he keep thinking?

—Thinkin' bout your las' day, huh? The skinny one, Mr. Bones, Arthur, now with the knife, agile with it around his eyes. —Las' glory day on God's green earth. Green ain't it? He cut a bush which fell over Thomas's eyes so that for a second Thomas saw nothing, did the knife go into his gut? Mary again, with the meat platter, and quickly, Mary in her bed, her breast, breath moist. The room dark.

Thomas tried to say The First Baptist Church of Harlem of the Body of Christ but blurblurblurb the letters saliva flowing onto his chin.

—Say what? the strong one asked. —Say, blurb? What you think he means, Art? That was the first time.

—Arthur, Arthur said.

—OK, mistah fuckin Arthur. What do you think he's saying?

—I donno, Arthur admitted. Where was Arthur lost to Thomas's line of sight. —I don't speak no fucking blurb. If I cut

43

his tongue he won't talk like that no more. He grabbed Thomas's tongue, he pulled it, he put the slick blade to it, he drew blood off its curled edge.

—You cut his tongue I cut your balls, the other one, not the skinny one, not the strong one, said. —He's gonna need that tongue to answer my questions.

Thomas didn't remember any part of their walk through the streets except that John appeared three more times then disappeared each time. The first time, John looked pasty as the dead, and he looked apologetic for having died. The second time, John dressed in a black tuxedo as though he'd come to invite Thomas to some grand dinner. Finding Thomas otherwise engaged, he disappeared. The third time, John brought Mary to have a last look at Thomas, but Mary turned her head away. Then John disappeared yet again.

Though his legs were numb, Thomas stumbled up the torn-up steps to the building. The plywood replacing the door came back from the opening when the skinny one pulled on it, and then the strong one pushed Thomas through, where the other one, not the skinny one, not the strong one was already waiting for him. The other one escorted Thomas to the living room of the vacated apartment on the left. There was so much garbage Thomas slipped in it, then Arthur pushed him down. Thomas sat into the trash, his head tapping against the wall.

Kicking open a space for himself in the garbage, establishing there a circle of command, the strong one, the big one, the one they called Atlas and Black Atlas and Big Atlas stood before Thomas looking at him for a minute. Thomas squirmed to sit up. —You ain't totally dumb. You're dumb, but you ain't totally dumb. Look at them eyes. Big Atlas turned to ask Arthur. —See the kid's eyes? They ain't dumb. He looked back at Thomas. —You want to die, boy?

—Yes, sir.

—Wrong answer, boy. Don't lie to me. Don't lie at all.

—No, sir.

—Don't 'no, sir' me, boy. 'Sir's' a white man's word from the white man's army. Hear? Round here we don't fight no white man's war, hear?

Trying to say 'yes,' it would not come out.

—Say 'yes' or I let Mr. Bones Mister Skinny Man Arthur here have your tongue, don't you know he needs more flesh. He laughed. —You ain't laughing you ain't talking. Better talk in a minute.

Arthur Mr Bones Skinny Man came over with the knife. He pulled out Thomas's tongue again with a jerk on which Thomas nearly choked.

—Not yet, Bones, Big Atlas intervened. —He can't talk with your hand on his tongue, now can he? Can he? Thomas gurgled. —Look at him kick. I like that, I like a boy that'll kick for his own tongue. Even if he don't know what it means to fight for a life he may not even want anymore. Does he?

Bones let go of Thomas's tongue. Thomas reached up but when his hand came to his mouth his tongue was already gone. Gone back into his mouth or was it already cut off?

—We're gonna rob you sure, Atlas said, kicking at the crap on the ground. —We might hurt you, we might kill you. Nobody'd care. You're in Harlem. You come into Harlem and you'll live by Harlem law. So you might just as well talk, might just as well tell me what the fucking deuce you're doing up here. Cause, pausing, Atlas paced. —Cause I'm a curious type. I like to figure things out. I like to know just who I'm messing with. Who are you? He looked right down at Thomas, right into Thomas's eyes.

Thomas found his tongue now, but it was too thick and it wasn't cooling. He pointed to his mouth.

—It's all right. Mumble, The other one said, the one who hadn't said much yet. —Mr. Warp can hear you just fine. That's me, Mr. Warp. I'm the warp and the woof. You know what that

45

means?

Thomas nodded his head. His tongue trickled spots of blood into his mouth. He swallowed. He may have pissed his pants but how could he know in a body alternating between being his and being so distinct from him it could have been another heap among the refuse scattered on the floor. —Try to say my name, now. That's a sign of respect. If you respect me you might live. You know. Tina Turner. Respect. All us Negroes want respect. You know that, don't you? If you respect me you might live.

—Mr. Warp. You're Mr. Warp.

Mr. Warp insisted that Thomas, looking straight up at him, repeat his name. Thomas obeyed: —You're Mr. Warp. In Thomas's acquiescence, Mr. Warp let show the genius that roamed his face for Thomas to see. Thomas's voice came thick with guttural weight. His words came out as objects: —You're Mr. Warp.

—You want to cut that boy? Warp asked the skinny one, Mr. Bones, Arthur.

—I'll cut anybody.

—Cut his ear, Warp said. —Just like I taught you.

The skinny one had stood by the boarded window. No daylight came in around the edges of the plywood boards. Thomas's body wouldn't stop rumbling. His brains shook. John's promise: —*I won't ever leave you. It's because you're scared and you need me.* The knife coming through Thomas's earlobe.

—Art!

—My name's not goddamn Art!

Mr. Warp kept looking at Thomas. —You think I care what your name is, Arthur? You think?

Pick up that piece of that ear.

—Arthur, man. You call me Arthur.

Mr. Warp looked over at Arthur. Arthur leaned for support up against what had been and still looked like the fireplace. Mr. Warp drew his voice out so it drawled. —Arthur, would you please, like I'm asking you, would you please go on over there and pick up that piece of that boy's ear that's right there on the floor beside him.

—I just mean it. I'm Arthur. That's all.

—Fine, Arthur. That's fine. Then Mr. Warp spoke to Thomas. —You let your eyeballs roll back into your eyes, you might still live. Might not. But might.

Thomas's eyeballs did roll down. The room reappeared to him as through blood, reddish and liquid. Mr. Warp's figure bent and rolled. —This used to be you, Mr. Warp held up the little piece of flesh he had taken from Arthur, —and now it's not. That's how we are, can be just cut off like that. Isn't that something! Now it's just trash. Meaningless. I'll make the rest of you trash, too. But if you talk to me and tell me the truth maybe I won't.

Thomas grunted.

—What's your name? Mr. Warp asked, still right in front of Thomas, filling his eyes. —Just your first name. I just want the name that people call you, when they call you. The name you hear.

—

—What did you say? Say it again. Mr. Warp couldn't hear you.

—Nothing. Thomas's voice did not come out as he thought it would. —I didn't say nothing.

—Your name ain't nothing. Mr. Warp smiled. —But it might be. Mr. Big Atlas told you no lies. Now. No lies. What's your name.

—samoht. A stammer. A stutter. A mutter. A fact drawn from pulling of the inside out of memory.

—That the truth?

—Yes, sir.

—That the whole truth?

—No, sir.

—Tell me more, then.

—Thomas.

—That the whole truth, then?

—No, sir.

—I'm nobody, sir. Nobody. Nothing to bother about.

—You ain't nobody, Mister Nobody. Maybe someday you'll be nobody but today you're talking to Mr. Warp you better tell the truth. You know what truth is?

—No, sir.

—Atlas here told you, no 'sir'. You're in the Black Man's Army now. What are you doing in Harlem at three o'clock of the a.m. in the morning, Chaos? That's my name for you. I'll call you Chaos. He rubbed the cut-off piece of the ear against Thomas's cheek. —Huh? On my streets?

—I was going to the bus to the church to the bus to the...

—Slow. One. word. after. the. other.

—March....Washington. Dr. King. I...was...

—You were going to save my Black ass and I cut off a little bit of your ear. Oh my Mama in her grave. Oh my Lordy Christ come down off his cross and be right here in our room with us boys! Mr. Thomas gonna save me. Save you, boys. March on Washington tell them cats. Tell em. Protect us boys down here on the streets. Need your help up there in Washington and we cut off his little ear Lord sew it back on sew that holy thing back on his bleeding ear! Mr. Warp laughed so Thomas's body, catching the vibrations of laughter, stopped trembling, finally. Mr. Warp threw the ear piece to Arthur but it fell on the floor. Arthur knelt down to find it.

—Find it, Mr. Warp said. —It is some holy thing, man. Find it. Mr. Warp turned back to Thomas, laughing. —Who's going to protect you while you're out protecting me? Huh? I'm worried about you, boy. Mr. Chaos. Thomas. Who's going to take care of you so you can take care of Mr. Warp? Huh?

Thomas's head hung. —John. John said he never leave me.

—Oh Lord what hast thou! Why and why! He had his John

to look after him but now he's got his little salvation self locked up in a room full of magic men going to eat his heart out like it was an African gazelle. That is what Arthur said, crazy Art?

—Arthur.

—See? Don't call him Art. He'll eat your heart I swear he's nuts. Lord oh Lord ain't that the coming of something or other, save me, Mr. Thomas Mr. Chaos Mr. Nobody is up to save me and all my African American brothers and sisters. And don't think I don't appreciate it. Mr. Warp knows how to give gratitude just as well as he knows how to do most things. It's just Arthur doesn't know too much but to hit and cut, right Arthur? Doesn't know about laba zabachtani, do you?

—About what….?

—Why it's the Ancient People's tongue, it's Hebrew, Mr. Warp said. —It means, 'my God, my God,' Mr. Warp quoted, —'Why have you abandoned me' Isn't that right, Mr. Thomas?

—I…don't know, Thomas said.

—You watch out for Mr. Arthur, though, Mr. Warp warned Thomas. —He knows what he's doing.

John appeared one more time, now as an evenly grey mist that surrounded Thomas, for a moment obliterating the room along with all of the men in it, for a moment, cooling.

—What I do? What I did do?

—You know what you did, Mr. Warp's voice tore the fog.

—John!

—There's ain't no more John any no more.

—What'd I do wrong? I. Please.

When Mr. Warp left, a flash of darkness came from the hallway, then a sliver of light cut through the front door as it opened then closed. Arthur closed the apartment door, sat leaning against the side of the tiled fireplace, keeping his eyes on the plywood-boarded front window. Mr. Bones, who had moved away from the window sat up against the wall, nodding off.

Morning light now seeped through the window's nailed edges. —I always hated that nickname, Arthur said. —If you've got a name, that's what you've been given, see? No need to change a name. Why would your Momma give you that name if it ain't what people gonna call you? It doesn't make sense.

—Uh-huh. I see. Everything in the room was stark. Things returned to ordinary proportions, perspectives. Even Arthur's voice seemed normal.

—What you're called, that's all you've got see?

—I see, Arthur. I see what you said.

—Good. People around here if they said, 'Hey remember that time old Mr. Warp and Art and Black Atlas picked up that white kid and took care of him? Remember how Art hit him so bad everything inside him gave up on him?' Nobody'd know it was me. If they'd have said 'Arthur', now everybody'd know it was me. See? See what I mean? I wouldn't call you Tom or Tommy. You're Thomas, man. You're no little kid. You're not nobody. You're a man. You're a simple dude. You got a man's name. It's simple. It's just an ordinary thing. When I mess with you again you say, 'Hey, man! I'm Thomas. You're messing with Thomas!'

—Yes, sir.

—No 'sir,' Warp told you, no whitey 'sir' shit. OK?

—No whitey sir shit, and no 'Art.' Call the man his real name.

Yet, when the knife had passed his ear Thomas heard Mary's sleeve at the dinner table. He thought when her sleeve brushed his ear it was the last sound of his purity with her. Life with her now was stained with passions. Arthur looked hungry, skinny, lost, like he wasn't anywhere, though anywhere he could cut that's where he'd be. That's why he could cut accurately, smoothly. They should call him Blade, or Mr. Knife, because that's all he was, was a blade, a knife, a sharp edge well aimed.

But Mr. Blade, Mr. Knife didn't cut him, because he

couldn't without a command from Mr. Warp.

—Going to Washington to march on down for me, huh boy? Arthur said. —Make all us Black folks free! I sure do appreciate it. Can't tell you how much. You're too good, boy, too damn good, ain't you! I know those people going down there to Washington, aren't they! Moses an' all. Red Sea 'em there. Let my people go. Atlas hit hard in Thomas's gut with his elbow, Mr. Bones now behind him with the blade unseen now tucked away but ready so that pulling it out would be part of the act preceding the act.

It was dawning. Thomas uncurled. He couldn't think the words that he might hold to for salvation, the words 'dawn' or 'light', the words 'John' or 'Thomas'. But the dawn and the light came through the wood, as through her door Mary's voice had come to call Thomas. He wouldn't see another day. He deserved not to, didn't he? Didn't he, John? Your sister's breast in my hand. I'm sorry. I'm sorry for ever being. I won't. I won't be. at being being what I won't ever be and never come close to knowing. Almost fainting, Thomas urinated in his pants again the cold urine waking him. How could there be so much cold? Was it only he who was cold, from the inside? How could Mary have called him from her sleep? Thomas tried now to call her: —Mary, he thought as loudly as he could think.

—What did you say? Atlas, Mr. Big Atlas, Mr. Titan asked from a corner. Thomas looked up with eyes that were falling back into his head. —What did you say about some Mary?

—You don't know what I said, Thomas said.

—You're a defiant little one, but that's good. It gives me more to work with. You don't know what I know, do you? You can't even see my eyes. Oh, I know. You can see Mr. Warp's eyes, can't you? Mr. Warp's eyes are all over his face. But mine aren't. So don't be saying you know what I know and what I might not know until I show you.

—Let me take his ear, Skinny Bones Arthur said.

—Mr. Too-soon, I call him, Atlas said. —Arthur Mr. Skinny Bones Too. Soon. He likes to do everything too quick, right now. He's got so many names because none of them count. See?

Thomas recovered from the first blow. His stomach muscles tightened to hold it still. He nearly blacked out but willed himself to hang on to at least see his own end.

Crossing through Atlas's old command center, Arthur sauntered backtoward Thomas, where Thomas leaned up against the wall. Where were Arthur's eyes? Where were they? —Don't think much about Mr. Cut, Atlas Titan said. —When I'm the one's gonna give the call, I'm the one's gonna take your heart home like it was the heart of an African gazelle. Then you'll know what you've done for my people. You will have fed them like they were back in Africa.

Thomas's arms jerked away from his stomach toward his face, then back to his stomach, his crotch, his middle, including his heart. Only two arms. He rolled to the left to roll away from Atlas came out away from the wall, stood, then, weak legged, fell back, falling so heavily the shock of hitting the wall knocked Mary's words into his mind, what Mary had said about John. —John! Atlas's knee at that very sound found its way into Thomas's kidney so that Thomas screamed dry air, waited for breath, found it, then screamed aloud, his hands having chosen now of their own accord: they covered his eyes.

—Good, Atlas said. —Scream. That's good. Now you're quieter aren't you? Ain't no John abandon you. Nobody abandoned you. You had to face me sooner or later. Come hell or high water. See?

Thomas let his left leg, which had come up with the blow, descend to the floor. He thought he urinated more from pain, but couldn't distinguish real from phantom sensation. Not dead, not but Thomas's body had disengaged from its own system of sensation and response.

—Sit down, my man. Sit. Atlas kicked some garbage away,

making a place for Thomas.

—What do you want with me? Thomas whispered into his own lap. —You want to kill me? Kill me.

—Decision like that's a bi-iig thing. Want me to kill you? Atlas challenged him.

Thomas searched through answers that surprised him. —No, he chose one.

—You were thinking about it though, huh?

—No.

—No more lies, white kid. No need. You're free now. Do you understand? You were going to Washington to free me, but instead now you're free, so far as freedom goes. Now ain't that something for a white boy on a cold morning? Ain't that for some Glory Be, huh?

—How do you mean, free?

Atlas twirled his lips around in thought for a moment. —Go get me a drink, he told Mr. Bones. Arthur slid off into the apartment. Mr. Atlas added: —With ice. Ha! That's good. With ice. You must be all ice now, huh Mr. Thomas? You cold? You scared?

—No, sir.

—Just no be fine. But you're lying and I told you not to. You ain't lying to me. You're lying to you. You're lying to the one you call Thomas. You whisper to that one in your sleep. You call him without using his name that unnameable thing that never sleeps. Now that's bad. Once before a man dies he wants to tell the absolute the dead honest the no hiding truth to himself, doesn't he? Then he can die, even though just then might not have to anymore.

—Yes. A small gurgle of blood came out the corner of Thomas's mouth. That's how we die, Thomas thought. A little blood comes. Something's broken inside and we're dying.

—So I'm going to help you.

Arthur Mr. Bones returned with a glassful. —Whiskey, Ar-

thur said. Atlas Titan took the small glass into his large hand.
—Finest whiskey in all of Harlem, my Homeland. You take a
drink, Bones?

Arthur nodded.

Atlas sat opposite Thomas now, on the windowsill which,
having lost almost all its many coats of paint, was nearly bare
wood. He sniffed the whiskey. —To my Homeland, Atlas said.
—And to my best friend, Arthur. Atlas drank, then he set the
glass on the window sill. He sat for a moment to let his whole
body taste the liquor. —That's right, Atlas said. —You know,
my last name sounds something like your first name. I wonder
if we're relations. Your people don't come from Africa, do they?

—No.

—Didn't think so. All the same. Didn't own no slaves back
in the high days, did you?

—My people have never owned slaves.

—No? Mine did. Then they became slaves. Now we're free.
See? Free. Except you're going to Washington to make us more
free. Mr. Bones, Atlas addressed Arthur, —talk a little bit to Mr.
Thomasboy.

Bones went over to Thomas. His knife, appearing as from
nowhere now, had somehow come into his hand without his
taking it from his back pocket, but it wasn't open. Bones swept
the closed edge of it along Thomas's neck, down his chest, poking it in immediately below his diaphram.

—Shaking? Atlas asked Bones for a report on Thomas.

Looking at Thomas, Bones nodded.

—How scared are you now?

Thomas had to shut his eyes in order to be able to speak. —
Mister Atlas, I'm very very scared. The words came from under-
neath the end of the knife, shaking Thomas's lips as he spoke
them. He hadn't spoken them. Someone else, using his mouth,
his tongue, his language spoke the words. Someone Thomas
feared. His lips went death-grey.

—Scared in your bones?

—Yessir. Eyes closed.

—Scared in your heart?

—Yessir.

—Scared in your mind?

—Yessss..sir.

—How dark is your mind?

—Darkest.

—How deep?

—Deep.

—Deep, Mr. Thomas? Or endless? You think, now.

—Endless as my voice. My limbs. My name.

—What is your name?

—Thomas. Means nothing. Just a name. It comes and it goes.

—Who are you?

—Thomas.

—Who are you?

Thomas spread his arms open to either side of himself. His body displayed. Exposed.

—What's your name?

Thomas didn't move or speak.

Eyes closed, so he hadn't seen or heard Atlas come up beside him until he felt Atlas's shoe crash into the side of his head. He didn't black out. He went into another country where all was dark but alive, the middle of a forest where he wandered between thick trees falling against one then another. When he came back to the room, Bones's knife was open very close to his opening eyes.

—Can I take out his eyes?

—Scared in your asshole?

—Yes.

Thomas felt a certain hormone, a specific juice within him released, as if from the center, in fact, of his asshole, something he'd held in since birth.

—Scared in the mucous in your nose?

—Yes. Scared to live and scared to die.

—Take out his eye. Just one.

Thomas's body gave up its final consciousness. He was first conscious again of his head amidst the trash on the floor, of the hard floor itself. The trash coldly putrid.

—See if you can open your eyes. See how many eyes you've got left.

Thomas's right eye opened, then his left eye.

—You are living, aren't you?

—Yes.

—I thought so. You disappointed Mr. Bones here. I hope he can get ready to forgive you. But you pleased me. You pleased Atlas. You answered to the gods.

—Atlas.

—See how different you sound already? You say it like it doesn't mean a thing. That way it means me. It means me.

There was no way to tell what time Mr. Warp came back. Time itself had warped and curved. The light from the seams of the plywood at the windows was that of just after dawn. A crust had formed at the tip of Thomas's ear. When Mr. Warp opened the door Thomas heard Mary's voice as though Mr. Warp brought it with him. Why hadn't Thomas yielded to the desire in his lips to kiss Mary, take her mouth to his mouth, and her whole spirit with it? Mr. Warp's words, which followed the sound of Mary's words.

—Good, boys. Everybody OK? It's almost time to move now. Wait for me. Don't move even if it's a long time. I'll be back with something for you.

—Shit, Mr. Bones smiled out of his sleep. —You ransomed that kid didn't you? You're slick, Warp.

—Why do you think I call me Warp, Bones? You think it's because I'm warped, don't you? More warped than you?

—That's it, Jack. More warped, more twisted, more cool.

—Don't call me Jack. That's not my name.

—Missstah Warp.

—Well, you're wrong. I call myself Warp because I'm the only thing's straight. You don't get that do you? He turned to Thomas. —Mr. Thomas, rise up. Your business is over and your time has come.

—Time for what?

—Oooh. You found some questions running around here while I was gone. That's not so bad. Now rise up.

Thomas thought he'd heard that last word — if not the whole phrase — before. The intonation of it reminded him of Reverend Hooper's voice, or even more, a voice he'd heard as a child, his own Priest's voice back in Cincinnati, Reverend Kearny. It was a tone he'd come to think of as merely officious. Now it had its originally intended, deeply steady spiritual effect.

A Buick LeSabre, midnight blue and metal, heavy, ran and hummed, dented, damaged, but pure in its engine. — This is Mistuh Mistuh, and it is 5:43 in the a.m. in Manhattan-BrooklynBronxandtheQueenoftheQueens Nooyoak right now. So right now I'm play for you.... Mr. Warp switched it off. The street dead quiet. John; Thomas thought. If they were going to kill him they wouldn't care if he saw the street where they were, right? Right, John? Mary?

Mr. Warp pressed on the gas lightly, pulled the shift lever so the car meshed into gear. They rolled on to the corner and saw the street sign: 137th Street. He wasn't a martyr. Then he said, —I'm no martyr. I'm just a stupid kid.

—That's not quite right, Mr. Mr. Thomas. You were dumb, but you weren't ever stupid. I told you that. That's the thing we share, you and I. We aren't stupid. When you're dumb about something you can learn. When you're stupid you're stuck with it. And you're no kid. So you're not stupid and you're no kid. You wait. You'll see.

A gold engraved sign on the dashboard read BUICK LE SA-
BRE MIDNIGHT BLUE : MR WARP. Left hand on the wheel, right arm
slung across the seatback, Mr. Warp guided the power-steered
car onto Fifth Avenue with limousine grace. —Turn around,
Mr. Warp said, —I want you to meet my wife. In the back seat,
against the opposite door, a young woman nursed a newborn
baby. —Mr. Thomas, this is my wife. You can call her Mrs.
Warp, he chuckled. —Truth of it all is I'm just the shuttlecock.
She's the warp and he's the woof. Right baby?

—That's what everybody calls him, Mrs. Warp said, —they
all call him Mr. Warp. —Nice to meet you, Mr. Thomas. I hope
you don't mind me feeding my baby.

—You didn't ransom me and you aren't going to kill me,
Thomas said.

—Ahhhhh. Mr. Warp sang out loud. —You found some answers tonight didn't you? And if you forget them you can always
remember when you look at that ear. Mr. Warp swept his forefinger across Thomas's cut lobe. A knife is a sleeve. All night
Thomas had traded the desire to live against the notion of death
until the confusion of hyperbole had grown into a subspinal
system holding him up, nerving him. He'd felt sorry for his parents, his grandparents his two sisters. He'd felt unbearable grief
for Mary. He'd felt rage at John. That all dissolved now in the
salt of the one desire to live and to go on living forever.

Warp had gone left on 110th Street, passed the spot where
they had picked up Thomas earlier, drove south through Central Park, then came out again at 96th Street as though they'd
been on a brief ride through the country.

—I've got fifty dollars, Thomas said. —I'll give you forty-five.
That leaves me enough to get home. Let me go here. All right?

—Mr. Bones already got your fifty dollars, Mr. Warp said,
—way back when we jumped you from the bushes. Don't worry
about no fifty dollars. Don't worry about no let me live. Don't
think about no ransom. Enjoy the ride, boy. This here's Man-

hattan in the morning. Greatest city on earth. You know that? He smiled over at Thomas. —Look, Warp slowed and pulled to the east side of the street, —there's *The Jewish Museum*. You got one of them in London? Paris? Huh? How about Buenos Aires? What have you got in Moscow? Warsaw? Think about it Thomas. This is some damn city huh? Some damn weird country.

Warp rolled down the front windows. —Smell that air, he said. —It's got a little bit of everybody ever lived here in it. See if that helps you to figure this city out.

They cruised all the way down the still empty Fifth Avenue, the park on their right, to 59th Street, then the hotels, stores, the stone cathedral great by proportion, the collected wealth of several ages, the inevitable new wealth asserting itself slowly into this landscape. They turned east on 42nd street then drove through the United Nations. A driveway, up past the African-American Institute, down to 42nd street again, past the Public Library where Warp pointed out the stone lions and talked about the history of the building. They drove through Times Square which Warp called the other United Nations, down 9th Avenue, the Fourth World. It didn't dawn on Thomas until they were already in the Holland Tunnel, while Mr. Warp was saying that above them somewhere out there stood the Statue of Liberty, but that that wasn't nothing, what was important was that also above them somewhere sat old Ellis Island, the real, true, grubby Statue of Liberty where Mr. Warp's people had somehow forgot to stop and check in.

—You're taking me to Washington, Thomas said.

—Baby, how would you like to go see your cousin in Baltimore tonight? Warp said.

—Washington doesn't need me to go to it anymore, Thomas said.

—That's just why I'm going to take you. Warp drove on, finding Route 80, the car cruising with the comfort it had been built for. In Pennsylvania, Warp pulled over to pick up two young hitchhikers with a sign that read 'March on Washington For Freedom and Peace,—Looks like some of your boys, Warp said, changing his mind, passing by the hitchhikers. —Everybody wants to march on that poor town like it was burning up again and they just want to put out the fire. I'll be eating up in Baltimore, but you boys will be marching down in Washington. I don't get it.

Mrs. Warp covered her breast, waking the baby, who cried for a minute as she rocked it into sleep again.

Thomas walked through a crowd of southern Colored farmers and rural folks with their children running around, all busy serving themselves lunch from long tables set up in the main basement social hall of the Church of The Body of Christ, Washington, D.C. Although it was certainly 1963 it could have been 1863, or 1865 perhaps. The men, smelling of fields Thomas could hardly imagine, all wore farm overalls and flat shoes. One group sang, clapping hands, off in a corner, quietly. Children ran about everywhere. As the swinging door of the kitchen fell closed behind him Big John stood in an apron, his hands in a tub of hot water, a pile of dirty pots on one counter, a few clean ones on the other. John hadn't heard the doors swing or Thomas enter.

—You betrayed me.

John turned, holding his rubber-begloved soapy hands away from himself. He watched Thomas for a minute. Then he said, —No, Thomas. You lied to me. Was it a certain sorrow in John's eyes now, was it John who felt helpless?

—So you're mad at me, Thomas asked, —for lying to you?

—I've been washing these pots, John said, —thinking about you. I told my mother and my uncle you could be dead for all I know. And you could have been.

—Perhaps I was.

—What? You're not lying now, you're mad.

—Do you know what we're doing here, John?

—That's what Mary asked me on the phone.

—What did you tell her?

—I told her to ask you if she ever saw you again.

—What did she say?

—She said that if she ever saw you again she wouldn't have to ask you. What's going on, Thomas? What was she talking about?

John, the church basement, the yellow rubber gloves, the doorway in which Thomas the Thomas now stood — all self-evident, never inevitable, each moment spiraled within each object. Behind Thomas, through the closed swinging wooden doors of the church kitchen the crowd of marchers and protestors-to-be-Black-and/or-White ate chicken with mashed potatoes and green peas. In their low song voices they sang, with their dayandnight hands they clapped rhythms in tune to the time which in their bodies they beat, they prepared themselves for the spontaneous effort to make some serious mark on the accidental flow of history.

Three

Born

I was born born was I without illusion, somehow. Oh I fall. into hopes. I did. I would be even for a time persuaded of them I needed to be. But I didn't, I didn't need those hopes. They were false, they were unnecessary. I was fine. Wasn't I? Only an I was necessary. And. It. Was. It was. But what did I know? I was? I knew. Did he? That one thing.

Was Lieutenant Colonel then. I'd made Lieutenant Colonel. Come a long way, son. With them now of them. Flesh blood and brains. Just as, so, ah, hell? Didn't want even her. Didn't want nobody to. Present for the new man. All the stories. Patton. Alexander. Last one. Last time. He was six. He was six.

I always knew he would. Some day. Even though it was obvious to anyone else that he wouldn't, still it was something I kept in mind, believed in more than hoped for, never able to give up on: that someday he would. When it would happen, when he would, all would be well, all would be at last and finally well. Worlds would open. Bodies of worlds. In this instant, less than an instant, powder flash of a millisecond's awareness, I see: he won't. Look at the world, then. Take it in. a long eyedrink of our world.

This lawn a vividly green. Watered. Tended, each blade, by hand, were. I did. Once. We were in Virginia. He was Lieutenant Colonel then. The steps in his career cooked into the family food. The very first time, I was terrified, poor thing. Momma'd said, —honey, you are the conduit for God's babies He'll give you as your trust. The boys be his and you've got your girls. And trust me, you'll need those girls you keep them close to you. You don't know him, honey. You'll see. You just don't. He is his own army.

He wasn't born yet. If he knew what freedom meant if he'd had to fight for it just once if he knew the price of it he doesn't. How can it be? Your son. The enemy within he'd said. I told him, son, the enemy within you now is me. Face your enemy. Join him, or defeat him. Then I told him, son, the only enemy within you is yourself. Find him. Know him. Then join him, or defeat him. You choose. Your freedom. To choose, I told him. You can. Defeat him. But you have to choose. I chose. I won.

Mother. is she awake? Is on the stairs now? Where? The sixth stair down? That's where the pattern didn't fold properly from the baseboard onto the next stair. She tried to get them to fix it. It's a blood-red rosette and the flower doesn't fold properly down so that the petal emerges onto the sixth stair as it should, descending from the seventh. Do you know what I thought about that, Mother? I thought, You/me really are a nut.

How can I love you so much?

His, I just hated him, no, I adored him and then I wanted to hate him. So much mixture of admiration in it, strong tincture of it, memory, whiff. To be him. So too much harder than to be just myself. So much easier to be anyone than to so to be myself. Living dying. I was able to be him and he was just himself who is that? Isn't that right, Mother? He doesn't deserve this. I didn't do it against him against his well-pressed uniforms. His dress uniform for ceremony. His fatigues for the soldiers. His combat boots stained with the muds of. Then, cleaned. Mother, I too long for the brotherhood. Just because I am doesn't mean I don't. I do. No. Not true I despise the brotherhood of it. I'm not for revenge on anyone. I didn't do it. It came to me in my blood it's that simple even I didn't know how simple my self-loathing. that's how people are the grass would be wet if I took my shoes off. his shoes filling with blood.

I think of myself thinking or of his shoes filling with blood. Then I think of his shoes. The heavy highly polished black shoes filling as with my blood because it was supposed to be mine. I lied, Mother. I don't just adore him, from a distance, I love him. I wish that I didn't but I do, and now I'll have to hold him up. Will you blame me I wonder? You might. Will I fall apart? How much guilt I feel, allowing myself to feel it or denying that I feel it. This is my body, mi cuerpo, Father. Sergeant. Master-Sargeant. Captain. Major. Lieutenant Colonel. Colonel. Sir, yes, too, I too yes am awed. A small boy from Makom California until you gained it. The history of those few great men. The same rosettes on the rug in the hallway. Maybe she crosses them now. Where we stood, Father, you and I, we stood there.

He, who never knew Joseph Stalin. Never saw Khrushchev bang that table with his shoe. Like a hick. Took off his shoe. Oh, Communism. He never saw America hurt, that's why. I saw my country bleed. Where is pride in him? What have I failed to do while doing so much. Go ahead, son, laugh at God & Country. Until you lose both of them and someone comes to crush you. We, he said, we are the enemy within ourselves. I am not the enemy within myself. They are the problem, I am the solution. I am Freedom. To? Be a man. Raise my son. You are God & Country son or you are no one. You are for God & Country or you are for nothing and whoever is for nothing is lost. I have seen it, son. The lost. They wander in a purgatory of their own making who cannot belong who will belong nowhere.

He told me: Communism it's the delusion the lie of power the perversion of power the warped mind of power. Democracy is truth, son, is true power. The only truth under God. It is God. The Argentine solution. He'd been there. To save Democracy for the Free World, he'd said. It wasn't the only time. Sometimes I thought, after the war, they'd made him into a specialist in Fascism, as though that were the job the United States assigned him: specialist in the Implementation of Anti-Communist Anti-Fascism fascism. What gurgles up within him that others simply cannot be who we are. Anti-Col. Witherspoon Specialist.

Like in Argentina, I told him, Democracy is truth and sometimes Democracy it's a hard truth. A pain-filled. To preserve Democracy, in Latin America, to create it, elsewhere, in Africa, in Arabia, that makes America safe, it makes him safe. He doesn't see the knife at his throat. How can I make him? Yell at him: TOMMY! Wake up, Tommy. You're asleep at the wheel. Your car's headed straight for that tree that will not be moved.

Tommy.

I was coming from the kitchen. We'd been talking. She'd giv-
en me a glass of her hand-squeezed lemonade. We talked for a
while. I was going up to my room to study to read history.

Then: —Thomas. He stopped me.

I stopped. The rosettes, red. There.

Two things I learned I tried to teach him: Honor, and Freedom. Without Honor, I told him, your Freedom is a slavery. Without Freedom, I told him, your Honor will never be your own. I hadn't read that anywhere. Not one of these books in this library or any other library in the world has that in it. It's the one true and original saying of Col. Robert Witherspoon. I invented it for myself back then when I was nobody when my Father was nobody when we were all nobody. I invented it one day sitting at that rickety desk at that rickety school to become the somebody I have now become. The somebody I would give to him, to Thomas, to Tommy, as his Mother likes to call him. Tommy. Tommy Tommy. —Without Honor, your Freedom is a slavery; without Freedom, your honor will never be your own. - Col. Robert Witherspoon.

I always knew he would. Some day. Even though it was obvious to anyone else that he wouldn't, still it was something I kept in my mind, believed in more than hoped for, never able to give up on: that someday he would. When it would happen, when he would, all would be finally it would finally be well. I'd go on. He is my dream. In this instant, less than an instant, powder flash of a millisecond's awareness, I see: he has, had long ago. Worlds do open we flounder in chaos ----- our complaint become flowers.

Do you think I like to watch men die, Thomas, my men? Do you think I like to hold their shattered bodies in my arms and take their last words home for them and never tell their family how they looked at that last moment? That's what it takes to defend Honor and Freedom son. Doing it teaches you to defend Honor and Freedom. I do it for your Honor your Freedom. Choose them. Just choose them over all else, even over your own desires. For they are your deepest desire, son, Honor and Freedom are your deepest desire. Find them. By Duty you will earn them. You didn't have to be a soldier, son. I told you that. I saved you from your Granddaddy's ignominy. From the ignominy of the dirt I was born of. I did that for you before you were born I did that, fighting in Afghanistan. Then I did it in Asia. Then I did it again and again. Where the hell are you now, son? Son. Where are you in some homosexual bar downtown? I know those places. I know every seedy rat-infested den of anti-American sewage from Juarez to Tierra del Fuego. It's my job to know. They scour those places looking for malcontents, Thomas. Have you already signed up with them? Against us? I brought you up right, boy. Right, to be strong. It's you I was always defending. It would be your America I would hand off to you.

—Yes, sir.

—Thomas, I have in my hand a letter—unsigned—from an alleged classmate of yours at the University. I will hand this letter to you. You are to read it. The only comment you are to make is to tell me whether these allegations against you in this letter are true, or whether they are false, and all lies. I have enemies. You are to say nothing more to me, son. Am I clear? Truth, or lies.

Hunting down those phrases. —Nothing to do with you, sir —No one's fault —Just a goddamn faggot —A goddamn Commie faggot —Not a crime —No taint on you, sir —You've been a good Father, sir —You don't even love yourself. For that millisecond of it self-anger surges as he had failed in courage, as life had caught up with him to do to him what he had intended to do himself, if only he'd acted. No time for remorse. I've held Miguel in ways you've never ever held Mother. Tearful and Tender. Held myself. Hold myself.

You don't love yourself, son. All love of God, all love of Country begins with love of self. That's what we gave you, your Mother and I, that was ours to give you, what we started you out in life with. Yes I remember your first heartbeat, and into that heartbeat I breathed love of self for you, because no one had done that for me. And if I, given no love of self to begin life on, could find his right way to God & Country and Duty, but mine own son, given love of self, can find his way only to a perversion of God's will, then dearly do I seek guidance for I am become blind and I linger in a nightmare of Chaos.

He raised his hand against his son's remark, but it didn't strike. Tommy might have looked at his Father, into his Father's clouded blue eyes, touched him, put his hand on his Father's shoulder, saying something, apologizing, —I didn't mean that, saying something comforting, warm. But it wasn't that way in this war now. Tommy either fought or lost forever. The risk of either silence or tenderness too steep, Tommy speaks.

—These are not allegations, not accusations, Father; there is no crime. If you're asking me am I a homosexual as this letter claims, I will tell you. I am a homosexual; I have always been a homosexual; I will continue to be a homosexual. I am not ashamed to be a homos....

—Thomas!

Tommy did look up. His Father's eyes blue yet ashen. A very light blue. His Father's face, toughened with age and exposure and desire to become toughened, but softened by a thousand secreted encounters with himself. He is not an ounce of homosexual I am all of it. Tommy avoided the acquiescent defeat that he would find in the glare of those light blue eyes.

Did his Father see the color in Thomas's eyes they way Thomas looked finally for the color in his Father's eyes. Did he see that Thomas's eyes were more distinct than his own. Did his Father see refusal in Tommy's eyes the way Tommy saw the nothings which ashened his Father's?

There would be time to reflect. To lie in a bed somewhere while a breeze blew across you. You could recall this when it might be absorbed.

She's a fine woman. Fine women have weakness in them as she has for Thomas. I could have never known about him. Was it something I did to make him that way? I never guessed at it but I know now that she did not even guess she knew because she doesn't miss a thing. The way she laid out this house. Not a thing missed. This room here, everything done because she knows me and she knows my needs. Like she knows everyone. She knew all along. What will I say to her what will I do with her now. That rosette carpet she put down for the roses I brought her every day when we first. We came up through the ranks together. I brought her with me up through the ranks. I would blaze the ignominy of her Father out of history, I told her. I would give her pride, which is the purchase of Honor and Freedom. And I've given her that. Pride.

Yes, sir.

Go into the study, Thomas. I've left something for you there, on the reading table. It's a gift. As you know me, you will understand that this gift abides by the way of life I have chosen for all of us. I have demanded of all of us. You will know how to use it. Perhaps there is no blame involved. You will truly be my son.

Thomas could not find his Father's eyes all the while his Father had spoken. When his Father stepped aside, there stood before Thomas only the two cherrywood doors into the study, easy to slide on their runners, with hand-carved scrolls.

When you go in, the Colonol said, slide the doors behind you. You will want to be alone.

Thomas's hand shook trying to find the wood of the right-hand door to slide it closed. His hands, his legs, his stomach, even his brain were surely incorporeal and of another world, yet he needed them to act in this corporeal and in this physical realm. With the door sliding closed, the room darkened, absent the light from the hall, light coming only through the draperied French doors leading to the garden. It was only noon, or just past noon. The clock in her kitchen.

Mother beginning to nap. Just after noon.

Will power is a corporeal thing, Thomas thought, so the thought would be a thing to hold on to. The Beretta was corporeal. Thomas's body corporeal now, Thomas's brain was. While Tommy became an idea. Against the blond wood table, the gun sat flat black.

Was the Open Book meant for Tommy? Only one Book left here now for Thomas, in his Father's library: the Book of Beretta.

When he first touched another man. He, who had more strength stronger than his Father. His Father who was Beretta. He would lie on the couch. He would lie on the floor. If he could lift the gun he would open the curtains to lie down on the floor by the French doors to the blue sky. He would shoot. Annihilate shame. Love honors; freedom plays; duty honors thy Father. I longed for the brotherhood. I long for the sonhood that now is of Beretta. I honor my duty I love my freedom I play with those things which for my Father preserve uphold protect and safeguard Democracy. Freefalling. I.

Virginia hadn't quite fallen asleep but remembered as if it were a dream, though it had been real, the day she'd said to her husband: It was my fate to marry you. It will be my fate to be undone by you.

What do you mean? he'd said. I'll make you into something. I'll make it to Colonel. People will respect you. I'll make you proud to walk the streets of any city in the United States of America. You'll know that we own this country that we bought our part in it with sweat and blood and duty and honor.

Virginia's Mother's words to Virginia: Robert is a man who will make you know that you own this country, that you will serve it in a way that will make you feel like you own it. I dreamt of that feeling, Virginia's Mother told Virginia, but you will have it. As she drifted into sleep, wanting sleep, Virginia heard her husband, then her Mother. She had wanted to tell her Mother that her Father wasn't weak, hadn't been a coward; but it wasn't so. If he'd been strong he wouldn't have been killed that way, leaving nothing. If he'd really served.

If she'd had the strength she would have called the dog that lay at the foot of the bed to come to her. Scot, she would have whispered, and the dog would have leapt up to her not for comfort, but for protection, hers, or his own, sensing a danger in the house that was beyond his power to attack. Though Virginia, already half asleep, formed the dog's name with her lips, her voice wouldn't vocalize it. She heard the dog's name like she heard her Mother's words, her husband's words. The very first that she dreamt was of her son, Tommy. He was near a window, his face bathed in sunlight.

What you've done, Thomas, you've done to yourself. It's no fault of my own. Maybe your Mother. I don't know. Strong Mother, weak Father, they say. Not this family. I gave you everything you needed, son. Son? All day the light changes. You can tell the time of day you smell it in the air. All night you don't know. The quality of darkness is constant.

You are defending a country that exists first and only in your mind.

Good. Let darkness fill that window. Let darkness fill everything I see. Let darkness be a quiet. I have enemies, Thomas. Now they'll come after me. His own son, they'll say. They'll use you against me. The Communists use everything. They use everybody. They have no grace and no mercy and no justice. But you, Thomas, I gave you grace and I gave you mercy and I gave you justice. You never knew to use them. I gave you influence and inroads. What you could have been! What you could have done! This is America, Thomas. A man can rise. Against darkness. Against chaos, I, too, am America.

Thomas lays his open palm over Beretta. This plain grey carpet it never occurred to me that the carpet in the study was different from the other carpet. Why hadn't Mother asked me about carpeting for the study? But Beretta was Beretta, a gun a gun, solid, also corporeal, on the table, here in the library: a Book of Beretta.

Library from Libro from Liber from Liberation.

Beretta comes from Beretta. Father, I.... Father. I fought this war against you many times and many times time and again I lost. I lost myself in my awe of you. In my love of you. In my desire to become you. In my fear of you. In my false indifference to you. In my rages against you. You, who spoke so often to me of grace and mercy and justice. Of duty, freedom. I can only lose that battle because I can't leave the field; because I need you? because I need the battle? how to lose it in my own best way? I will not live a battle the rest of my life against me. Thomas.

These pictures in my head. You, Thomas, dancing in those dives. Some guy with his chest vulgar-bare. What you could have been! What you could have done! Your lips. His. Dear God, do not stain my mind trained to serve with these visions. I turn back to you, Rev. Quincy. I turn to Christ Jesus the way that you taught me. I promised to guard this Christian country of ours for all of us, Rev. Quincy. I told you I would. Dear Christ. If I have sinned, if this be punishment for my sin, tell me my sin that I may repent it before Thee. His hands on him. Dear Jesus. Redeem this your worshipper on his knees with his hands pressed toward you upwards through the darkness of his night. Lift me into light, Lord Jesus, into the light of Thy love. Raise me beyond the sins of the offspring of mine own loin. Is the sin of the son visited a thousandfold upon the father?

You are the bravest man alive, Robert Witherspoon. That is your calling dear Robert. Good Robert. You make life clear. But when it comes to the things that are beyond you, in that realm, turn to me, I will protect you. For those things you are not meant to understand, Robert Witherspoon, listen to me, I will guide you. That's why we are brought together into this couple that is my joy and my burden. I bear the heaviness of your duty for the sake of our faith, not just in God or Country, but in life. Only together can we see our way and make our way through this bountiful life. After all that you have given to Tommy, for Tommy, he is not your son. Leave Tommy to be my son. You have a myriad of sons in your command and you have loved them with a manly love and guided them and led them. You don't need to see it or know it, but in me we are one, in you we are one in Tommy also.

I'm defending you, dear. My son. Myself. Freedom. Look at us, sweetheart, we are America. Isn't that enough?

The war you're fighting was over so long ago and you lost, but it's all right. I lost also because through you I was trying to prove that my Father wasn't a failure. And he was. But no man who serves his country is a failure, no matter how he dies, coward or hero, no matter what he leaves behind, wealth or debt. He was no more and no less a man than you are.

That's wrong. It's wrong.

He served the same men you serve: arrogant rich men who pretend to be patrician, men you think God appointed to be rich and to control small men, like yourself, to make those small men believe they are as large as the rich man's wealth.

You're tired. You're not strong. Childbirth was too much for you. We won't have more children.

I am tired of this life. I wish I were a pauper some where, a simple woman with simple pleasures, a peasant in some backwater in Brazil.

You're prophetic, my dear. We'll be going to Latin America, but you'll be no pauper there, believe me. And I'll rise so quickly you will forget unhappiness. We belong in this life together, you and I. We belong in this war.

falling Father were it a unison Father & freedom no fascism
lost at the juncture where failing falling is a faintly a whisper
a howl freely & falsely & a furious fascism falls inwardly to
through is as into the doing to raise the demons of duty of the
panes in shattering visions failing nor choking in Chaos democracy is freedom to be who is and is not free fall fall falling freely
into lost loss nobody nowhere who are you he was seen he'd
asked it of me blank face asks blank face answers that day rage
oh rage until it's nothing as it free rage a raga of nihilism not
nothing before he was born fire rage cool heads prevail let cool
heads prevail into cool colors into cool coolness your face before
he was born cool you were not born anywhere else but into a
rage and a joyous body of teat-sucking a rage and 'til now oh
Colonol Father & in Witherspoon I'm who paradise in Chaos
hell is mine riven in a river of honor in soaring falling in & furious to love is an honor to serve the other what runs deep runs
calm a frightened laughter breaks in the cornfield get away from
me out! out! slaves to countries that live only in his mind in my
mind a slave to my body to flesh it to whose voices are these anyway am I yes I am I hear voices Father and they want to kill me
they prophesy war they falling out of the thickness discovered a
slackness in your Fatherheart not for me I drink my life in the
sunshines of histories what is human he asked me touches my
skin touches my sex into terror where there is the crossroads
of a soldier lays in his memory lies in the bosom of an Abraham
that is a Father again Father I am your Isaac I breathe in courage in fear I who do honor honor and I who disdain the prison
of power and I yield to the scales of justice one truth on one of
them another on the other I hope only to desire to yield here
to the wheat & to the corn on this earth to which you in your
power you brought me through the Grace of the womb of my
Mother think of her once in her communion with me inside of
her Communism is the phony dream of communion democracy
has become a license to steal you who have never stolen a shirt

off anyone's honor nor a bullet from anyone's name you Father please Father there is a noose on your neck Chaos can release it tightens it it even it moneys arrogant rich men pretending patrician pretending your freedom onerous falling of faintly country god give me wholeness beauty and the radiance of a beast give it to me now my demon lover while my Father is away to our salvation where he cannot see we are saved hallelujah Father whose voices are yours are these Father & that someday I swear it without honor or freedom or duty or justice or grace beyond fascism & communism & democracy I will save you far away will I save you neither with love nor with anger neither with only with the being we share I do Father I do love freedom I do in ways I will teach you when & whenever I find you within me or without me where you were born to ignominy I do not and only my laying in bed with a man of my reality will I see how without seeking it without finding and but driven by the force that burned you and you gave me you gave me you gave me you gave

To sit here in this chair to have sat in it reading and thinking and planning and to refuse sleep, to refuse it all this night. Sometimes, when I close my eyes, I see her Daddy run away, up that hill. I see that bullet like it was in slow motion come from that perfect Nazi soldier a perfect shot from his perfect German rifle spin its way uphill after the nape of his neck. I even — I confess — I see him as if running naked because of his shame because of the guilt of his cowardice. I told her there will be no more nakedness in this family. I told her the U.S. Army would rise me out of all poverty and would rise her out of all shame, the way her Father shamed himself in it. I sit here and I refuse succor. My eyes are open. I will not flee this ruin of my family and my name I will see how to turn this ruin into victory. We won that war.

Tommy lifts his hand from the gun. Before he moves he sees himself moving and then he is motion. After he crashed through the locked French doors to roll outside just lightly bleeding — from his arms which he'd raised to cover his eyes—after the afternoon breeze of Caribbean air hit the little opened wounds, he wondered how hard it would be to break through the wood between each window pane. Yet already he knew the answer he had answered himself.

His own legs had propelled him. Mother would be proud, would lean out her window he would turn and look up at the house to see her. Miguel and he would celebrate in hiding, laughing. He would love to hide from his Father, with Miguel, and he knew where and he knew how. He knew a great deal. Hiding is cowardice. Hiding is preservation.

I wrote that on my application essay to West Point. Honor, and Freedom. Without honor your freedom is a slavery. Without freedom, your honor will never be your own. He stared at the plaque photograph of his West Point Class, with that motto engraved on it. I gave them that motto. I live by it myself you've sold out honor, Thomas, one term of the Eternal Equation. I can't help you anymore where you are where you have gone to be.

Colonol Witherspoon walked to the broken glass French doors to watch dawn come. Is a man, left only with Honor and Freedom, enough?

Tommy's Mother looked out the window. The noise from the shot of Beretta's gunfire reached both her and Tommy at the selfsame instant, in which instant Virginia froze before running downstairs, so that Tommy, who ran instantly into the study, was the first.

Father. Sir, Thomas said. He led his Father, holding him up, to the red leather couch above which the bullet had gone into the wall. The Colonol allowed himself to be led.

You should have done it, Thomas, Col. Witherspoon said.

Neither could you, sir.

Look, Tommy's Mother said from the doorway, my husband and my son sitting on the couch together. What a fine sight for a woman to see. Thomas walked over to his Mother.

Oh, Mama, he said.

Don't worry about me. Even if I do nothing at all for the rest of my life but worry about you.

Thomas left the library, packed up his things, left that house. The Colonol remained in the library. He did not come out to say goodbye. He did not protest when Thomas drove off in one of the family's two cars. He spent that night alone in the library. In the morning, he came to breakfast. As he did every morning, he gave his schedule for the day. I will be back by supper, he said. We will have company for dinner. The Ambassador and his wife and their daughter. Thomas should be here to meet them. They are interesting people. We live among great people, Virginia.

I'm packing, Virginia replied.

Is that what all these people are doing here at this hour of the morning?

It will only take a few days. We'll be in California by the end of the week, Robert.

I would like to be in California. You think I've gone mad, don't you, dear?

–

I haven't gone mad. I'm in your care for the moment, yes. I understand that. But I haven't gone mad. I could go mad. But a man of my powers does not go mad. He lives with every limitation that God and life place upon him. He looks out on the truth with whatever eyes God has given him. I know that you love me.

Virginia smiled at him.

That is not a bitter smile, the Colonol said. That, he said, is the smile of Grace.

His words released her smile so that it blossomed full on her face.

And.... the Colonol added.

And Grace, she finished for him, is a quality co-eternal with Justice and Honor.

These are not empty words, the Colonol said.

Yes, dear, they are.

Then I'm empty.

Let's say this. Let's say they are empty, and they are all that I love in you. All that I have to love in you.

You are a mystery to me.

I, Virginia said, am a mystery to myself. Everything is a mystery to me but Tommy. Somehow, Tommy I understand.

I can't go on talking. I can't stand to talk. I will never talk again.

As you see fit, dear.

Tommy waits for Miguel, in the meantime tells his story to Roderigo, Gustavo, and Osvaldo, adding details to each telling. He keeps talking as each of the friends in turn get up to go for another round of beer, go to the bathroom, distract themselves talking to someone else, then come back to the booth with Tommy to re-enter his story at whatever point in its meandering urgent circularity. They are in the Café Rage. Roderigo, Gustavo, and Osvaldo offer reactions and good advice, proffer help, guidance, support. When Miguel arrives, Gustavo, rushing forward, tells Miguel that Tommy's in a bad way, on the upside-down, then leads Miguel to the booth.

Miguel stands; Gustavo sits.

I don't hate my Father, Tommy says.

I do, Miguel says.

Don't. Tommy, reaching out his hand, touches Miguel's arm.

You fucking Americans, Miguel raises that arm. You swallow up everything in your path. You parch this fucking earth.

Don't.

Sorry, Miguel says. I hate him; you don't. We can go on together. You stay with me. For a while at least. Miguel looks around the table at Roderigo, Gustavo, and Osvaldo.

I believe in freedom, of course I do, Miguel says. They've never brought us freedom. We've bought our own freedom.

You're like a trio, Thomas laughs, pointing one at a time to Roderigo, Gustavo, and Osvaldo. You're Freedom, Grace, and Honor.

Me? Miguel asks.

You? Thomas says. —You're Duty. The five of them, they all laugh together. The afternoon's drink taking effect, the laughter becoming more infectious raucous silly disorderly chaotic desperate and happy.

No one notices his Mother just as no one notices the Beretta in her right hand that falls at her side. Terror had passed through her only because over the years her body had learned to be a conduit for anything that came at her. Not even Roderigo Gustavo Osvaldo Miguel notice much until Thomas stops laughing. None of them make a move for his Mother or for the Beretta she places on the table in front of Thomas.

Had anyone, even God, told me I would have to choose, Tommy's Mother says, I would have said that I cannot live without him because I have no idea how to do that and that had I chosen you I would have taken this Beretta to my own self next. That he waited until you were surely gone is a sign of his great love for you, Tommy. His enormous courage in the face of what he could not finally face. And so, even though I cannot look at the him that I see in your face right now, I will never abandon you, Thomas, and when you give me time, I will look again. And I will say to him as they bury his body that I, his wife, have renamed you, his son, Freedom. And only Freedom. The Beretta is empty now. He wrote that he wanted you to have it, empty. It's his blessing on you for all that you are, for all that he was and was not. Come home when you want to. The house will be cleaned of blood, the French doors repaired, and it will look like a house again. Then, please, Thomas, explain this all to me. I cannot understand, my beautiful Tommy, the mind of men that is so strong and so weak and so terribly confused—and so fragile. So fragile.

Thomas rises to catch up with Mother.

Not yet, Miguel says. Give her some time. She asked for that.

Did you really hate him, Miguel? Please.

How could I not?

Insurance

Around

2:00 a.m., coming from the party at a Columbia University student's apartment on 112th Street, Thomas waited, alone, at the 116th Street subway station for the #1 or #2 IRT train, downtown. He would switch at 42nd Street for the downtown N, Q, R or W train to 8th Street, then walk three blocks back to his dorm. At 2:07:17, the #1 train pulled in. The clatter of its doors opening echoed off tile walls. Thomas stepped into an empty car. On the seat next to him, someone had forgotten or discarded a large brown envelope. As the train pulled out of 116th Street, Thomas opened it. Unable to discern anything from a glance the top page, Thomas took out the whole sheaf of pages.

...and so Thomas read:

SAMPSON, KIMBLE & WORTHY
Attorneys at Law
717 Figueora
Suite 2500
Los Angeles, CA 90017

November 24, 2016

Nettleton Insurance Company
47 Broad Street
515 Brattle Building
Omaha, Nebraska 09909

Attention:Mr. Ron Askworth

RE:Your File: 89562
Our File   8917762
Insured: National Meat Markets
D/L: 5/13/16

Dear Ron:

I am in receipt of yours of the 20th. Having done preliminaries I believe the following:

1. We should defend for the sake of your image (Nettleton cannot be easily sued) and because of obvious reduction possibilities. This guy's not worth that much. Not worth much at all.

2. Medical question (Zampao v. Great Chain, 17 Cal 455) arises as to rehab. Right hand single finger loss can be retrained to cut meat; triple finger loss can be retrained in other areas of same industry. NO THUMB LOSS THIS CASE.

3. I should depose:

1. Plaintiff;
2. two fellow employee witnesses;
3. supervisor;
4. expert medical;
5. expert technical

Please approve as per our standing agreement. I will proceed unless otherwise notified by 12/1/16.

Very truly yours,
Wm. H. White

WHW/em

104

SAMPSON, KIMBLE & WORTHY
Attorneys at Law
717 Figueora
Suite 2500
Los Angeles, CA 90017

December 8, 2016

Nettleton Insurance Company
47 Broad Street
515 Brattle Building
Omaha, Nebraska 09909

Attention:Mr. Ron Askworth

RE:Your File: 89562
Our File: 8917762
Insured: National Meat Markets
D/L: 5/13/16

Dear Ron:

I am in receipt of yours of the 6th. Depositions in January set for:

1. Plaintiff;
2. Jack Carlson, meatcutter at National;
3. Dr. Robert Shaw, Plaintiff's personal physician;
4. Dr. Stanley Moss, their expert technical.

I will advise, as usual, following each deposition.

Very truly yours,

Wm. H. White

WHW/em

P.S. Saw Frank and Herb last week. Played together in Long Beach. Frank top of form. Vivaldi. Gives the fingers a workout. Herb wants to try some Debussy. Told him, give me a year.

P.P.S. Merry Christmas, old boy, and my best to yours.

SAMPSON, KIMBLE & WORTHY
Attorneys at Law
717 Figueora
Suite 2500
Los Angeles, CA 90017

January 5, 2017

Nettleton Insurance Company
47 Broad Street
515 Brattle Building
Omaha, Nebraska 09909

Attention: Mr. Ron Askworth

RE:Your File: 89562
Our File: 8917762
Insured: National Meat Markets
D/L: 5/13/16

Dear Ron:

Deposed, this date, Plaintiff in above-captioned. Subsequent to denial of Plaintiff's request for deposition at his counsel's office, deposition held at our offices.

Plaintiff, Ronald Lemans, white, 42-year-old French male, appears clean, adequately dressed, working class. Will present credible. Speaks articulately, with French accent which may charm jury. However, he is not overly intelligent and can be confused. His testimony's credibility can be prejudiced. Emotionally stable, but easy to anger. Emotionally charged about loss of fingers, hence an area of vulnerability to consider — i.e., to jury, imply that his anger betrays guilt. It was at least partly, perhaps largely, his fault, etc.

Plaintiff married, two children, 17, 19. Little sympathy value. Wife (in attendance in waiting room) a bit roly-poly. Good appearance, but fortunately unattractive.

Plaintiff testified had not been drinking on evening prior to loss. Admits to social drinking, can be confused on this issue, perhaps angered. Plaintiff claims amicable married life. Plaintiff testified that on morning of loss appeared at work on time, performed functions as usual, no unusual conditions at plant, except high absentee rate.

Q: Did the high absentee rate cause you to go faster than usual?

A: Of course. Meat's gotta move.

Q: Did anyone tell you to cut faster? Your supervisor? Anyone.

A: Why should they have to?

Q: So you felt you had to work faster to get more work done?

A: Yes.

His own decision to speed up. Opposing counsel did not object.

Plaintiff testified to frequent machine malfunctions, reported to both supervisors and union.

Plaintiff's record at National is good. No arguments with superiors, colleagues. Plaintiff on this job six months. Prior employment: Safeway, one year; Richardson Meats, one year; Samson Bros., eight months, An unsteady record.

Evaluation of Testimony:

Believe this plaintiff drinks more than he will admit, and believe I can coerce this testimony from him. Believe he felt pressure to work faster to make up for absentees on day in question, particularly as he was trying to prove his worth to employer. He needs money. I can get that out of him after supervisor's deposition. It will not be hard to do by inference alone.

National Meat and Nettleton owe little if anything in this case. I'm convinced liability belongs with machine manufacturer and plaintiff, himself. The French drink wine like we drink water. Look at their GNP, it shows there. We saved them from the Nazis, now this one wants us to save him from his own sloppiness. If they want welfare, let them stay home.

This is not a difficult case. Plaintiff will have trouble proving because:

1. Unsteady work record;
2. drinking, which I will bring out;
3. competence as meat cutter, evidenced by job-jumping.

Regarding number three above, why has he changed jobs? Why, at 42, has he not become supervisor, opened his own shop, worked non-union, higher-wage jobs? These are the beginnings of admissible lines of questioning to establish incompetence. Let's see what his cronies think of him, as well.

<u>CONCLUSION</u>:

No negotiations: go to trial.

Very truly yours,

Wm. H. White

WHW/em

P.S. Roger home for school break. What a kid! Hot on the basketball court. What breaks! Girls love him, dates, friends. Bought him a Z for Christmas. You should hear it in the driveway. He drives like me.

P.P.S. Divorce final. I did damn well. Men can still hold sway in California. Told you.

SAMPSON, KIMBLE & WORTHY
Attorneys at Law
717 Figueora
Suite 2500
Los Angeles, CA 90017

January 12, 2017

Nettleton Insurance Company
47 Broad Street
515 Brattle Building
Omaha, Nebraska 09909

Attention: Mr. Ron Askworth

PERSONAL AND CONFIDENTIAL

Dear Ron:

Am in receipt of yours of the 8th. Thanks for congratulations and kind words. Your account helped this promotion, believe me, buddy.

I have one rule in this business: don't pay lawsuits. That's the only line. Spoke to Roger on phone today, told him to study like that, there's only one line, that's an A.

Working on Debussy. Don't like it. The guy was a nut, totally weird.

Thanks again.

Very truly yours,

Wm. H. White

WHW/em

SAMPSON, KIMBLE & WORTHY
Attorneys at Law
717 Figueora
Suite 2500
Los Angeles, CA 90017

January 19, 2017

Nettleton Insurance Company
47 Broad Street
515 Brattle Building
Omaha, Nebraska 09909

Attention:Mr. Ron Askworth

REYour File: 89562
Our File: 8917762
Insured: National Meat Markets
D/L: 5/13/16

Dear Ron:

Hold everything. Deposed Dr. Robert Shaw, Plaintiff's personal physician, this date, our offices, Los Angeles.

Dr. Shaw will make a better than average witness. He appears clean-cut, well-dressed, speaks very articulately. He is intelligent and sober.

Dr. Shaw testified that plaintiff has shown a heart murmur since 1979 which will shorten his life by 20-22 years. This caught Plaintiff by surprise, as it did me.

EVALUATION:

Prior to Dr. Shaw testimony, Plaintiff could have sought $1,897,400 damages. Subsequent to said testimony he might seek a maximum $600,900. Given the likelihood of his contributory negligence, which I suggest will be large, we could offer $200,000 and settle for $230,000 maximum.

This man has 11 years to live, actuarially. They'll never go to trial. Also saves us costly x-complaint on manufacturer.

Bravo! I keep a tally of money saved to clients and this will make a very nifty contribution to that statistic.

Very truly yours,

Wm. H. White
WHW/em

P.S. Susan is <u>appealing</u>! I relish the fight. She has a *stupid* lawyer.

P.P.S. I recommend joining. Play indoor tennis in winter or you are jelly by summer. Expect to beat you across the net this summer often. Be ready!

P.P.P.S. To answer your question, yes, I can get my hands to do the Debussy. Good God it's weird. Where's the melody?? We're playing it Sunday. Can train these hands of mine to play anything, you know that. It's not whether I <u>can</u> play it — never doubted that. I don't <u>like</u> it.

SAMPSON, KIMBLE & WORTHY
Attorneys at Law
717 Figueora
Suite 2500
Los Angeles, CA 90017

January 22, 2017

Nettleton Insurance Company
47 Broad Street
515 Brattle Building
Omaha, Nebraska 09909

Attention:Mr. Ron Askworth

REYour File: 89562
Our File: 8917762
Insured: National Meat Markets
D/L: 5/13/16

Dear Ron:

Hold everything! Got to the wife! She'll testify. Waive rights. Guy's got a kid back in the old country, in Marseille. Abandoned the old girl-friend and the kid but she's got him by the balls because she works for his brother. He sends her money via the brother. Fled when he got almost caught in heroin ring on the Marseille docks.

I'm on hold to his lawyer. Back to you right away. Permission to offer they drop all charges, we don't report him for extradition!

Very truly yours,

Wm. H. White

WHW/em

SAMPSON, KIMBLE & WORTHY
Attorneys at Law
717 Figueora
Suite 2500
Los Angeles, CA 90017

January 23, 2017

Nettleton Insurance Company
47 Broad Street
515 Brattle Building
Omaha, Nebraska 09909

Attention:Mr. Ron Askworth

REYour File: 89562
Our File: 8917762
Insured: National Meat Markets
D/L: 5/13/16

Dear Ron:

Gotcha! Frenchie's lawyer's an old buddy of mine. Tells me the guy's sad story. Poverty family in Marseille. Loses job in layoff on the docks. Gets in with the wrong guys. Cops breathing down his neck. He flees. Has to. Loves the girlfriend, the kid, but he's got no choice. Whole sob-story, soap opera.

I made him the offer, he jumped at it.

How does Sampson, Kimble, Worthy & White sound?

Very truly yours,

Wm. H. White

WHW/em

P.S. No, Roger will not play basketball for them. I told him to stick to a white man's sport. He's going for tennis this spring.

SAMPSON, KIMBLE & WORTHY
Attorneys at Law
717 Figueora
Suite 2500
Los Angeles, CA 90017

February 19, 2017

Nettleton Insurance Company
47 Broad Street
515 Brattle Building
Omaha, Nebraska 09909

Attention: Mr. Ron Askworth
PERSONAL AND HIGHLY CONFIDENTIAL
EYES ONLY

Dear Ron:

Have received this date most gruesome thing. In the mail, in a box, second and ring fingers of adult male.

ANALYSIS:

Surely this is the grotesque joke of that disgruntled French meat-cutter from last month. Heard his wife threw him out. No wonder she did.

CONCLUSION:

I have destroyed same. Nettleton does not want publicity, I'm sure. It can only happen once, so I recommend no suit, no police, no criminal charges. One for the books, just between me and you.

Very truly yours,

WHW

P.S. Where did that jerk get those things? Off the floor of his shop?

P.P.S. Susan told me she wrote to you. Called absolutely hysteri-cal. What is wrong with women? Expect her letter, expect her to be crazy. She's not the same Susan we knew.

SAMPSON, KIMBLE & WORTHY
Attorneys at Law
717 Figueora
Suite 2500
Los Angeles, CA 90017

February 26, 2017

Nettleton Insurance Company
47 Broad Street
515 Brattle Building
Omaha, Nebraska 09909

Attention: Mr. Ron Askworth

PERSONAL AND HIGHLY CONFIDENTIAL
 EYES ONLY
REGISTERED MAIL

Dear Ron:

Sorry about that last letter. It was a nightmare. See? A dream. But it seemed so damn real. I woke up and I was in the damn dream and I wrote you that letter. How can you wake up inside your own dream? These guys are after me. I beat them and now they're after me. Don't worry about me. I'm fine. Anyway, Ron, I was just kidding about it, old buddy. Drink up. Forget it.

All best,

W

SAMPSON, KIMBLE & WORTHY
Attorneys at Law
717 Figueora
Suite 2500
Los Angeles, CA 90017

March 5, 2017

Nettleton Insurance Company
47 Broad Street
515 Brattle Building
Omaha, Nebraska 09909

Attention: Mr. Ron Askworth

PERSONAL AND HIGHLY CONFIDENTIAL
 EYES ONLY
REGISTERED MAIL

Dear Ron:

Received this date little finger, adult male.

ANALYSIS:

This meat cutter is crazy! He cut off his own remaining finger! He has now only a thumb. I told you this was a no thumb loss case. It is now a thumb only case! Where does the world get these madmen?

CONCLUSION:

He wants money, Ron. Quite clear. If we go in the open, he hopes for sympathy, a trial, money. No way. Let him cut off his thumb if he wants. No way. Hold firm.

No publicity. Nettleton is clean.

Very truly yours,

Wm. H. White

WHW/

P.S. Yes, Susan has gone nuts. Maybe I should send her these goddamn fingers.

P.P.S. Yes, Debussy coming along. Still hate it. Was he crazy?

SAMPSON, KIMBLE & WORTHY
Attorneys at Law
717 Figueora
Suite 2500
Los Angeles, CA 90017

March 12, 2017

Nettleton Insurance Company
47 Broad Street
515 Brattle Building
Omaha, Nebraska 09909

Attention: Mr. Ron Askworth

PERSONAL & HIGHLY CONFIDENTIAL
EYES ONLY
REGISTERED MAIL

Dear Ron:

Am in receipt of yours, undated. Thanks for the suggestion, but Roger is just going to have to sit here and take it like a man. It'll be a lesson to him. Believe me, he could use a few. I got the same advice from a psychiatrist here as you got, but I don't believe those birds any more than I believe goddamn gypsies. I'll be fine. I am fine, Ron. The kid'll be fine. He's going back to school. Business as usual. She'd love us to fall apart now, wouldn't she?

And let's not forget <u>she</u> divorced <u>me</u>. Susan's suicide is on her own hands, and you and I both know that.

I love you like a brother, too, Ron, but I'm not hallucinating. I can take more stress than you can. Thanks for your concern, but it's not necessary.

We're doing a full run through on the Debussy in a week. You see, pal, life does go on and because some people won't, others can't stop. Right?

I never told you out of simple respect for Susan's privacy, but after we got married, she showed incredible weaknesses. She was <u>so</u> high spirited in school. Remember? Well, there were days when she just lay in bed. I hired a maid to take care of the house. Paid a lot of money. That's not the beginning. I put up with it. You just go on. That's it. There's one bottom line I always say and that is that you better go on.

I'm at work and you know how busy that is these days, so I can't write more. But I'm fine. I'll just make sure Roger doesn't falter here. He's got a hell of a future, I'll tell you.

Very truly yours,

Wm. H. White

WHW/

SAMPSON, KIMBLE & WORTHY
Attorneys at Law
717 Figueora
Suite 2500
Los Angeles, CA 90017

April 9, 2017

Nettleton Insurance Company
47 Broad Street
515 Brattle Building
Omaha, Nebraska 09909

Attention: Mr. Ron Askworth

PERSONAL & HIGHLY CONFIDENTIAL
EYES ONLY
REGISTERED MAIL, RETURN RECEIPT REQUESTED

Dear Ron:

Am in receipt, this date, of his ring finger, <u>left</u> <u>hand</u>.

Same procedure, no discussion.

Very truly yours

Wm. H. White

WHW/em

P.S. I can't play this damn Debussy any more. Have you heard it ever? It's a trio from 18-something-or-other. My damn fingers won't move. Stupid piece, but Herb insists. He just loves it. The guy's nuts. Herb is. Any suggestions for playing it? Give it a listen.

SAMPSON, KIMBLE & WORTHY
Attorneys at Law
717 Figueora
Suite 2500
Los Angeles, CA 90017

April 23, 2017

Nettleton Insurance Company
47 Broad Street
515 Brattle Building
Omaha, Nebraska 09909

Attention: Mr. Ron Askworth

PERSONAL & HIGHLY CONFIDENTIAL
EYES ONLY
REGISTERED MAIL, RETURN RECEIPT REQUESTED

Dear Ron:

Am in receipt, this date, of the second finger, left hand, of adult male.

ANALYSIS:

This sonofabitch has gone mad. Who the hell does he think he is? Thinks he can scare us, spook me. No way, Ron, no goddamn way.

This is criminal matter. Must be another person's hand. Whose? Murder? What? Jesus Christ!

CONCLUSION:

If we blow we lose. I keep fingers as material evidence. It is criminal only to harbor the man, withhold evidence. No arrest, no crime on our part. Trust me. That's what you pay me for. Nettleton could have thousands of these jerks sending them parts of bodies if we let loose now.

Very truly yours,

Wm. H. White

WHW/em

P.S. Personally this makes me sick, Ron. You should see these fingers. He must send them frozen, so the P. O. doesn't smell them. By the
time I get them...I'm telling you, it's not pretty. But neither is life. Not
pretty.

SAMPSON, KIMBLE & WORTHY
Attorneys at Law
717 Figueora
Suite 2500
Los Angeles, CA 90017

May 14, 2017
Nettleton Insurance Company
47 Broad Street
515 Brattle Building
Omaha, Nebraska 09909

PERSONAL & HIGHLY CONFIDENTIAL
REGISTERED MAIL, RETURN RECEIPT REQUESTED

Dear Ron:

I'm typing this myself, but I'm a good typist as you will remember from college.

I received in the mail this date one <u>female</u> thumb, right hand. Goddamn this asshole when's he gonna quit? No one here knows any of this. I can't tell them. I can only tell you.

He's trying to get to me, but he won't. I swear that thumb looks like Susan's but of course that's crazy. Just because it's a woman's it does, you know, red nail polish. It's sickening. He did freeze it, cause the blood begins to flow a little when it gets here. It's on the desk now, and it trickles just a little. Bizarre.

I quit the goddamn Debussy. I hate effete music. The whole point of music is its beauty. Its drama. Or its goddamn power.

I'm staying at the office a lot. It's easier. On the couch. You know, quicker. I'm at work by 7:00 after a run at the Athletic, breakfast there. So don't call me at home, I'll probably be here. Call my private line here.

When are you coming?

Very truly yours,

Wm. H. White
WHW/

SAMPSON, KIMBLE & WORTHY
Attorneys at Law
717 Figueora
Suite 2500
Los Angeles, CA 90017

June 4, 2017

Nettleton Insurance Company
47 Broad Street
515 Brattle Building
Omaha, Nebraska 09909

Attention: Mr. Ron Askworth

PERSONAL & HIGHLY CONFIDENTIAL
EYES ONLY
REGISTERED MAIL, RETURN RECEIPT REQUESTED

Dear Ron,

Am in receipt of yours of 27th. Thanks, buddy, but I don't need help. That's not why I said that. Thought you'd like some sunshine, that's all. Sunny Southern California.

Listen, Ron, I got a woman's finger in the mail today. What should I do? I think it's time to expose this asshole. Maybe we shouldn't have postponed it. I didn't think he'd go this far. He's a sore loser — you know I hate that. I'd like to get him bad now. Put him away. What do you think?

If you're in New York, check up on Roger. He hasn't called, I can't get him in his room. Of course, he's probably called at home, and I'm never there, that's all. So many cases to work on. I've got the best insurance case record in the entire city's history. Insurance Board wants me to talk on Tuesday. Wish you could be there, see your old pal.

I talked Herb into some Strauss. Good old boy he is.

Very truly,

Wm. H. White
WHW/

SAMPSON, KIMBLE & WORTHY
Attorneys at Law
717 Figueora
Suite 2500
Los Angeles, CA 90017

June 18, 2017
Nettleton Insurance Company
47 Broad Street
515 Brattle Building
Omaha, Nebraska 09909

Attention: Mr. Ron Askworth

PERSONAL & HIGHLY CONFIDENTIAL
EYES ONLY
REGISTERED MAIL, RETURN RECEIPT REQUESTED

Dear Ron:

    Receipt, this date, one <u>female</u> left hand ring finger. Susan's wedding ring! Fuck him! Fucking madman. I'll get him. I'm William White!

Very truly yours,

Wm. H. White

WHW/

SAMPSON, KIMBLE & WORTHY
Attorneys at Law
717 Figueora
Suite 2500
Los Angeles, CA 90017

June 25, 2017

Nettleton Insurance Company
47 Broad Street
515 Brattle Building
Omaha, Nebraska 09909

Attention: Mr. Ron Askworth

PERSONAL & CONFIDENTIAL

Dear Ron,

Herb may call you. He's worried about me, he says. Bullshit. I couldn't play the Strauss. Fingers wouldn't move. No more time for music. Time to grow up, we're almost 50. These are our power work years.

Fuck Herb. Hear?

Very truly yours,

Wm. H. White

WHW/

SAMPSON, KIMBLE & WORTHY
Attorneys at Law
717 Figueora
Suite 2500
Los Angeles, CA 90017

July 9, 2017

Nettleton Insurance Company
47 Broad Street
515 Brattle Building
Omaha, Nebraska 09909

Attention: Mr. Ron Askworth

PERSONAL & CONFIDENTIAL

Dear Ron:

 Yours of the 3th. I told you to fuck Herb. I do not need help, I do not need a vacation. You think it's those fingers, don't you? To hell with that. Sometimes business is war. War is gruesome. Right? Buckle up, buddy. You haven't even seen the fingers, yet. Want me to send you a few?

Very truly yours,

Wm. H. White

WHW/

SAMPSON, KIMBLE & WORTHY
Attorneys at Law
717 Figueora
Suite 2500
Los Angeles, CA 90017

July 16, 2017

Nettleton Insurance Company
47 Broad Street
515 Brattle Building
Omaha, Nebraska 09909

Attention: Mr. Ron Askworth

PERSONAL & HIGHLY CONFIDENTIAL
EYES ONLY

Dear Mr. Askworth,

It is my displeasure to have to correspond with you in this fashion. Sampson, Kimble & Worthy will continue to fulfill Nettleton's defense needs as assiduously in the future as we have in the past. I have advised you, this date, under separate cover, of the names of attorneys assigned to your open cases.

Per your request, I give you the following for your personal information only. This letter is not to your file.

This morning the first attorney in the office, Mr. Greg Kimble, discovered Mr. White in the following circumstances. Upon his desk were ten small boxes, each addressed to a different recipient in a different city. Your name was on one such box. Upon the desk also was a small cutting board and a meat cleaver.

Mr. White was apparently about to cut off at least some of his own fingers.

Mr. White is in stable condition at Our Lady of Vanishing Grace

Hospital, Los Angeles.

Any light you may shed on this terrible and, I'm afraid, even grotesque, event will help the police. I am afraid our firm will undergo severe unpleasant publicity. However, any information you might provide us in the nature of your personal relationship with Mr. White will not implicate Nettleton.

We suspect the untimely, unseemly nature of Mrs. White's death this year may have led to this tragedy. We all know Mr. White to be a dedicated member of our team, loyal and hardworking. His wife's death must have jarred him disastrously. Despite their divorce, I am aware of his love and continuing devotion to her and to their son.

Asking for your cooperation, and assuring confidentiality, I remain,

Very truly yours,

Robert Kimble

RK:mk

Nettleton Insurance
47 broad street
515 Brattle Building
Omaha Nebraska 09909

from the desk of Ron Askworth

July 21, 2017
Robert Kimble, Esq.
Sampson, Kimble & Worthy
717 Figueora
Suite 2500
Los Angeles, CA 90017

Dear Mr. Kimble,

Receipt yours 7/2. Agree re not to file. Accord this letter same. This correspondence remains unrecorded.

Sorry, I know nothing to help. Have not heard from Bill in other than professional or casual personal matters for some time. Believe we played tennis last summer, played music on his trip Omaha in August.

Can't help on the wife. Knew her in college. That was long ago.

I leave business correspondence to business letters, as do not want to compromise this strictly personal matter.

Very truly yours,

Ron Askworth

RC/

Ron,

Last night Jesus kissed me on the forehead. It was no dream. I was in my office. On the couch. He opened my office door. It woke me up. I was awake, Ron. He wore that white robe we always saw in those pictures. We shouldn't have made fun of it like we did. You remember. He walked ever so slowly to the couch. Not afraid I. Waiting just watching. Him. In the dark of the night of my office. He bent down. He kissed me on the forehead. He left. I sat up. I sat for hours. Now it's 5:17. I'll go to the Athletic. Until you know that life's a brutal, awful test, Ron, He won't come save anyone grace them and kiss their forehead.

JAZZ

He

wore a speckled grey-white silk suit as though it were draped on but didn't touch him. It was the way he ate, as well.

The bartender, a young man who cared little about jazz, but who was busy working his way into New York, brought the diner at the bar on a white plate on which lay two ribs thick with meat covered in a red sauce. Three paintings by a famous Indian painter hung on the wall behind the bar—payment for someone's unlimited drinks. Somehow, partly by keeping himself at a distance from the plate, partly by holding the fork and knife practically without touching them, partly in the way he wore his suit—or let it drape around him—he managed to eat these beef ribs as though they hadn't really existed. He ate without appetite or hunger, eating a rite to be performed of an evening, as late as possible so as not to interfere, and done well, with good food.

He cut the meat without pressure. He held the fork with a certain delicacy. He half sat on the barstool, half stood. Thomas watched him, without being noticed. But out of anxious habit, Thomas would glance down quickly at his own tenor saxophone at his feet, then look back at the diner. This elegant brother, also from Harlem? Thomas, inelegant, now made lonely anew, with his talent turned from playing to seeing, from blowing to listening. The man breathed without air as he saw without eyes. When he finished his meal, he spoke with words that had been waiting in the wings, and, the appropriate time come, he called them onto the arranged stage of a social interaction.

- It's all taken care of?

- Of course, the bartender said. Mr. Cross said it was all taken care of.

Having wiped his fingers on the cloth napkin which he let lie on the bar next to the plate, the man slid his right hand, loose at the wrist, between his shirt and the silk jacket of his suit, barely touching jacket nor shirt, and withdrew a thin leather billfold. The wallet opened not with a flick but with a mere unadorned turn of the wrist. He took a ten dollar bill, folded it in two, laid it in front of the plate with a nod to the bartender—who had gone down the bar already—and left. He disdained the money as much as the food. His disdain for the material world was exquisite and complete. It was a form of power a man like Thomas would never know. Had Thomas been more powerful, less vulnerable, might he have kept her?

Thomas settled against the bar. With the distraction of the gentleman gone, Thomas concentrated on the music. He had come to hear, not to eat nor to drink nor to pass an anxious hour or two. He'd left the jam session early up in Harlem, riding the A train downtown to the village. Horace Silver. Silver keys. On which Mr. Horace Silver wove a complex composition of all the instrument's elements into harmony and discord, impossible to disentangle one from the other. Horace committing himself so that each note was clear, perfectly articulated, in tune with every other note, in order to establish the world of musical order, an order abandoned and lost that the musician created out of love for the non-existent fabric of time. Thomas needed to hear that. It lifted and carried him. But he himself would never be on fire again, never enlightened or enflamed again. He listened until all hours, afraid to let go of the music, until he could walk to the subway, or just walk around, holding closely to himself the last opportunity for night and sleep at the very edge of the beginnings of a clean, rising dawn. Turning up 7th Avenue, the tone of the music an undertone to the tone of the City: expectant, the buildings all hit with the light of dawn. And then, the very City he had just given himself to, this fulsome and indestructible Metropolis he might name Jazz, the image of Horace Silver working at the transformation of his piano inside the articulate skill of his horn players, beside his subtle drummer, the bottom of it dropping away so that it all sank or dissolved or disappeared.

Had his fertile imagination now abandoned him, the way that Margo had, abandoned him, abandoned himself? Was the only thing left him now the image of the man in the grey/white speckled silk suit, eating meticulously, elegantly, beautifully outside of the beast of this world, eating itself not a process of the beast. Or the elegant diner and the bright light of Horace Silver as images remaining.

Thomas walked with a quickening fear. My God, he said on this empty 7th Avenue, what kind of verdant soul have I given myself to believe in?

The Liberator

Investigators trying to determine who broke into the tomb of Juan Péron and sawed off his hands have arrested six people in recent days, only to see five of them cleared by a judge.

New York Times, September 6, 1987

When

I went with them I never thought it would be like this. They told me we'd ransom them to the crazy Péronistas for millions and even though I was young I'd get a hefty cut. I believed them. I was poor. Hell, I was nearly starving and they probably knew they could take advantage. Bastards! They didn't tell me about this part. All they said was that the Péronistas were stupid. Anyone stupid enough to follow that thief Péron and his madonna/queen/high priestess/goddess-of-sin would be stupid enough to pay the ransom. Hell, they said. Argentina is full of Péronistas. That's all we ever had: Péron. I'm not a fool. I know what it means to dig up a body from its grave. I know the consequences. The ghost can torment you, give you nightmares and day visions, but I was young and strong and I could ignore that crap. I needed the money. And I wasn't selfish either. I thought of Mama, Papa, of Juan Luis. They told me I'd get a big share since I was doing the hard work, the digging, breaking open that amazing coffin made of African hardwoods so dense you thought it was stone, then lifting out the body of Juan Péron with its unbelievable stench of putrid gas and rot, then cutting off the hands and putting everything back. Cutting? Did I say cutting? I put each hand up on a stump I'd brought. I knew it wouldn't be easy, even with the time he'd been dead. Bone doesn't dissolve quick. I know that. And I slammed that axe into each wrist accurately. I made a clean cut in a rotting corpse. Not easy. They didn't hire some buffoon. Or maybe they did. Where's my money? Where's theirs? They haven't got not one stupid peso. What've they got? A bucket of ice with a pair of dead hands lying on top like two dead fish, one palm up, the other palm down. Every now and then when you look you imagine they want each other, two hands very close but can't touch as if each one were in an adjoining cell, or came from families of different classes who weren't allowed to see each other.

So they gaze. They talk in a secret language. And each day they change the ice, careful not to damage the goods. It started at night. I guess I could expect that. But why didn't they just come in a dream choking me, slapping at me, with a gun even? Why did they have to come stroking my forehead my head my face so I began to weep like a little child begging forgiveness. I never felt anything like that, circles of tenderness. Péron has soft hands and he can be so gentle with them. He has been gentle with me each time. Always. Not asking for anything, but giving me. I didn't wake in a sweat screaming as if in a nightmare. No, I woke up and lay on my back trying to recall that sweetest caress. There are no rings on the fingers. If there had been, they're gone now. Nothing stands between my anguish and Péron's forgiveness. He understands why I did it. Forgive me, but Jesucristo had not such gentleness in the flesh of his fingers, in the gaze of his suffering eyes as Péron has in these dead hands. They're grey, but not ghoulish. They're dead, but they're not repulsive to me. One day they'd sent me out for food. I'm tied to them now and can't get away til I get my money. What money? Do I still believe that? His hand came, taking hold of mine. It was a narrow street, no one there. It walked with me like a girl at first, his fingers between my fingers. Soft. I felt light and I wasn't alone and I wasn't angry, even at them. What did I care about them anymore? I walked easily like there was more room to walk in, more air to breathe, plenty of air even though it stank like the air there in that neighborhood always does. Who cared about stench? You could breathe. How does he know what I need, Péron? He was a bastard. You think I'm one of those Péronistas? Péron the God? Never. They're all crooks, I know that. I'm one of the people starving in this city. I'm stuck with a bunch of thieves.

One night I woke up with a lonely hard-on. You think I'm going to say something dirty about Péron's hands now? No. His hand came, it was his right hand, and it soothed me. It didn't get me aroused or wild with some hopeless passion. Even Péron's hands are not a woman. He soothed me, calmed my fires till my stiffness relaxed and my desire calmed and I was all right. I lay in that darkness, then I went and sat in the street for a minute in the middle of the night. It was very peaceful under a dark sky, the streets were completely silent, the stones cold, everything felt still, even my brain which is usually on fire, even there I felt still. I went inside to look at the hands but that gangster Gregorio never really sleeps. Waking up, he pulled a knife on me. I could kiss those hands, believe me. I'll tell you why they didn't tell me it would be like this. I'm the only one in the hideout who knows. Me and the one boss, the top guy they left here in charge. The bosses never told these thugs whose hands these were. About the ranson, about nothing. They didn't have to tell me. I could see it was Péron's body. They don't see it. They think they've got some hands, that's all. They could be the hands of that guy Roberto who died last week. Bunch of really dumb thugs.

Nothing special. They have no idea. Sometimes when I see the hands they look to me like they're in pain, yearning for their body again. I can feel their urge to slip off the ice and re-turn. If they can come to me why can't they return to him? Is there any reason?

Who was Péron? What happened after he died that his hands have become like the hands of a saint. You'd think maybe he's guilty, but his hands—you could tell if you felt guilt in them. I don't. Why not? What's he learned in his death, that's what I want to know. One night I did wake up—this was last week— and I thought those hands were coming after me for vengeance. But Péron proved himself. Those vengeful hands I saw were creatures of my own frightened mind. Péron's true hands came and took those two demonic brothers from my dream ready to pounce on me and dissolved them into dust. Then he caressed my brow again. My cheeks where they were sore with fear.

He ran his fingers lightly over my eyes. Then that strangest dream happened and that was it. I followed those hands down a street. It was cold out. I moved fast behind them. They sailed in front of me down where my knees are. They didn't have to beckon or convince me because now I'd do anything. I followed them out to the cemetery. My heart was beating like crazy when we passed the gate. It was over. He wanted his due. Why not? I had desecrated his body. You think I don't know words like that? Desecrate? Sure I do. I know a lot of things. You think I don't know who Péron was, how he stole from my country to build his fortunes? Sure. He stole from me to dangle furs over the white shoulders of that loser actress. It was cold in that cemetery. He'd murdered, tortured, probably cut off men's balls, but those hands gave me something I never had, ever. When I got to the grave the hands started clapping. Can you believe it? Like a bunch of gauchos at a campfire, clapping in a great rhythm. Duh ta-ta-ta ta-ta-ta, over and over. I danced right on his grave. I sang that same rhythm, Duh, ta-ta-ta ta-ta-ta. I never danced in my life. I threw my arms over my head and waved them in the air. The sky spun. I sang and he clapped. We had become some wild pair of maniacs, Péron's hands and me. I kicked up dirt still loose from the digging. Where were the guards they were supposed to have put here? Out fucking some whores on the money they made that's for sure. All I saw was the moon, mid-day. The sky ice-blue. The world thinking about freezing up. Another hungry winter in B.A. for me. What the hell were these hands doing? I was laughing so hard tears came down. What a crazy world where you cut off someone's hands and they caress you, they cool your fires, they make you dance on the grave of your dictator who stole everything while his people starved, clapping in the cold air while you feel the first joy you ever felt in your miserable life, the first time you felt some wild freedom. This isn't the Perón we knew. Are these his hands? He's learned something there, in that death, that's for sure. The other day I was walking down the street fast because I'd just stolen an apple and I knew one of his hands took me by the arm like an old friend. We walked on like that for a while like we were two rich gentlemen types who had known each other long and were having a quiet talk about our families or business or something. I don't know where this is going. You think I care? These hands...I'm telling you. If only they knew. I'm sick of this, watching Roderigo and Gregorio and listening to these fools talk about spending their millions and lying on that hard pallet each night listening to the boss stick it to that low-class whore of his. I'm on my own.

Let them dream of their money. I won't turn them in, but I might do something for my poor country. At least something for myself. And anyway who cares what happens now to a starving peasant? I'm the man who liberated the hands of Juan Perón from their death. Even from their life. Even if no one ever knows it, I'm that man.

Cool

——Cool, he'd been gone all day that

day. When finally Cal ran into Cool, Cool was lying under a tree by the creek. As Cal came up on him, Cool took off downriver running more like a deer than the hound he was, leaping logs, turning into the woods, back to the river. Then, jumping into that lazy, nearly inert, muddy thing, Cool swam hard upstream while Cal hollered at him I mean screamed out for him like if he hollered loud enough the whole Jefferson Davis Parish would hear and they would all drop what they were doing and turn out like a herd of posses to find Cool.

—Cal's voice penetrated the woods. Then it died into the heavy foliage, fell into the riverwater and was mute. Cal stood there in the silence. Not a breeze crossed his face.

—You know, Hot was Cool's Daddy. Now, if Cal would have gone back to the house and got Hot, Hot would've run Cool down and brung him home. Oh, Cal had done that before. But it had been a couple of years at least since Cal had used Hot that way. Cool had cooled. He should have, he was about three and a half years old now, when all this happened. Born in March. Funny how dogs don't have a rut like cows do, like a deer. A season. They're like us. No. Nobody's like us, we do it day and night. All day long.

—Breaking into that hot summer silence that surrounded him right then, Cal hollered again downstream: 'Cool!'

—How'd Cool got out? Had to be something in Cool's head to take him off like that. Did maybe Hot get too hard on him, too rough? Did some fool kids poke at Cool through the fence? I don't think so. If they had've poked at Cool, Cool'd've scared them so's their pants dropped — they couldn't run fast enough away from there. Something in Cool's brain, though. Something in his heart.

—Maybe the heat even got to him. Jesus hell this heat now'll kill me before I know it. Same kind of day today as it was then. Just a year ago. Last year, July twenty-eight, two days short of a year exact from today. Fall dead right into the river from this heat, right here under the bridge. Then that bridge'll fall on me, sure to. I won't cross it myself anymore. Look here, the trees themselves are sweating. These tall weeds over there are. The grass is.

—I know everything about this whole thing because I heard Cal when he was yelling out for Cool. Then, later, I made Cal tell me every little detail of the whole day. Something there is about Cool. Something unique something quite beautiful that gave everybody, well me, it gave me a joy to be around Cool. Play with him.

—Cal went back to his truck, drove down the highway, turned onto Sawcreek. Right there he caught a glimpse of Cool as Cool ran back into the woods by the trail. Quick, Cal turned, spun out back to the highway, hauled down the road to the other end of the trail at Hanson's. Now Cal was laughing. Now he had that silly dog. He liked Cool better than he liked Hot even, and Cal loved Hot. Maybe we all did. Like Cool better. Cool was funnier, had more guts, more charm, more play about him. You could look into Cool's eyes and just about know what he was thinking. Then, if you were right about what he'd been thinking, he'd turn away like to make you chase him, like maybe you'd seen too much, seen what even he didn't like to think about. But he'd shown it to you. He'd wanted you to see.

—Like the time Billy was born. Year and a half now. Everybody was in the house, people coming in by in cars and trucks. Hell, Mama Savoie was long a grandma already and here she's having little Billy boy. No wonder—her age. They all thought it was a miracle so everybody come to see the baby, yes, but to see the miracle, maybe even to see some angel like that angel in the Bible who came to Sarah but then Mama Savoie was only 52 and Abraham himself was, what? A hundred and ten? So Sarah must've been ninety at least. People believe in awfully funny things but why shouldn't they after all?

—So after little Billy was born and everybody could see he was OK and Mama Savoie was OK and everything had settled down, Cal had gone out to give some water to the dogs, Hot and Cool. Those two stately Pharoh Hounds in the light spring air. Hot pranced about looking for a treat, but Cal had forgotten to bring anything. Cool was just about crazy. He stuck to Cal's feet like tar from the minute Cal walked in the gate. Stuck and licked and cowed. And when Cal stood, while Hot drank his water, he saw it in Cool's eyes. Cool-sad. He'd seen it before. But just now young Cool was so Cool-sad was because everyone was inside fawning over that baby, that miracle, and Cool couldn't be in there with them to see it happen. Cool wasn't jealous of that baby. Oh no, Cool's something else. I'm telling you.

—It wasn't that Cool wanted the attention for himself. He wasn't like that. That miracle, that baby born healthy and strong to that 52-year old woman and she too was healthy and fine and strong and everybody feeling it was all so grand and Cool had to be just a dog in a dogpen when he understood so perfectly well all about what was going on. 'Look,' I told him, 'it's like if you wanted to be there when God created heaven and earth in six days because it was all so grand but you couldn't be there because you are just a human person but even though you're human still you want to feel you want to understand the glory of it. See? Now there's Cool. See? That's just what Cool is. He wants to be in there like a human being feeling all the glory of the situation, of God, as it were.

—'I see,' he told me.

—So I went on.

—'Oh Cool,' Cal had said, giving Cool a good scratching up and down his back. Cool wasn't hardly mollified, and he didn't drink. He lay down by his house. There were two separate houses, one for each dog. Cal always took good care.

—'So you see what I mean about Cool,' I said. He nodded like, 'yes,' he understood.

—So now to go back to where we were to that day just a year ago when Cool'd run away & Cal was in his truck headed for Hansen's cause he knew Cool would come out of the woods there. So now Cal was laughing as he sped out the highway because he knew he'd catch Cool unexpected by the end of the trail. Turning up the dirt road, Cal drove down about a quarter mile, parked, jumped out of the truck. Knowing he'd beat Cool, he ran 50 yards to the trailend. Just as he got there he almost bumped right into Cool running out. Cal threw his arms around Cool. But Cool kept running just slipped right out of Cal's arms like they were greased. 'Cool!' Cal called.

—Cool, running still, shot a look back at Cal. Cal yelled out down the dirt road: 'Cool! What is in your heart today?'

—Cool stopped, turned. Cal saw for an instant that he had Cool's attention, that he became, for much less than a second, Cool's master again. He yelled the one word he knew might work: 'HOLD!' Cool stood and Cal had him if he just moved towards him talking steadily, 'Stop, Cool. Hold. Stay, Cool. Cool stay. Stay.' Then Cal added his own favorite phrase: 'Be cool.'

—When Cal got up to Cool the laugh he expected to share with Cool at Cool's expense was not to be had. Cal patted Cool up behind the ears, scratched him there, then Cool shook himself out. Putting Cool back in the run wasn't so easy. Cool came hard, pulling back against Cal. When Cool got back into the pen, Hot came over to lick Cool like Cal hadn't ever quite seen Hot do before. Hot licked Cool's head, his eyes. Cool loped around the pen. When Cal petted Cool hard on the ribs before turning to get Cool's food, Cool stiffened up against Cal like Cool wouldn't have let God touch him.

—'What is it, Cool?' Cal backed away a step, muttering as

he turned, 'What's got into that dog?'

—Cal put out feed, then rose up from the feed bowls, lifting his back against the damp air as sweat fell in drops from his forehead onto the ground, turned as he rose to go out the door into the house to get a treat for poor Cool. Cal took two steps, still raising his body, kind of spiraling it upright as he strode out, and saw, turning his head over his right shoulder, the specter of a large beast coming up from the ground to his neck, right to his jugular which was now covered by his turned-out cheek and jaw. Cool hit, Cal thought at first with his paw, grabbed Cal with his clawed paw and pulled at Cal's cheek. Cal was smart enough to keep going right out the gate pulling it behind him in one motion and then when he was on the path toward the house when he saw the blood dripping onto the ground so that he looked down and saw his white T-shirt stained with a little blood he realized he'd been bit. The heat drained him. His feet came out from under him so he stumbled.

—Right then up the walk here come all three of the kids home from swimming, Jesus! just now with Cool like that, dangerous. Cal couldn't yell to them. Tried to call —Mama but just barely graveled it out of his throat but what good would that do anyway. Damn flies to the wound. *Why me!?* he thought but then he knew. *'Who else but me?'* Cal turned just then.

—Cool ran across the pen, hit the top of his own doghouse and out over the fence. Crossed the yard with that yelping. The kids didn't know. Hurried into the house. 'Mama!' Cal called her. She by the front letting the kids in. The kids safe? 'Mama.'

—Cal, he was leaning up against the sink now to hold himself up, he grabbed a rag to tie it around his neck as Mama came in. 'Cal!' she let out a little yelp, her hand up to her mouth. I'm telling you just the way Cal told it to me because I wasn't there and I'm glad I wasn't there though I should've been there to help Cal, wish I had been.

—'Tie it,' Cal told Mama Savoie, and she did.

—Mama insisted they drive to the hospital, even while she kept asking what happened. She couldn't imagine what would tear Cal like that. A tree limb? Hit with it? Somebody did it? 'Tie it,' he told her, and she did.

—Cal came out the back door, the blood staunched. The shotgun behind his back so Cool wouldn't see it. *Tasted human,* then Cal's thinking. *Oh Cool,* he's thinking. *You soul. Delicate. No, not delicate. The opposite of delicate but not brute the opposite of brute fine or refined but not weak the opposite of weak exposed but not helpless the opposite of helpless independent but not cut off connected interwoven entwined interlaced. The only beast can't be a beast that it is. That sees a moment of glory that drives him insane. But you know what, Cool, I'm a human and I see the glory of God but just a few shadows of it now and again or just a few lights of it flash in those shadows don't even see those shadows but every once in a while. And I don't go insane, Cool. I don't. Beast you. I gonna commend you. Got to. Have to you know that. I understood but you understood. Cool. Moping down there by water like it was Babylon. What's the matter with you, dog? You're just a dog beast.* Was it tears even into his blood? No. Just blood. His jaw hanging. He just began to feel it. *Cute even. Look at it. Like the day after the day Cool was born. Cool Cool. Hot Cool.* Cool in the pen playing with his Poppa. *Playing like a damn puppy. Batting around. Up on their hinds. Rolling. Sweet like. I'm gonna. Think of those kids.* The 12-gauge behind him.

—Now Cool knew where Cal was. Cal knew Cool knew and Cool kept playing with his Daddy, but then Cool jerked away from Hot. Cool ran around the pen then ran across just like before, leapt onto the doghouse again then over the fence for the second time. Cool turned to run down into the woods behind the barn, down that hill. Cal didn't follow — knew he didn't have to. Cool was in Cal's heart now like whatever it was had been in Cool's heart. Cal wasn't controlling Cool, but a kind of being with Cool in Cool as Cool as Cool ran in the woods, ran in circles right up to the barn then ran down through the woods again then back up that hill and if you didn't know what was happening you'd think Cool was being real cool, was having fun, was running like he was excited to see you, like he was all wound up with happiness.

—When Cool came back out of the woods he came straight toward Cal in the yard by the circle. Ran up the hill now like a serious dog no more frolic.

—*Why, Cool?* Cal's thinking now. He wants Cool to tell him. Cal doesn't move the shotgun. Sweat on the hard trigger. *Beast of my. Something into him. Babylon. Ran. attacking. straight on.* When Cal pulls the shotgun from behind and lays it up against his shoulder so he can see just right, get Cool just where Cool has to be got, Cool stops.

—Cool's tongue curls out over his teeth, his body fills with breath, his trim ribs pumping. His eyes up at Cal, and one look in them. No saliva on Cool's tongue it all burned off in the heat. No sweat even. Cool as if dry in this wet damp limpid sluggish day. As Cool's head comes up to look at Cal, Cool's front legs go down. *Crossed that line. Crossed it.* His front legs down, Cool knelt.

—Then Cool's head followed so Cool gives his bony shoulders to Cal, and Cal quite did what he had to do. Hot, staring at them from the pen, tongue out and panting in that heat. Mama standing on the porch watching.

—In the morning a man from the State came to examine the dog. He wanted to open the belly, take out the liver and look at what was there, look into the brain.

—'I bet you don't find a thing,' Cal tells him.

—I spent the whole night that night with Cal. He never slept, neither did I. I spent the whole day with him the next day, too. Everybody was all very upset by it all, shaken.

—Cal said to me more than once that night and the next day, 'You and I know I did what I had to do. But why?

—I told him, 'Cal, I think you know why every bit as much as I do.'

—He told me, 'I guess. I'm not saying that you being a doctor means you're supposed to know anything more than I do.'

—'No,' I told him. 'Just because I'm a doctor,' I said, 'doesn't mean I know any more about it than you do.' That's how I told it to that fellow, Thomas, if you want to know. And I guess you do want to know, because you asked me to tell it to you just the way I told it to Thomas. And I have. 'So, now, Thomas,' I said to that fellow, 'you know all about how it happened with Cool. Satisfied?'

—He nodded his head as if to say, 'ok. Satisfied.'

—'Then let's get a drink,' I told Thomas. And we did. We went and got a drink, and he told me all about himself, and you know what we did? Me and Thomas, we drank to Cool. Then to Cal.

—And when I told it to Thomas that day I met him when he was passing through we sat here on this bench under this birch tree and by this bridge just the way you and me we're sitting here now, you and I. But even if another stranger passing through, like that fellow Thomas was, and he'd heard somewhere down the line about the story about the dog named Cool, and he asked me to tell him about it, I would. Or, if someone else like you, who was away when it happened but who knew Cal but were gone out of town for a while—you were gone for a good long while almost three years wasn't it?— if someone else like you were to come back home after a long absence like you did and had heard about Cal & Cool but didn't know the details of what happened, I'd tell them the whole story, just like I told it to that Thomas guy, just like I told it to you just now. Hell, even if you yourself asked me to tell it all over again from the beginning, I'd tell you again. Hell, if that Thomas fellow came right back through town and asked me to tell it all over again to him I would. Maybe it's just me, something about me, but

I can't ever get enough of telling that story I'll die here telling that story. Something about it but I love telling that about Cool. And Cal. Does me good. And I have to tell it, because Cal won't talk about it. And there's no better place I love to sit than right here by the slow river by the useless bridge right here among all these willows and these oaks and the squirrels and the birds and whatall til the stars come out but there comes a time in the afternoon so let's go get us a drink. I could use a drink and you look like you need a drink. Heavy kinda story, about Cool and all. Needs a little lightening up. C'mon. You're OK.

The Utterance Of Names

Bodi

less. Dark? Yes, it emanates dark, though the street he had come in from had been also dark. Which street was that? Walking, he'd turned left, then left again. And finally, left once more. Into what kind of dominion had he wandered? It isn't the darkness so much that stuns him. Is it the dark chaos? Disorder? That it is old, worn, tattered? Isn't there a vulgar grace in the wood splintering from the rounded edge of the bar, and, behind it, a sort of a stage? What darkness this, red-tinged? And what grace in the smell, sharp, acrid, urine-scented, of something so repugnant as to seep into the fiber of the wooden floor from which it nonetheless seeps back out, permeating not only the air but the name of the place he'd seen on a sign outside just as he entered but what had that been?

On the stage a woman, big, hardly dressed, grinds out the movements that, even so defiantly formed, could cohere into the lure of what we might call an erotic dance. Below this dancer-of-sorts, behind the bar, another woman, similarly undressed, wanders back and forth across wooden pallets, peering into the reddish darkness to discern once in a while if anyone needs a drink, or if any of the girls needs water or actual liquor.

So it isn't the darkness that gets to him, nor the tawdriness of the place, nor the odor, nor even the performance of contempt—sexual contempt? self-contempt? life contempt?— of the woman dancing. Snow outside. Two hours wait. A gnawing restlessness? a rawness? Frightening and promising desire? is it erroneous? is it authentic? is it misplaced? A certain hunger traveling from behind catching him now.

He shuffles through the indoor darkness guided by the footlights on stage. The bartender more senses than sees him. He takes in her mélange of sweet perfumes, the gait of her legs, her thin belly exposed beneath smallish breasts displayed in a halter top. She wears white short shorts and high high heels. It is the dead of winter in what we know of as the city of Boston. Hard, his heart beats. He orders beer.

His hand shakes in taking out money. It shakes also in raising the mug to his lips.

On stage the performer dances; gravity, pulling her down into inner secrets eventually will win. Contempt cannot save her. Blue lights bouncing off the mirror behind the stage highlight the hot run of sweat with heavy make-up together forming little rivulets.

A woman on the stool next to him has edged her way in before he'd seen her coming. She has her hand on his crotch before he can blink. He moves his hand over onto her bare leg, one crossed over the other. Her skin, fresh in this dim steamy place brings memory to the surface of his hand.

—Buy me a drink?

The ugliness of her teased-up hair, her lips, her rounded brown eyes are all lovely now, so close. He could sit here just so for hours, looking straight ahead into the hell of a nowhere, caressing the inside of her leg warmers, her hand so slightly on his sex. Lightly, drawing her hand from his erection, she rubs his inner thigh then comes back to rest her hand directly on him.

—OK. Yes. Of course.

—Take it in the back room?

—How much?

—For what?

He leans over not to whisper, but to taste her ear, for hunger has raised a terrible anxiety in him. Or is it anxiety has raised a terrible hunger in him.

—For everything. For all that you've got.

—For all I've got? Two hundred dollars, sweetheart, plus the drinks.

The jukebox music stopped. No other customers sat at the bar. Sunday night. Mid-January's bitterest. How will he sleep on the long stuffy Greyhound ride home ahead? Dreaming against a cold window of loss, of a void he cannot cross but only reach out into, of rest, of hope.

—How much for a blow job? He pulls his face from the side of hers to look again, but closer. —Eighty bucks?

—Sorry sweetheart.

Another record comes on. James Brown. Another woman hovers over the jukebox in the back. The woman draws back away from him, sits upright on her stool, sips from the glass the bartender had set down in front of her. Leaving it three-quarters full on the bar, she smiles a twisted mouth at him, half warm, half cold. —Let me send you a girl, she says, —Maybe you can talk to her. Make her an offer. She slides away, disengaging looks, hands, bodies all at once.

He draws in one breath. What does he want? Nothing short of everything? He can go wait in the yellow light of the bus station. Or a few drinks and some titillation? To relieve what? Something larger than he might imagine? Something as small as a quick two hours between buses? The same woman dances on stage. Clear the night outside. Biting cold the air. The moon, gibbous, all there for the watching. Swift sharp night, able to cut and cleanse. Or unable to do anything. How meager beside what the prostitute had offered of herself. A heat flushes through his body, inexorably kindled anonymous desire composed of lust and shame.

The one who came next gives a name: He knows that name, just as she flings herself into his lap as he flings back his head as she chases it with her mouth into his ear: —Buy me a drink. I know. Just buy it for me buy it for me.

The bartender sets down her drink, neat and stiff: scotch. She holds it between herself and him, sips it loudly, sinks into his lap. She throws her head back. A wildness splits her eyes from left to right of each eye so they cannot not stay still to see. The wildness pounds trembling in her body as he holds it; it pulls her toward him as he pushes her away to have a look at her. He wants the flesh, madness, griminess, the running scar of her mania gone nearly beserk.

—I dreamed about you last night, you know? I dreamed us.

—What were we doing? He looks for something, some way in or some way out. What could she want from him now? Uncounted years. He could ravage her, enter her with a full with a desperate tenderness, struggling to find the end of her, where she keeps hidden his name, and she would actually say it.

She leans into him again in the dark, leans back, then in again, still in his lap, one arm around his neck, the other holding the scotch, bringing it up to her lips. —No. No. I'm not telling you what we did in the dream. We weren't doing anything. You know. You know, don't you? We were dreaming in the dream.

Was she so drunk? What drugs ran through her, little deracinating needles? Or was she this mad, she, who had always lived on the far side of an edge, hanging on, looking at everyone else, cursing them their lives? Was she, who used to pray every day all day to Jesus or Yahweh or Buddah or Allah and to obscure gods to dim goddesses whom she had called up from dead faiths to rechristen into her own pantheon, was she still praying, with this job now her new her most true her most articulated prayer?

—No, he insists, urging her. —No, I don't know the dream. Tell me. Where were we? Here?

—Not here, fool. Here's for fools. Here I am, fool. Not here. Never here. Wanta go inna back? Whadya want? Blow job? Nice. She runs her tongue over pouted lips.

—I don't know what I want. Tell me your dream. I don't have much money. Eighty bucks. I dunno....

—Eighty bucks, forty bucks, four thousand bucks. For ten thousand gold pieces you can screw me in Paradise. Ah.... She laughs a soft laugh whose edges pull at her hysteria to contain it, to push it into her eyes so it splits right through each one, the left one off in the distance, on the sidelines.

He holds one of her breasts. She pushes into him. —You like that, dreamer, man o' my dreams? Come to me in my dreams. C'mon. She undoes the one button which holds the top of her low-cut thin white blouse. He takes her in his mouth to suck with eyes closed, one hand around her breast. She, squirming in his lap, her eyes closed, gives all her ecstasy to him. Behind the bar the woman dances; in the back, beside the jukebox, the first prostitute sits, glancing at her and her trick.

—Ah, She hums, —I'm good. You like my tits? I be good to you. Where were we last night? Huh? You know? You remember? She takes a drink, orders another.

He coughs up a ten.

—You gonna run my money on booze or your body? His own coarse words explode out of his mouth pulling him up short. These are not his words, not his. If it all falls away, then a Where am I? The night outside raw. Her hand on his penis. The dank apartment on Dennis Street. A waif like a helpless in chaos a girl-child. —…on booze or your body! A barrette holds her brown, thick hair. Right where it rises off her temple he sees her face as the face of her as a child. He touches her there. Now.

Oh. Don't do me like that I'm a lady. Oh fuck me. Oh you I'll fuck you to kingdom come. Gimme a million. Buy me a ticket. Like my tits? I dream of you don't I? Do I? Always did always. Who the hell are you? Cold night in Beantown. Cold boring fucking long dark boring fucking night. These tits wanted a little sucking and the sucker pays for the suck doesn't he? Jesus sucked these tits. Sucks em every now and again. Gets needy. Gets lonely. Gets hungry for a mama. Gets human lonely or gets human cosmic kinda lonely maybe both at once don't we all, baby? My Body? What you got? She says you want to spend eighty bucks. Eighty bucks. He takes his hand down. His lips move to form her name: she cuts him off. —I'm a professional, sweetheart. You dream about me? I dream you. Know what we did? Do you ever remember? We didn't do what you're thinking. Notatall. not. at. all. alter. thought. all. Remember? Go on. I hate blow jobs. Forty bucks I'll fuck you honey what?

He closes his eyes. For a moment no clarity, but a borderless boundless darkness comes with visions that inhabit it, random and senseless, analogous to nothing but themselves. Mysteries.

—Yes, he sighs. His hand slips up her short skirt. Finding no underpants, he slides one finger into her.

—Inna back. Gotta go inna back, she moans. She strokes his hair as she squeezes herself against the finger inside her.

Any crispness the night held has dissolved into just cold, just a biting at his cheeks, his nose. His hands, gloved, fall by his sides. His feet crunch into crusted snow. A shiver courses through him, his body relaxes up to a point, then, lost, embittered, anger. Himself inside her, the pleasure. no. Had she really dreamt of him? No, fool, of course not. The way she'd put her lower lip to her upper teeth to form the word earlier: —fool. Sloppily she had done it, carelessly.

He walks the row of Greyhound busses parked, each at a 20° angle, each in its nominated, designated stall. Finding the 02:37 with its destination-sign above the large front window scrolled to NEW YORK CITY, he climbs aboard, up the five steps. In that bus, empty, he takes a window-seat two-thirds down the aisle. On the seat beside him, the sports section, detritus from the Sunday Boston Globe.

Ten minutes later, the bus leaves precisely on time. He is its only passenger. The large and dark blank night outside the bus window large, dark, comforting, enveloping and distant across fields of wheat stubble. As he's about to slip into sleep, a flash of fear and self-hatred illuminates the curative silence, an explosion of his body. But hadn't he gotten what he'd wanted? That bright flash dims and suffuses. His eyes open once long enough to engage the darkness outside, the bus rolling forward on the two-lane highway, cold bracing the window against which he lay his head buffered by the sports section. He sleeps.

What was to have been light when he awakens, is yet dark. The bus idles, parked on the diagonal in a stall of the terminal. The sign on the wall, unambiguous, says it: BOSTON. He sits in the bus for a minute, waking up, peering out again at the sign. Checking his watch, 02:14, he stumbles down the aisle. Each seat, empty. The driver, gone. He climbs the steps down onto the concrete. The bus's destination sign, unambiguous: NEW YORK CITY. A young man, a boy really, comes to clean the bus with a dustbroom and trash sack.

—I'm in Boston again? he asks.

—I'm in Boston, the kid says, —so it looks to me like you're in Boston. Whether it's again or for the first time in your life is something between you and yourself, my friend.

—It's Monday night? he asks.

—It's Sunday night for me, I'm off Mondays, the kid says. —Whatever night it is for you is between you and your calendar. The kid gestures toward his head.

He waits. At 02:37, the bus leaves for New York City.

—No Monday papers? he asks at the newsstand.

—What'm I? A prophet? the newsvendor says. —Ain't tomorrow soon enough for Monday? Soon enough for me oughta be soon enough for a guy like you.

He wanders the maze, familiar, unrecognized. When he passes the club, its inner rankness drifts out to the street. Passing under its name-sign over the door, he enters the same dim room, its warmth. Something he can almost put his finger on, nearly distinguish, leads him back to the bar. He sinks down on a stool. Altering his drinking habits, he orders scotch. It's a different woman now behind the bar, tightly dressed. Onstage the dancer is as thin now as the dancer had been ample the night before. Her thinness as asexual as had been the other woman's corpulence. When the one, the old roommate from Dennis Street, sits again on his lap, he neither refuses her nor does he welcome her. Resting his hand at the middle of her back, he keeps her from falling backward.

—You buying?

—Drinks?

—Sweet sweet flesh, honey.

—Don't talk like that. No more.

—Don't tell me, honey. She leans into him, her breasts at his mouth. He licks them, one, then the other. —Buy em, she says.

—With what? He answers, his mouth so close to her his speech reverberates in her body, in her breasts.

—Take me, she says —I want you and I want you and I want you.

—In the back, he says, —like before. We have to talk.

—Talk here, fuck there.

—Don't mess with me. His voice now coming from some other avenue through his body, travelling through his brain and his belly and meeting at his mouth. —Yes, he says, —in the back, but no bullshit.

Dim light from a covered lamp, old as Boston. A couch not even a bed. She lies out on it. —Come, she says.

He stands at the door.

—What's the matter, honey? Pay me and fuck me. One, two. You know how.

—No.

—You want me you want me. Look at me. She opens her blouse. —Come take these they're yours now you paid for em.

He walks over to the couch. He kneels beside her. Her eyes are closed her head flung back against the couch. His cheek against the cold bus window rolling into that night. He rubs her neck she moans. —Pay me, she begs. He lays his one remaining hundred-dollar bill in her lap. Without looking, she runs her hand over it. —A C-note.

—You're not so drunk as you look.

—I'm drunker than that. What do you care? I dream of you. I see you know what we do? Not that. No. No no no you know nothing you're stupid but I like that come to me stop talking.

—And your eyes, he says, —where I see them split, right through the middle I see something else. Beneath your words in your breath I feel you. You're kneeling at the altar of the Virgin Mother saying my name to her like a rosary. She listens to you, doesn't she?

—Fuck me you-son-of-a-fucking godless-mother-fucking-whore. Fuck me inside of me. Stay. Linger. Safe.

—And the Virgin Mary leans down, I see that. She kisses you on the mouth, not like a god like a woman like a lover. She goes into you deep with her tongue. And there, speaks my name inside your mouth.

She has the hundred-dollar bill under her raised skirt, between her legs rubbing herself with it. —Put your cock where your money's already gone.

—And my name expands inside your head, doesn't it? Even as a nameless name as a name unnaming named names or unpronounceable the yod/yod name of the one God of the Hebrew People spoken by the Virgin Mary to you. And my name. It fills you and it fills you, it comes up and out through the top of your head, and there's a little baby there, and the Mother Virgin but you call her Pallas Athena and you call her Lilith she takes the baby she dips it in water. Isn't that how I feel you, in your dream?

—I dreamt you, she gasps. —That's what we were doing. The Virgin takes my baby.

—You're pregnant from last night, he says.

—There is only one night in all of our life not two. You're crazy from drinking, she sits up.

—You're sober.

—Get out.

—Too late. You shouldn't have dreamt that my name filled your head. I wouldn't have come back to you. It's not by choice. None of it. It's because the dream came out on your breath that covered me, and then I dreamt it so fast I didn't know. I dreamt your dream. Now I'm going to stay with you. I inhaled this dream through my pores. You called me.

—I'm just a whore, she begs.

—I'm a coward. I'm afraid of your call to me. Look at me.

She puts a whorehand on him. —You're trembling, she whispers.

—Am I always trembling? he asks her.

—She died, didn't she? Up north. That's why you're here, isn't it? I can't leave here. I'm a drunken whore.

—It amounts to the same. You're a whore to men. I'm a whore to trembling. We've both gone too far. We've gotten away with much too much you and I. We've each paid a terrible terrible price.

—I couldn't tell you the dream, she protested. —The Virgin made me promise not to tell you.

—Yes, he said. —I heard her.

A History Of
Zero

—Thomas.

, must have been dreaming. Sleepy then the room dark. But I hadn't been dreaming, had I?

When the ambulance came, Thomas had been at home working on essay, —A History of Zero, revising some aspects of Aspeto Enada's notion that *zero* (originally, *nfr* [beautiful] of 18th cen. BCE Egyptian) was a purely functional discovery required for certain mathematical, and especially architectural, as well as musical, computations. It's a fiction made up from the [beautiful] imagination of mankind, who does not see it in nature. Before even the beginning of counting, mankind understood one stone, two stones, but not zero stones. It was Enada who first articulated carefully the idea that *zero*, a value which cannot be the empty cipher so many think of it as being, and yet not a material substance, required a definition of another order. We cannot say, Enada argues, that zero books is a meaningless amount, whereas one book is a meaningful amount. Insofar as zero books has meaning, it is not an empty *thing*. Enada admitted he'd been unable to successfully accomplish a definition that incorporated both of these concepts of zero's [beautiful] purely functional, fictional existence. He'd left off with the question: what is zero? Thomas would answer it.

Thomas didn't want to turn away from his work; the sirens weren't jarring, but actually soft, muffled, melodious, inviting. Looking out the upstairs window in the back of the house, reflections of the red lights bounced off other houses on the street, off of trees, off the pavement. He had to go, didn't he? He couldn't sit writing about zero while his own house might be on fire.

He looked out, then dashed over, sliding down the stairs that ran outside the house from the second story, ignorant of his own safety. In the less than a minute that he crossed the street, they had Raphael on the couch, instruments attached, a needle in his arm, lights humming and bleeping to signify methodically arithmetically the chaos of a human body in crisis, trying to organize it into diagnosis then action.

Raphael, though fatigued, had good color in his face, although his wife, Maryanne, might not be able to contain all her anxiety one more minute in her thin/aged/bony frame. Thomas went right to Maryanne. Though nearly voiceless, she talked faster and more rampantly than usual. Even in the dark I can see it. White cloth hump on the rag rug on the wood floor. I was afraid of that girdle. The way I imagined it. What it defined, hid. Am I now? I can't tell. I'm tired. Be careful, Thomas. Don't leave. So what? My body looks at itself in the mirror of her body. I have done a saintly thing. I feel vastly strange, I'm afraid. It's dark and I love being afraid just like this, as though this were the gateway the awakening of some small nodule of absolute knowledge, maybe a kind of zero even.

Thomas put his arm around Maryanne's brittle shoulders. Though Maryanne worked hard in her garden and around the place, she was brittle, very precarious. —This time, Maryanne said, —I married a younger man so he'd outlast me, the last husband would be younger. And look at him. He is younger, you know, by eight years. We fell so very much in love when we met at a. . . . Maryanne ended: —How are you Raphael? Talk to me just a little. Then the paramedic said Maryanne should let her husband gain his strength. The paramedic thought it would come back. Did she want something? the paramedic asked. —Oh God no, she said.

—Would you like to sit?

—God no. There was that chair. The little living room overflowed with seashells Maryanne and Raphael had collected from seacoasts around the world, imbedded in their driveway as sea patterns, hung on the walls, displayed in boxes, set out in a glass case. They had told Thomas the story one by one of each shell, of where they'd been, how they'd found it, how they'd had a dinner that night of sole meuniere where the maitre d' had spoken to them as though they were young lovers when God knows they were already....well, you know, he's younger than me, by a few years. Raphael has the only blue jay in the world friendly to man. Comes every morning and Raphael teases him with a few morsels until he sits right on Raffy's shoulder, pecks at his hand, then Raffy opens it up, don't you darling? Raphael is the most amazing man with the birds and the squirrels. It's because you're gentle, isn't it, darling? It's his teasing they love, isn't it, darling?

One word goes through my head. Darling. Quiqui, I've lost you, darling. Now I'm alone, Quiqui. The day never comes to any conclusion, to any single point of resolve. Why? There's nothing I could have done to have held you, is there? Nothing I should have done. It was all circumstance. Do you remember when Maryanne brought us shells from Mexico? I teased her I said, —who wants these they're just the remains of something that isn't here anymore. You'd said, —you and your zero. I said, —Darling, you are my zero. You said, —No, darling, I'm your one and your two and your three and your four. And then you were gone. And then you left because you had to, to go back, and you were right to go back. Fate had it pulling you that way and there was nothing you or I could have done about it. And I watched it on TV. On BBC. It wasn't Channel Zero, was it? I couldn't tell. I might've seen you go down. I saw so many. Is what we were then now zero? You can't make a Square without zero. You can't make a bullet without zero. Quiqui. I couldn't have made you without my zero, you made me without your zero. Is this now my life without zero? Empty without zero. Oh, yes. One bullet is not zero, it is one. Quiqui you were not zero. You were so much one.

The radios crackled with static and voices. The day was awfully warm. The small room, dark. The house was of small rooms, all dark, and all cluttered. And everywhere there were mementoes from Maryanne's life, from her days in the 20's as a *bonne vivante* in Greenwich Village, friend to painters and poets, from her childhood in Connecticut, from her marriage with her second husband, the one who walked out one day and got lost somewhere and never returned. In the months after the death of Raphael, Maryanne would go over these photos and drawings, books and trinkets with Thomas. And they would talk of Quiqui.

Thomas loved the youthful portrait of Maryanne done by her Romanian painter-friend-admirer. Something in her eyes, in the line of her mouth eager and vulnerable. Something almost too accessible.

Blame it on the vodka. They always do. I never have. Won't now. Don't stir someone's darling. Grace will carry us. No?

When they moved Raphael from his couch to the wheelchair, entubed, he said to me, —I hope I'm coming back, and he laughed. Raphael's laugh which was a combination of the wicked blue jay he had tamed and the raucous squirrel he hadn't tamed. —If you don't, Thomas answered, —don't worry, I'll be following along, eventually. That made Raphael laugh all alone, his own laugh, without the aid of other creatures.

Now that bottle was half gone! More. How she could do it. When we had her over for Thanksgiving and we laughed and drank and sang songs and got very drunk and danced — she loved Keung-Kung, dancing with Keung-Kung. And she said it had been the perfect break for her, all the strain of those long long days in the hospital with him, even with his humor intact, still, how long could you keep that up? His dry humor, its wicked eye on life which maintained at the same time its gentlemanly pose, as Raphael himself did, making you feel that a carriage had just passed by and a gentleman within had just said hello with a formal tip of his hat, but had said something in the way he tipped it that was appropriately sardonic. Raphael was as skinny as Maryanne. For all they ate! That Thanksgiving while Raffy was in the hospital. They did have a grand time that night.

The way Maryanne waved the bottle when I walked in. Raphael two. . . three days. Three days gone. You're still here though, aren't you, Raphael, still in the room? Yes.

Shall we do it again, she and I? Can I stand it? Take me to bed, she said. We, singing and shouting and calling out to you and she promising me the farm and all. I'll just tell her no, that's all. I don't want it, surely. I don't want anything from you, to intrude on this. My God. You did her a favor that's all. Why're you feeling so protective of it? A memory you're already harboring, some precious thing. I thought of you, Quiqui, I thought of you like crazy. You waited on the lawn for me and I looked out the window. I'm thinking of you now. I want you. Here I'm in bed with a hag. The greatest hag who ever lived. You hear? Raphael, can she hear me? Yes? The sheets so sweaty. Look, the wet spots still. My God I must be crazy. I've never been so goddamned happy in my life. What will I do in the morning? Fulfilled. It must not be so late. We didn't again. Yes, we did we did. I could see everything. Her old face, fantastically old. Her bones, each one. Now I know why that girdle, it practically holds her up doesn't it? She doesn't have a spine left I could've killed her she wouldn't have cared she's got the grace not I. She'll do it. Somehow. Morning coffee, good cheer. Could you believe it there with me in that chair and her slumped on the couch where he'd been and she said take me to bed and I thought at first of course not, of course she's drunk drunk, so very terribly and totally and thoroughly drunk, and she misses him and she says it. But she said it again like it wasn't a request or a command or a desire but a fate. Take me to bed. I'm 29 years old Maryanne! Can you hear me? No? Don't die tonight. No. You won't will you? Your brittle bones have a hunger to survive and I felt that against my pelvis. How dared you? I'm dreaming. I'll wake up now. I'll put my arm across your back and hold your breast and wake up. I'll never tell you I love you. You'll always

Lovely. Falling. Sonata.

Moon. Into. Bleeker bakery, Darkness around me us. Bleeker door, concrete steps, brick. Prison. Smiled. Him. Him scarred no war Bleeker bakery morning. Darling. Darling and painting and smelling. No war no mamma falling darkness around me us pop. Lovely and falling darkness. Michel we called. Michel Michel

Michel Michel Raphael. The painting and falling and Bleeker and darkness. Find one. . . I one . . . They're here in the darkness. I'm falling surrounds me. Huh? Around him. Men paint smell. As long as you're falling. No, Raphael, no, not your eyes your mouth lost muscle lost speech last falling lost stop me stop.

Sleep is. Now again and or different falling. Watching myself at it always. I keep it from dying. Falling . . . mama . . . lovehate . . . lovehate Connecticut lovehate the garden into the garden Raffy. No one on the porch. Es Esther Estartled Astarte in the garden no one on the porch. His nipples. His mouth all fallen. His name gone. All fallen. Still falling. Still night. Good good night no dawn. Come to bed with me. Vodka falling eyes fallen no! No peace. Open your eyes. I can't there's only this darkness I'm falling I see everything in darkness darling I see my legs belly spine hardly spine toes laughing Thomas no we. I didn't. Shells darling mama. At the shore. Where water rolls into the darkness. Where the sleep rolls where the fish scared me and mama was. No war. Raffy. Mama's gone, Raffy. Long gone mama we drank enough vodka like babies its bottle cold. Oh and oh. Oh. I'm unhappy Raffy. Keep falling mama. Into Bleeker. Lovely and lovely and falling and lovely and not lonely loved and be loved Roumanian. On the ground the beasts arms beast mouths. Receding into falling Esther is falling and take me take it's yours. Oh. Is Esther gone? Unbreathed? I can't see me. Where 'm I? Darkness no falling. In me INRI they say some parade today its down Figueroa piñatas. For the tomatoes the sweet basil for Thomas. Don't say Quiqui. No more wars are bad for the country everyone and powerfear and so many machine oil cogwheel doing it Raffy you and I we worked in that factory we met in that factory we beat the Hun we had dances every night like this is a night like this. Oh, I loved her together we became a world the myth of ourselves. a falling and I'm in my body's sleeping I think and I see my thoughts thinking themselves my arms my body wrapped around them dear Thomas you go home now you work on your zero you have you have graced your friend, Raphael, he smiles down on your Maryanne is alright she is alone and her thoughts wrap around to embrace her.

Uncle Apu

Thomas

grabbed the phone as the electrical impulse surging through the wires set into action the first ring.

{Thou beleeuest that the Plants haue a kinde of Soule, that is to say, a certeine inward power or vertue which maketh them to shoote foorth in their season.[1]}

—Apu's back in the hospital, his mother said.

—Where have you been? I've been trying to reach you.

—Working, Thomas said. —Many deadlines.

—They amputated his leg, the right leg.

{The sensible Soul of a vast Whale exerciseth its regiment to every part of that huge structure with the same efficacy and facility as the Soul of a Fly or a Mite doth.[2]}

—Christ. His leg? Thomas sat down on the white couch.

—Yes, his mother said, it's unbearable.

—Certainly is. Thomas rested his left hand on his left leg.

—Where? he asked

—Mercy All Angels. Room. . . she rifled through pieces of scratch paper. —...Room 895.

—Same place?

—Not quite. The south wing. his mother said.

—You haven't gone yet?

—Later. This evening.

—It's not like a human. They're taking him apart piece by piece.

{King Henrie. . .his saul commendis to God, and his body to the clay.[3]}

---

1 Golding. *De Mornay* i. 11. 1587.
2 Hale. *Primitive Origins of Man.* 1677.
3 Dalrymple. tr. *Leslie's History of Scotland II.* 1596

—Like a crazy puzzle. How much could we take away and leave Apu?

{*The absence of the soul is far more terrible in a living man than in a dead one.*[4]}

—I'll be over today. Thomas hung up the phone. What would I do? Strong Apu. The very strength of it all. That laugh. Uncle Apu's face, ever about to break the surface.

{*Sir, as I haue a Soule, she is an Angell.*[5]}

Good Apu, strong Apu. Hardly walk now across the room without dragging along a stored-energy-battery-powered-ever-humming machine

{*subtracted like the soul we never knew we had. . .*[6]}

from which he inhaled pure, mechanically regulated draughts of compressed oxygen. Apu's face ever tanned by a long history of outdoor winter days.

Going to the hall closet, Thomas took out the toolbox with the electrical drill Uncle Apu had given him, the power driven circular saw, hammer, a green wooden-handled screwdriver, odds and ends. —Stupid, Thomas said aloud, —sentimentality.

{*subtracted like the soul we never knew we had. . .//Just so. . ..some still are/ nurtured by their innocence. . ./something is lacking,/some point of concentration around which a person can collect itself/and be neither conscious nor uncaring, be neutral*[7]}

Getting up, Thomas paced. As if his own legs

{*I know many people have doubts as to the existence of souls in small boys of this class.*[8]}

were on loan to him now. How strange, a man made up of these things, parts.

{*Louis Armstrong declared that 'Anything played with beat and soul is*

4 Dickens, Charles. *Barneby Rudge* iii. 1841d
5 Shakespeare, William. *Henry VIII*, IV, i. 44. 1613.
6 Ashbery, John. *Flow Chart*. p. 11. 1991
7 ibid.
8 Kingsley, M. *West Africa* 441. 1897.

jazz.[9]}

In his mind, Thomas was telling Bavna: Can you imagine? he was saying to her. A heart attack, an asthma, a leg! What would I do were it me? Kill myself? Die of exhaustion?

{I could not from my soul but fasten the buckle in return.[10] My father was an eminent Button-maker…but I had a soul above buttons… I panted for a liberal profession.[11]}

Apu, just one month ago at Uncle Ravi and Aunty Indira's anniversary party lumbering around dragging that stainless steel oxygen machine attached to himself and gasping, even so, for air. Oxygen.[12o] Elemental. Irreducible. Relatively stable. So moved by the sight of Apu's persistence that Thomas went over to him where Apu sat in a big chair, wheezing breath.

—Uncle Apu, Thomas had said softly, — I've got to tell you. You've got a hell of a courage.

Apu smiled up at him. —What courage? he huffed. —What choice? Apu laughed. Now a leg! The man will go mad. All this sitting around has been driving him crazy as it is. Reaching down Thomas rubbed his right leg, then stomped it on the ground. He looked out the window at the midsummer brown hills. White clouds hovered steadily over them.

_____*{The problem which concerns me most…Is, bluntly stated, 'Have I got a*
9 Grove's Dictionary of Music (ed. 5) IV.600/2. 1964
10 Sterne, Lawrence. *Sentimental Journey, Temptation.* 1768.
11 Colman, G. *New Hay at Old Market.* 1795.
12^0 Oxygen: Symbol: O. Number: 8 on the Periodic Table of Elements. Atomic weight: 15.9994. Atomic volume: 14.0cm3/mol. Boiling point: 90.2K. CAS Registry ID: 7782-44-7. Group Number: 16. Group Name: Chalcogen. Periodic Number: 2. Block: P-Block. Standard State: Gas at 298 K. Color: Colorless as a gas; liquid is pale blue. Oxygen is the third most abundant element found in the sun, and it plays a part in the carbon-nitrogen cycle, one process responsible for stellar energy production. About two-thirds of the human body, and nine-tenths of water, is oxygen. One-fifth of the atmosphere is oxygen gas. There is not normally any need to make oxygen in the laboratory as it is readily available.

soul?' And, soulhood granted, while millenniums roll, Will it inhabit some congenial clime. . .Anonymous in what we name 'the Whole'?[13]}

Inside and out, in the heat, a certain shimmering stillness prevailed.

Thomas opened the front door so a rush of air, even warm air, might come through, but the air too lay still. Thomas stepped outside onto the stone path.

That indomitable man is going to die.

{To hold opinion. . .That soules of Animals infuse themselues Into the trunks of men.[14]}

Thomas stood with that thought for a moment. Had Uncle Apu thought much about death? Had he reckoned this day always into his life? Had he lived with it, the way that I do, failing to grasp it. Letting it go. Failing to grasp it. Failing to grasp it. It grasping him. Letting go. Failing to grasp it.

{My senses, and my saull I saw, Debait a deadly strife.[15]}

This dismantling.

Thomas, hungry, hadn't eaten yet today; Bavna was on her way. Returning to the kitchen, Thomas put up bacon, started eggs. As the eggs sizzled, and Thomas put two slices of bread in the toaster, Bavna came in with her sweet smile, her face surrounded by the dark hair that hung down to her back. Those days were gone when Thomas would chase Bavna, while she would withdraw to a point where he could still just reach her; then he might withdraw to that same point in himself, so that she would have to chase him. They had never caught each other, but they had somewhere each agreed that they must find it possible to stop running.

{The best method of arranging his oil-skins to keep the water out. . .known as a 'soul and body lashing.[16]}

---

13 Sassoon, Sigfried. —A Traveler to His Soul, in *Satirical Poems* (ed. 2) 68. 1933.
14 Shakespeare, William, *Merchant of Venice* V.IV.i. 132. 1596.
15 Hume, A. *Hymns* i.21. 1599.
16 Protheroe, C. *Life in Mercantile Marine* 150. 1903.

Bavna came into the kitchen. From behind, she put her arms around Thomas, who let go of the spatula he held, turning to embrace her, kissed the curve of her neck as she offered it to him, her face below the eyes, her eyes, and finally her mouth, pressing her body against his own.

{*Oh, no! No picture of miserable, vicious, Parisian life. This is beautiful; there is soul here.*[17]}

Bavna, with the simple happiness he drew out of her, kissed him back. Then, smiling, backing away, Bavna said, —Your eggs will burn.

Thomas turned off the flame under the eggs and the bacon and held Bavna again. —Want coffee? he asked, biting her ear.

—Noooo, she moaned.

—Beer?

—Noooo.

—Whiskey?

—Um-um.

—Tequila?

—Maybe.

Downstairs, undressing,

{*My Father lou'd Sir Roland as his soule.*[18]}

they got in under the sheet. One window was open, but only a still, warm air stood out and inside the house. The dry heat of southern winds. The dry heat of brown hills. A heat they reveled in.

{*Slouch could hardly call his Soul his own.*[19]}

They played, laughed, bit, teased, kissed, sucked until finally Bavna whispered —I want you inside me. It was exactly—already half on top—what Thomas wanted, just then, to hear, to be needed by her. He en-

17 _____. Lytton. *My Novel III. IX. iii. 22. 1853.*

18 Shakespeare, William. A.Y.L. I. ii. 247. 1600.

19 King, W. *Old Cheese* 8 Wks. 1776 III. 144. 1712.

tered her moist body

{He that gaue the vnreasonable soule sense, memorie, and appetite; the reasonable besides these, phantasie, vnderstanding and will.[20]}

which encompassed him entirely. Slowly he came into her, more and more deeply, as she called to him, —Thomas, oh I've missed you. Missed you so much, so many times, my Thomas, losing her face in his body, taking his body into her body. Thomas moved faster with her until without forethought they found themselves moving furiously with each other creating more heat and finally sweat to pool in the dry day.

They lay side by side for a while, body by body, body by heat,

{Africans were being disposed of as Europeans were by their princes not long before, when the Congress of Vienna. . .distributed them in lots of so many thousand 'souls'.[21]}

breath coming going and coming unforced. —I feel, Thomas muttered, —as if someone had injected my brain with some secret solution. My brain is floating, my body is limp.

{It has been said, that 'common souls pay with what they do—nobler souls with that which they are.[22]}

—You didn't hear me, Thomas said.

—How could I hear you, laughed Bavna. —I'm not in my body. I'm having an out of body experience.

—Remember, Thomas whispered, —that all out of the body experiences occur in the mind, inside the body, electricity jumping ganglia producing sensation.

{The idea was that the soul was a little bloodless, fleshless thing.[23]}

—Is that what we just did with our bodies? Bavna smiled, turned facing away from Thomas.

—No. Thomas mused. —That's something else altogether.

---

20 Saint Augustine. *Citie of God* V. xi. 1610.
21 Kiernan, V.G. *Lords of Human Kind* vi. 225. 1969.
22 Emerson, Ralph Waldo, *Ess., History Wks.* (Bohn) I. 7 1842.
23 *Daily News.* 17 April 1899 4/3. 1899.

—Yes. Bavna agreed. —It is.

—Yes. Thomas said. —That's nerves, blood pumping, heat rising, oxygen rushing in and out: oxygen: number 8 on the periodic table of elements. Atomic weight: 15.9994. Atomic volume: 14.0cm3/mol. Boiling point: 90.2K. Melting point...

—Stop! Bavna, laughing.

Thomas Kissed Bavna's shoulder.

{*It's just really rough what the colored entertainers have to go through sometimes... That's why the colored people sing the blues; that's why they sing with soul.[24]*}

Thomas went upstairs, got two beers, stopped to taste the three salty strips of meat bacon he had abandoned in favor of lovemaking.

—Hungry? he called down to her.

—No. Just thirsty, just beer.

—OK.

A familiar owl called from the oak in the yard, though barely audibly. As Thomas entered the bedroom he found Bavna lying back, one arm under her head. —What are you thinking? he asked.

{*The principle of the animal Motion of a Brute has been likewise call'd a Soul, and we have been taught to name it the sensitive Soul.[25]*}

She sat up.

—Have you heard that owl yet?

—Yes, I have. Just faintly.

—They're faint. They don't hoot loudly. I swear there's a pair out there. It's their mating season.

—Oh?

—Yes. Really.

—And how do you know, he asked her, —that it's the owls' mating season?

Handing her a glass of beer, Thomas sat beside her on the

---

24 *The American Folk Music Occasional. New York: Oak Publications. 1964.*
25 Watts. *Logic.* I. vi. §3. 1725.

bed. —I've got to go across town this afternoon. My uncle. Uncle Apu.

—Uncle Apu? With the heart attack last year?

—His leg....now....

—What is it?

—They had to amputate it.

—Oh my God, she said, —poor man. Poor man. She stroked Thomas's thigh.

—Gangrene from the diabetes. He's just going down the tubes. I've got to see him.

—Sure. Want me to go with you? I won't go up. . . I've never met. . . I could just wait somewhere, if you want. You know? But if you'd rather go alone...

—Yes. Please come, Bavna. There's a cafe just down the street. Quite nice. This isn't the time to meet him. But if I know you're waiting for me it won't be so hard. I think it's going to be tough. Depressing.

—That's fine, Thomas. I'll get the Sunday paper. It's no problem.

{*Peculiar to the medicine-men of the Haida, Tlinkit, and Timshian was the use of a special 'soul-catcher', a bone tube, generally carved, for capturing the wandering souls of the sick and restoring them to their bodies.*[26]}

—Yes.

Thomas and Bavna showered and, dressing, they teased each other again.

The cafe, as it turned out, was not just down the block, as Thomas had remembered. It was about half a mile. He dropped Bavna there. They parted on the street. —I won't be an hour, Thomas said. —I love you. You know I do.

{*Sir, as I haue a Soule, she is an Angell.*[27]}

—I know, she smiled climbing out of the car. —Take your time. Don't rush it.

---

26 Jenness, D. *Indians of Canada 333.* 1932.
27 Shakespeare, William. *Henry VIII, IV. i. 44.* 1613.

—Then we can have dinner around here, later.

—Whatever, she said, —don't worry about me. I'm fine. Don't apologize. There's nothing to make up for.

Thomas drove alone to the hospital enclosed in the metal car; he shifted gears, listening to the sound of greased metal slide past greased metal. The car's motion made him brace himself against the spinning of gears and turning of wheels. Why Apu? What the hell.

{That the soule dyeth with the body is an old and despicable Heresie[28]}

Work hard, be strong, and that death comes to take hold of you.   Like when you sit back and watch the sun set over those hills as you see your life gather and at the same time see it going away from you. Paradox. Gather, go; go, gather.

{Aerial music. . .breathed such soul-dissolving airs, As did. . .[29]}

Thomas pulled into the parking lot of the Mercy All Angel's Hospital. It was a small side lot with only fifteen or twenty cars. Thomas had to wake the sleeping old man dreaming in the ticket booth. Saying — Thank you, Thomas took the ticket, drove into the lot, the tires squeaking on pavement making Thomas suddenly aware of the weight of the car, the weight of his own body, the rhythms of his breath.

Parking in this side lot,

{No writing lifts exalted man so high, As sacred and soul-moving poesy.[30]}

Thomas had to walk all the way around the chain link fence of the main parking lot to the hospital to the front entrance. Refuse in the street. A trash can. A changing traffic light.

{I guess it's real soul-inspiring to work in a ritzy layout like this.[31]}

Over there, the big shopping center. The streets here empty but for Thomas.

28 Pagitt, Ephraim. *Heresiography.* (ed. 2) 139. 1645.
29 Thomson. Cast. Indol. 1. xxxix. 1748.
30 Sheffield. (Dk. Duckhm.) *Wks. I.* 87. 1721.
31 Hailey, A. *Overload II.i.*106. 1979.

They used to go often to Apu's for dinner or, Apu driving him once in a while to school. Apu's truck, his weather worn work torn hands. A certain kindness and tenderness Apu had about him. His teasing. Or lying in bed at night wondering in the dark, the kind of sharp expectation you got to think of uncle Apu. —Oh phemeral thoughts, Thomas said aloud. —Oh you vain and necessary sentimentalities.

{*The word 'soul' probably originated with Ray Charles... Soul is the music of experience... It's one person's heart speaking to another person's.*[32]}

On the streets surrounding it medical support services, pharmacies, medical supply houses with artificial limbs in their windows, operating tables, examining tables, hospital beds. Oxygen tanks. Wheelchairs. Medical and surgical tools, stethescopes, probing mirrors. Machines. A medical bookstore with, in the window as Thomas passed, the several volumes of Lamberti's Complete History of the Medical Sciences.

Thomas, lost

{*From that moment he could not call his soul his own.*[33]}

in the maze of hospital corridors which radiated angularly one from another, asked a guard for room 895. Elevator to the eighth floor,

{*Shakespeare...became in soul one with the mighty prince as with the lowly peasant*[34]}

straight to the second corridor, turn left all the way to the end, and then right. Go down two hallways, turn left, and you're there.

Thomas got off the elevator and walked straight. The city had fitted the new medical complex with a prodigious art collection whose unusual context gave one to contemplate the relationship between the healing arts and the fine arts, or art and

---

32 *Radio Times.* 19 July 60/1. 1979.
33 Corbett. *Monk. xi.* 155. 1889.
34 Creighton, Mandell. *Historical Essays and Reviews i. 1902.*

disease, or the relationship of beauty and pain, or artifice and nature, or the creative and the degenerative, or the soul and the body. Thomas stood for a moment at a Claes Oldenberg large soft sculpture of an ice pack. Art talking about medicine and its tools. Art making you laugh, making you remember that muscle strain in your leg you iced, and then remember Apu's leg, and then stop, and refuse to think of what happened to the leg itself. And then art, insignificant? More significant? Along the wall hung a series of Deanne Belinoff large stones, black, flat, polished on the outfacing surface only, placed so their jagged grey edges jutted at each other, each stone inscribed with a hair-thin circle and a hair-thin line.

{*He uses a bewildering, unorthodox technique and his playing is full of what jazzmen refer to as 'soul'.[35]*}

Thomas staring, held the line and the circle, each in one hand. He looked to see what the series was called, but then as he walked down the hallway, he couldn't remember the name.

Thomas passed one nursing desk, kept walking, watching the room numbers. 800. 805. All the rooms had children in them. In one room an infant lay in a crib bed with a plastic tent suspended over its body. Thomas stopped, gazed in perhaps for an inappropriately long moment, then walked on. In other rooms babies and young children, two and three to a room, waited for or recovered from treatment. From one room came the crying of a young girl, and then, walking past that room Thomas saw the child's young mother soothe her.

Thomas walked slower now, turned a corner, passed a window behind which several new-born infants in dangerous condition drew Thomas's fascination, their tiny, tiny bodies, and their closeness to the physical origins of life. Thomas peeped into room after room, walking slowly down the hall, until a nurse approached him. —May I help you?

35 *Ebony.* September. 34/2. 1946.

He was startled. —... my uncle. . .

{I swear to myself I will be the best writer, the best Soul Writer[36]}

—He is a very young uncle?

—Sorry. No. An embarrassed laugh. —Room 845.

—That's in this corridor. But these are all children under four, You'd better find out where you're trying to go.

Thomas reached into his shirt pocket. —Room 8.....oh, he smiled, —room 8-*ninety*-5. Oh, sorry, I guess I...

—Right behind you, the nurse pointed, —down this hall, first right, then the first left.

—Yes. These hallways were deserted. Not a soul, except for one hospital guard. Thomas walked on, took the first right, then the next left, then again.

{They basted him with a mixture of Aqua fortis. . .which smarted to the very soule of him.[37]}

Staring at one art photograph, Thomas found his own image in the glass. The photograph was Brassai's, 1932, 'Bijou of Montmartre', the camera, very close, filling the frame with the fabulous Bijou at the long end of her middle age, seated at a cafe table. A glass of dark wine. Circles of pearls wrap around her neck, fall down her breast. Pearls on both wrists with thick bracelets. A big obvious ring on each finger. A veiled hat with a bow, the veil held up around the hat's close brim, but shading her eyes. Her face square with age, her eyebrows thick, beneath each eye a broad straight swath of eyeshadow. Lipstick all over her lips. Her unashamed gaze, clear. Lightly lying around her neck, a collar of fur. The mirror behind Bijou reflected the plain back of Bijou's hatted head, and not Thomas's face.

{One invariably sees a face in the centre of a soul-catcher, a tube of hollowed bone into which the shaman sucked the soul of a sick man—to keep it safe from

---

36 Malamud, Bernard. *Tenants* 63. 1971.
37 Nashe. *Unfortunate Travels V.* 168. 1594

harm while the illness lasted.[38]}

Gazing, Thomas steadied himself with a hand on the wall. He wanted only to see Apu now, his old uncle Apu, as though Apu sat next to Bijou in the photograph where she leaned toward her left and the photo was cut off, as though it were Apu's face Thomas saw reflected in the mirror in the photograph, as though he could hear Apu asking for him.

In Room 895 there was only Apu, ashen in limp and fallen sleep. Thomas stood at the doorway. The upper sheet fell in where the leg would have been.

—Oh, Apu.

Another nurse appeared. —May I help you?

Thomas had to clear phlegm that had collected in his throat. —....my uncle here. . . He gestured towards the room. —I guess everyone, I mean, has anyone been...

—They left just a while ago, she nodded.

—A note?

—A note?

—I mean can I —write a note for him?

{Anna Wulf is sitting on a chair in front of a soul doctor.[39]}

—Sure. Ask at the desk, the nurse pointed down the corridor, —they'll give you pencil and paper.

Thomas wrote: —I came by. You were sleeping. No one around. I watched you for a while. I'll come tomorrow. Much love and more strength, Thomas.

Thomas turned again down the corridor. On the walls were more photographs, among them a close-up of Igor Stravinsky at rehearsal with sheets of music spread on his lap and a bottle of whiskey to his lips.

{'The voice of women...is a special soul-force in the struggle for a non-violent world,' the 36-year-old pacifist leader from strife-torn Northern Ireland

---

38 *New York Times.* 22 September 14/2. 1969.
39 Lessing, Doris. *The Golden Notebook* I. 202. 1962.

declared.[40]}

Another was of the poet Robinson Jeffers. He walked down the hallway, took the elevator to the first floor, then walked around the hospital again to his car, going to meet Bavna.

{With soul force we'll look to the needs of our brother In a world that's our universal home.[41]}

Apu woke. He called for the nurse. When she came Apu asked was he in the Phillipines again. The nurse assured him he was still in America.

—Oh. Apu said. —Good. Was my nephew, Thomas here or did I just dream it?

—Someone was here, the nurse said. —He left a note.

—Tell my wife to call Thomas, Apu huffed. —Tell Thomas to come back. I'm not near ready to die, but I've come very close this time and there's some things I have to tell him now. He's my best nephew. My very best, Thomas.

Thomas rolled his car up to the parking lot's toll booth. No other cars. No one but the toll taker the same sleepy old man. He was tall, bald but for a rim of hair around the sides and back of his head. He wore a white shirt with brown stripes. His eyeglasses with oversized lenses and thin rims had slid down his nose.

{Soul music belched from windows where Black women wearing tired faces gazed impassively down at the hopeless street.[42]}

Thomas handed five dollars over with his ticket. The toll booth attendant took the ticket, the five dollar bill, inserted the ticket into a machine. When the ticket machine read $2.85 the attendant entered $5.00 on the number pad. The cash drawer sprung open.

The attendant turned toward Thomas with the change,

---

40 *Arab Times.* 14 December 2/5. 1977.
41 *It.* 4 - 17 July 10/4. 1969.
42 *Black World.* March. 57/2. 1974

$2.15, leaned down, said, —wake up, man!

—What?

—You're asleep at the wheel, kid. Wake up!

Driving up 3rd street Thomas muttered aloud to himself, —To what? Thomas asked himself. —Wake up to what? What was he talking about? How does he know? What the hell was that all about? Where the goddamn hell did he come from? Who the goddamn hell is he? Wake up! Wake up! That old man, half-asleep.

At the Café Dialogique, suspended by circumstance between what has been and what will be in whatever is, Bavna reads an article

{She calls him exciting and lets him soul-kiss her.[43]}

about a court case on abortion. She grows furious that these judges, the rational courts of irrational men, would rule that a girl under 18 years of age, immature, needs her parents' permission for an abortion; yet, if if she can't get her

{Heraclitus...considered fire as the primary force and 'soul-substance' because it moved and transformed matter.[44]}

parents' permission, then she, not mature enough to decide on her own whether to have an abortion, is mature enough to become a mother. What of the child? That's a mother's question. A woman's. A girl's, even. But a judge? Quoth the Judge, in the newspaper: —Insofar as the soul enters the body at the moment of conception.... Bavna looks down at her body. Her hands on the table. Her chest. Her belly. Her thighs. She has seen her face so often in mirrors, daily. Where, this soul that entered this Presumptuous Judge. If your sole soul, your one and only soul, Judge so-and-so, entered your body at the moment of your conception then wouldn't you remember that? Wouldn't you remember your birth? Your ges-

---

43 Waugh, H. *Last seen Wearing.* 55. 1953
44 Eysenck, H.J. *Encyclopedia of Psychology.* II. 57/2. 1972.

tation? Wouldn't you know if your soul is the you who knows? Oh! This whole nonsense. If Apu has a soul is it made of what elements of the periodical table or any other table earthly or divine? My body my soul. Perhaps and perhaps now. Perhaps and perhaps not. Yet it is significant, and Bavna makes note of the significance, that if she had read this article five months ago—before Thomas—she would have burned with anger and isolation, while now, the anger doesn't burn and the isolation is not only in her but everywhere. Because Thomas. Isn't one like that. Is he? the one? Is there such a one one? Do I? Do I want one?

{*Soul Sleepers is the name of a new religious sect which has recently made its appearance at Fairfield, Iowa... They think that the soull is a mortal substance, and sleeps within the body until resurrection.*[45]}

Many I and always them. Not theses. I'm not waiting to stand up. Ach. not smart enough, strong enough? well, smart enough? am I? Married. Mother's voice.

Her mother's mother's mother's voice. All the way back to the villages of India. Way down there. This is the one. Wait wait Bavna. You let yourself in for. But something I know I know. Because I just want to know? No I know I know. Help me I said this morning while we were and he did. With everything he did and he has. He keeps asking me

{*I can hardly get so much for mine as will hold soul and body together.*[46]}

like that who are you looking at me like who are you? He said I enter you he said this is mine he said.

{*Like every king..., the queenmother has her elders, among whom are several spokeswomen, female akrafo or soul-bearers.*[47]}

And me?! Who welcomed

---

45 *Southern Entereprise.* 13 June 2/5. 1860
46 Scott, Sir Walter. *Cast. Dang.* ix. 1831
47 Meyerowitz, L.R. *Sacred State of Akan.* ii. 51. 1951

him like a conquered city: liberate me! Who does by God.

{Our vulgar notion that they do not own women to have any souls, is a mistake.[48]}

      I can't fathom. a place for himself. As I do claim his his.. ...that's mine then.

{Soul stuff is the spiritual power with which every male in primitive societies seeks to enhance his prowess and standing in the tribe. It can only be gained by special feats. ...It is also thought to be found in the hair.[49]}

      Thomas. Thomas. You need a new last name. We both do, a new one together. I. Let's go to Europe he says already this summer he says. Let's Go on Five Dollars a day. What's happening to you girl? Goddamn judges.

{That all their Thoughts, and the whole of what they call Soul, are only various Action and Repercussion of small particles of Matter.[50]}

      Got to stop eating so much the pleasures we've been on in three months! The taste of that sushi of the first sushi we always eat: fresh tuna! on the tongue! sucked slid in. Funny girl.

{I never saw so much soul in a lady's eyes, as in hers[51]}

      Make him laugh. What do you want to start with, I'll say? Oh my God I don't want to do this. He doesn't really. Am I right for him? It's not that I'm not good enough God knows but that I'm different, strange. I need funny things. Really believed I wouldn't. Was content. Things he couldn't ever understand. I have what I need? Bavna, you make yourself crazy. You'll make him crazy. He says he's too much for me I'd never be able to give him all he needs I say I'm too much for him he'll never be able to take all I give out all I hold in all I....my ontological insecurity. What

48 Montagu, Lady M.W. *Letters*. I. xxxix. 1716-18
49 Davies, D. *Dictionary of Anthropology*. 165/2. 1972
50 Bentley, Richard. *Boyle Lectures*. i. 13. London: Printed for Henry Mortlock. 1692
51 Richardson, Samuel. *Clarissa VI. 169. 1748*

a phrase. I love it. So hard to say it like it too is ontologically insecure. My crazy life. Ach. I can't believe I even floating I who've taken root who've grabbed hold. Nevermore. No kids for two more semesters. I can't believe it. I was reconciled. I really was. But then......and then. What's his new last name? Thomas _____? and Thomas _____? You who were content you're jumping the gun. You are my myths, he said. He wrote that. On paper. I have it. even if. Even when. Oh I'm so pessimistic and so romantic in the same breath. Aaaah. That cheesecake. There. Third from the left. That piece. How much? Money? More calories than money my dear.

{If aught that the...hand of sculptor has wrought in marble of soultrans-fiured and soul-transfiguring deserves to live.[52]}

The way he. ravenously.... as though I were....he's so hungry I fed him I filled him. we. Maybe he'll want some. Together we'll indulge. I'll wait. In just a minute he'll be here, I'm sure.

---

52 Joyce, James. *Ulysses* 138. 1922

Faith

W hen my father walked in an angel accompanied him. If, when I was young, I had continued my religious education I might have known which angel it was. But having abandoned my Rabbinical studies in its early stages, long before I might have even gotten to the sophisticated, restricted, esoteric studies like Angelology, I had no expertise with which to discern among the various personae who make up the Angelogical coterie, no key to the taxonomy of the assemblage of Other Worlds' characters, be they physical or supernatural, be they manifest or imagined, be they dream or vision, be they tradition or experiment, be they divine or demonic, be they mystical or spiritual. I was ill equipped. I was unprepared. I was a naïf.

With my mother visiting her sick aunt in the heartland of the country, my father and I talked about things we wouldn't have approached had my mother been with us. We ate at one of my father's favorite restaurants, a simple cafe with ample if ordinary food which served a regular crowd of retired people on fixed incomes. The pace of retirement from his post as Professor of Mathematics at Princeton allowing my father to breathe easier than the pressures of a working life ever had, he was opening up, With just the two of us free to wander, we meandered through the broken lines of his experience.

We ate simply, of a crisp head-lettuce salad, baked chicken, a melange of rice and vegetables.

My father ate with gusto while the Angel in our midst sang in Yiddish: —My'n zun, my'n'a ty'er ay'ner, a song my father used to sing, often nearly secretly. Alone, late at night, sneaking downstairs, I'd find him in the dark, twirling in a trance around our living room, dancing and singing this tune someone must have carried over from worlds now gone, cultures not meant for public display in our new world. The song means something like —My son, my beloved one. Had I only known more Angelology! Who was this angel – a union of distinctly dark and light almost-substance swirling within the hardly defined boundaries of his being. This Angel sang with a passion of extreme beauty I'd almost seen my father achieve in his secret nights alone.

Is that what attracted the Angel to my father? Song? My grandfather – my father's father – had been as pious as a disciple. Frightened in a frightening new world with opaque societies, he clung to the strict Jewish laws he carried with him from Russia, lashing out with a frightened-harsh hand when his children showed signs of straying. He kept *kashrut*, kept the prohibitions and obligations of *Shabbat*, kept his house, life, his prayer in an observantly arranged in a piously ordained order. He kept his children under his now stern eye. America, a safer home to his hard work, yet roiled with temptations: Jewish gangs thrived in my father's neighborhood, young Jewish kids going off to college coming home assimilated, wearing baseball caps, listening to jazz, opening hearts to chaos. Jews were marrying Protestants, Catholics, Episcopalians, Baptists. My grandfather hadn't ever heard of half the dizzying disorienting number of sects Christianity had spawned in the wild freedoms of this New World.

My father rebelled against the old ways, but lacked the anger or the strength or simply had too great a sense of humor to sustain radical departures, so my grandfather found it reasonable that my father go to university, locally.

First born in America, my father was the first in his family to get a higher education, a secular education at all. He married a Jewish girl, but they eloped early to have sex, and then, a year later, they had a proper Rabbinical marriage. My brothers and sisters and I were brought up in the faith: synagogue on *Shabbat*, Hebrew school after public school – Jewish history, Jewish philosophy – Jewish reason, Jewish mysticism, Jewish poetry, Hebrew lessons, Bar Mitzvahs, Jewish books on the bookshelves, Jewish youth groups where we would find Jewish friends, and more importantly, mates. We were Jews to the core of the spirit of that name. That spirit which suffocated me, had a brilliantly lit fire at its core. The fire caught me, if obliquely.

Our lives were rife with Jewish symbols, the history of the people, the recent memory of the Holocaust not only taught and discussed, but lived. Many of the older generation we grew up with had numbers on their arms. There was a recent time when we were, to others, a threat so total to the fragility of their psychic disintegration that we were vermin, a filth, a disease, the target of a well organized, bizarre, absolute, unreal and unrealistic, physical extinction. Yet, not even for the first time. So I studied, so I learned, so I dreamt, of victories.

At this dinner, absent my mother, my father confessed to me that he had his own ideas about our monotheistic God. What were his own ideas? He went to *shul* every *Shabbat*. My brothers and sisters had married Jews and were raising their children as Jews. I was the first to stray. In my youth, I had gone to Rabbinical school, but for two now abandoned reasons. The first, man has a consciousness so magnificently so dangerously wild that only the received structure of an ancient code has any hope to wrestle with it; and, I wanted to please my father, from whom love was a difficult gift to wrench out.

So what now were his —own ideas about the whole thing? The Angel stopped singing. My father ate. Did my father offend the Angel?

My family had been emotionally too quiet, but I was an emotional outrage, a thunderstorm, hurricane, a dybbuk born onto a quiet block to a quiet family. I went to Rabbinical school in that desperately earnest quest to attain my father's love, and it was the desperate attempt of a young man alone, with yet no fire of his own. I would do anything to fortify my meager sense of being bound to a hunger to know a greater, even sacred being. I would study, sing, try, I would be noticed by my father in his tower where he dwelt with his own sacred loneliness. I would shaken and awaken him, I would rebel so violently he would scream, or I would perform so brilliantly he would shine within the shrine of my brilliance. Neither happened that way. So I left Rabbinical studies with an awakening: I had all the love I would get. It would suffice. Being a Rabbi would bring no more illumination or approbation than being a pimp.

And something displaced my desire for love: a parched thirst for for knowledge, for knowing, fot the debased and the exalted experience of life. Was I premature? I walked, in my student days, down Broadway from the Seminary where I only spent days on end in a cauldron of waiting, past the University where I took my secular classes. At a local coffee shop, I stared in the window a long time. The mirrored reflection of my own face at the border of liberated meaningless/ identitylessness looked back at me in total longing in a spring afternoon. Walking in, crossing the threshold, I sat down adamantly to break the laws of *kashrut*. I ordered a hamburger — unkosher meat to begin with — and a milkshake, the insanely forbidden combination of milk and meat at the same meal. I shook as I sat at the little sandwich shop. When I turned to look, there I was again, an innocent out on the sidewalk looking in before the act, at the moment of the irrevocable loss of all childhood, of all attachment to my father, my search for love, my inclusion in community. What's next?. What's left? I may as well become a junkie. I'm lost. I may as well sleep with vestal virgins, steal, murder.

Liberation was not exhilarating. It was at worst dark and empty and terror-ridden, at best banal, its banality its most pungent consequence. People passed in the street. What could I do? Should I shout out to them that I had broken the Jewish laws and my ties with my past, scream that I was abandoned and excommunicated? Damned to non-being? Worse. Damned to life without meaning?

So I listened, maybe even more attentively than the Angel. My father, done chewing, spoke simply: —I don't, he said, — believe in any of it.

—What do you mean 'any of it?' You believe in...

—No. I don't believe in God. Never have. Doesn't make sense at all. The idea of God is a romance, a diversion, that's all, told by lost, small, frightened people who know that life is difficult and fear their death that is unknown, and they can't bear it.

—But, Pa. You go to *shul* every *Shabbat*. You're an officer in the Temple, an official in the services. They couldn't have services without you doing your job.

—I know I like it. It's part of the diversion. I feel comfortable.

—Are you still trying to please *your* father? I asked.

— Does it matter anymore? The God my father believed in was a Demon. A true vision. If I could, I would believe in his DemonGod. My father was deeply an enigma. I am just human.

As my father spoke, the Angel grew. The matter of which he was composed quickened in its spiraling whirl, expanding, becoming violent, storm-like.

—You don't believe in God?

—No. Do you!?

—No, I can't.

—But you want to?

—Of course, I said. —Don't you?

—No, my father said.

—You're lying, I told him. —I know you. Faith gives you meaning.

—Faith, my father said, —destroys meaning.

The Angel screamed. He bellowed, threw up his arms, enveloping the whole booth we sat in. His voice deepened to a more guttural, more resonant depth. He sang out something in Yiddish or Hebrew I couldn't understand though it sounded like an Angelic or a prophetic or a demonic formula.

My God, he is *Moloch Hamovet*, the Angel of Death. That's why he sang so laconically, why he sang Tatele My'n Zun. He called my father his little one in his song. He had come to take my father and on my father's last pronouncement, a denial of God, my father would die. The angel swelled, filling the entire room. Now I screamed. I jumped out of my seat threw up my arms and screamed.

—Thomas! my father yelled at me. —Are you crazy? Sit down! I did.

At the bottom of my scream lay my father's death. Beyond that, my own. Beyond that, only a pure something else.

—Don't say that, I said.

—Don't say what?

—You don't believe in God.

—Why not? Don't tell me all of a sudden you're religious again. *Frum*. A believer.

—No, Pop, I never really was. It's just... The angel sang again, holier now than anything, an aria echoed through a Great Hall. He sang the Jewish declaration of faith, what many Jews had sung as they went to the gas chambers, what all pious Jews in every age want to be their last words: —Sh'ma Yisroal Adonai Elohanu Adonai Echud. —Hear Oh Israel. The Lord our God, the Lord is One. That enigma of a chant declaring God's oneness, singularity, a being of wholeness on fire continuously and silently. Every religious Jew would hope to ascend to God's lap with those words on their lips. Surely this was *Moloch Hamovet*. My father was dying. I cried.

—Why cry? my father asked, —surely you don't believe any of that do you, in God or...

—No, Pa, that's not why...

—Well? What's the matter? Are you choking? Are you alright?

—No, Pa. I love you. I took his hands on the table, soft, familiar, those hands whose approval and small affections I prayed for as a child I could now take with affection myself at this moment of our mortal life.

The Angel sang deeper.

—Yes, my father said, —I love you too, but what's the big deal?

Then, the Angel was gone. Vanished. His voice still echoed, that enormous boom. His power lingered. But his visage was gone. Could I just not see him anymore? Was his work done? Would my father drop right here, now? I held his hands.

—Hold still, I told him.

—So?

—Don't move.

—What's with you? So I don't believe in...

—Neither do I but be quiet. We sat like that for 5 or 6 minutes, a long time. Death would now be no more of a revelation to me or him than had been my adolescent breaking of the laws of my faith.

The next day I searched through the city library in the Judaica section. I read through tomes of Talmud, tracts of occult Jewish texts, books on Angelology, until I did find something early in the evening. I hadn't eaten all day. I was swirling myself. I was right about that, it was dark and light swirling together. I found the reason, and the reason that when my father said he didn't believe in God the Angel swelled to enormous proportions and sang the famous *Shma*.

He is not *Molech Hamovet*, the Angel of Death. He is an obscure angel, little needed for thousands of years. His name is Achmuda, an almost perverse angel who chooses to flaunt God by caring more for mankind than God, with mankind's best interests at heart. According to one esoteric tradition, Achmuda intercedes with God on behalf of people who don't believe, have exchanged the beauty of of belief for the, only potential and fleeting, beauty of freedom. In this particular tradition, which emanates from ancient Hebraic sources, predating the exodus into Babylonia, predating Talmud, Achmuda is the highest of angels. One esoteric writing claims Achmuda created God during an orgy of Angelic Beasts. Created he God who is all of Him the body of sexual reality.

Conventional believers are blinded in their need to justify the presence of evil in the world. The man of no belief, the skeptic, has the greater opportunity to understand the marriage of light and darkness, the nature of Achmuda's appearance. The unfaithful have the more difficult path; according to these esoteric Rabbinic traditions, faith (—milk) is easy, so that unfaith is a kind of much stronger achievement (—meat). One cannot have milk and meat at the same meal.

Since this tradition was concocted by a group of the faithful, luminous Rabbis including the famous Rabbi Ashtoreth and the one Rabbi who was said to be closest to the angels, Rabbi Aliyah, I have no doubt they were intensely aware of the consequences of their statement and the limitations it offered their own positions. It is heretical. It is an astonishing recognition for men of faith to declare that the way of no faith is more difficult, more trying, and more true than their own. Was it not particularly prescient of Rabbi Aliyah to recognize the existence of Achmuda as God's nearest Angel, one who, as Rabbi Aliyah put it over a thousand years ago, (I quote from text, *A Tract on the Bliss of Contradiction As Known Only Through Contact with the Speed of Time*), Achmuda was the only being in the universe of any essence or any substance to have immediate access to God's attention. When Achmuda sings on behalf of the unfaithful, God has to listen God has to consider His own lack of faith. God gave Achmuda the most richly beautifully haunting voice in order that God would hear it instantly when Achmuda sang. God knowing well the travails of the unfaithful trusts them more than any other.

I couldn't decipher, through the entrails of this doctrine winding back on itself, whether it proclaimed the existence of the Divine, of God or the non-existence of the Divine. Each position – existence, non-existence – became increasingly impossible and inherently self-contradictory. Either that difficulty developed naturally over centuries of inquiry, or centuries of inquiry have obscured our ability to hold true and untrue the same thing at the same time. Maybe those clever, cultic, esoteric Rabbis were trying to force us with a kind of intellectual whirlwind down the byway of their own unknowledge. I wanted to know whether that Angel I saw was a reality. The Rabbis described him but then in their perverse logic, in the inescapable but truly seductive maze constructed of an irresistible language or languages they refused to confirm him, they even negated his existence.

I copied that passage out for my father.

—What does this mean, Thomas, he asked, —are you through with doubt? Are you going back to Seminary? I told you long ago you don't have to please me. Now you know I don't even believe in God.

—It's just something painfully interesting, I said, —something I found fascinating, maybe impenetrable to the modern mind.

My father, closing his eyes, recited from the Medieval Jewish poet, Reuven: —Oh I move you away Mountain, Oh I bring the City forward. He asked me had I heard of Roch Lahakot. His new book, *Swift Zero*. Rosh's theory that, while numbers are relatively stable, zero is never the same. Every time you see it, zero is a new zero.

—Lahakot? I said. —I haven't heard of him. Should I? A

friend of yours?

—Yeah. His family goes back in mathematics to the Middle Ages.

—Don't go crazy in your old age.

—No such thing as old age, he said.

—Or madness?

—Or madness. I'm looking beyond faith and meaning. Into this beautiful void I see but that I'm not sure exists.

—That's why I can't believe. How many times I have reached out for faith, OK, even for God, and touched only a void, and fallen back!

—I said the beautiful the extraordinary void. And I said I'm not sure even that exists.

—Does anything exist?

—Oh, my father said to me, —everything exists.

Idiot Child

—OPEN the window. —It's

freezing.

—Just a crack. I can't breathe. I need even frozen air.

—What if the baby comes?

—He'll do well in his winters, Jebii closed her eyes.

—Breathe. Breathe.

Thomas looked to the midwife but before she could offer any, Jebii said.

—Don't worry. Our baby's coming in exactly 20 minutes. Then you can shut the window. OK? Open it now for a while.

The midwife nodded. Thomas let the freezing air of Manhattan's blue dawn into the room.

—It's good to have a child at dawn, Thomas said, —it's the day's elegance.

—Such a romantic, my darling.

Jebii heaved and bit.

Thomas put a fresh damp towel on her forehead.

—I'm not in pain, Thomas said. I can afford to wax romantic.

Thomas bent to kiss Jebii's lips. Straightening up, the cold air hit his dampened lips leaving a layer of thin frost on them.

—Thomas, said the midwife, —you step out now.

—No. I'll stay.

—It's not seemly for a man to see his wife like this.

—Our lives are not seemly.

—Then be quiet and stay out of the way.

—Is he coming?

Jebii groaned.

—You heard her, the midwife said. He will come in eighteen minutes. That would be, she checked her watch, —at 5:55. Wait in the livingroom.

—No, Thomas said. I'll stay.

Jebii nodded her head for Thomas to stay. Jebii's hand squeezed his. Her thin fingers might have broken his bones. Lightly, Thomas squeezed back. Jebii screamed. Drawing in air, she screamed again. Her narrow hips cracked. She screamed once more, for the third time. It was 5:49. Then she was quiet, occupied.

The midwife prepared herself and prepared Jebii. At 5:55 the baby's head showed. Jebii was on the verge of being ripped open, but her body would tolerate any upheavals her child might challenge her with. She gave in, the birth occurring from behind her closed eyes down her spine into her womb pulling up through the muscles of her thighs calves feet soles of her feet her toes stretched out. The head came out; the shoulders forced an opening. The torso slipped through. The tiny fat legs the small purple-pink feet as they followed into open air. Jebii saw it all, then saw it again as image in the dark behind her closed eyes.

The midwife, first to see the baby, was the first to know, and she knew right away, he was what they called in Africa, an Idiot Child.

Thomas was the second to know. He looked for confirmation from the midwife.

Taking the child to her breast, Jebii felt it in the cherished way he sucked at her. They all three knew.

—Something's wrong with this child, she said.

—That depends, the midwife said, —on what part of Africa you come from. In many villages—my village—something is wrong with this child. We would leave him in the jungle to die.

—This is not Africa! Jebii said.

—Where you come from, Jebii, the midwife glanced over at Thomas, —in all of Tanzania, *all* of Tanzania, she repeated— there is nothing wrong. He is special. They call them a Roho Mtoto or a Mtoto Mzito.

—We'll call him David, Thomas said. —That's the only name for him now.

—But your Grandfather, Jebii said. —Masinde.

—He needs a name stronger than even Masinde.

—But David, the midwife protested, —was a King, a King of Jerusalem. Don't mock the poor child.

—Far from mockery, Thomas told her. —Far from it! Our boy needs a powerful powerful name. So he'll be King of Idiots. The great wide world of Idiocy will belong to him. Within this realm he'll do whatever he pleases. What Kings do. We'll all obey him from here on out. In Jerusalem, they would pronounce his name Dahvid. Or even Dahvid Melech! King David.

Jebii, pulling him down to her whispered

—Don't be bitter. Please. I can't stand it if you're bitter. Please, Thomas. I too will crumble under any bitterness.

—I'm not bitter. I'm proud, Jebii. We've given birth to a King. Descendant of a King. I'm not joking.

Long after the midwife, having finished with Dahvid, had gone home, Dahvid sucked at his mother's breast in that tender way as if he too knew what had happened to him, as if he knew the kind of world he would face, while Thomas sat on the windowsill watching them. Not one of their friends had come in from the livingroom or even knocked at the door. Thomas, taking Dahvid, heavily wrapped into a yellow blanket, carried him to the window. He described everything he saw to Dahvid, newborn, so that Dahvid would see and understand:

—Out there, this is what there is this morning: a truck has parked in the middle of our street, I don't know why. Already I've seen a few cars have tried to go around it. Some have made it, others have backed up down the block to go another way. Do you hear them honk their horns? That's their anger. The snow is piled up quite high now. A few cars, snowed in, look like they won't get out until spring. But of course their owners will come with shovels at the first chance they get to dig until they free those cars. That young boy from our block — I've seen him before —is walking a dog which their family probably keeps against the rules of the building they live in. You can hear the traffic moving on the Avenue. You can almost feel it. Maybe you *do* feel it, Dahvid. There are five trees on the two sides of this block. I'll count them for you they'll be an incantation over your Idiocy. One.....Two.....Three.......Four........Five. A pentangle of trees for Dahvid. And they're pretty good size, but I don't know what kind they are. They aren't oaks, Jebii, they aren't maple. Do you know?

—No, Jebii said. —I don't know.

—Your parents come from Africa, David, from Tanzania. But we're city people. From Nairobi. We don't always know the names of nature's things. Don't touch the cold window, though here in our room it's too warm. A little while ago, while you were busy with your eyes closed sucking at your mother's breast, people all up and down this block went off to work. What do they do? Clerks. Salespeople. Mechanics. Lawyers or Professors. Poets. Every morning during the week they walk out early into the snow on these streets to go off to work. Later in the evening, they'll come home again. They all have ambition. I work for all of them. I'm a union organizer. Thomas smiled. —Like a good Marxist, Thomas laughed, —I don't believe in God, not our old, tribal gods, and not our Christian God. But no, he laughed again, I'm not a Marxist. I don't believe in utopias. Just a little social justice. In the power of the people. Especially the power of the Idiot People. I wanted to be a musician. That's a kind of faithless faith that seeks to climb over ignorance in order to breathe more widely. But I needed a lot more education to do that. I don't want to talk about me. I want to talk about that, out there.

—Sing for him, Jebii asked.

—A lullaby?

—Sing *God Bless Africa.*

So Thomas began: —*God bless Africa / Bless its leaders*
—In Swahili, Jebii said. —He'll come to know it in Swahili.
Thomas sang https://www.youtube.com/watch?v=vhHM-cleuiEg :

Mungu Ibariki Afrika
Wabariki Viongozi wake
Hekima Umoja na
Amani Hizi ni nagao zetu
Afrika na watu wake

Ibariki Afrika
Ibariki Afrika
Tubariki watoto wa
Afrika

Mungu Ibariki Tanzania
Dumisha uhuru na Umoja
Wake kwa Waume nawa Watoto
Mungu Ibariki Tanzania na
Watu wake

Ibariki Tanzania
Ibariki Tanzania
Tubariki watoto wa
Tanzania

David slept. His eyes twitched.
—What does he dream?
—Does he dream already?
—Let's say he does.
—Then he dreams of his own tongue.
—Or he dreams of his own breath.
—Or of my breast.

—He believes that it's his, a part of himself.

—Yes.

—Or he dreams of your womb.

—That's another world altogether lost to him now.

—To be factored in to the equation of his readiness?

—Yes.

—Already.

—Immediately. In an instant. He takes in his first breath he exhales out the world of the womb gone.

Their friends had all left.

Thomas brought food. He kept Jebii comfortable. When Dahvid woke he would lie still, he would cry or he would suck. Then Thomas would carry him for a while talking to him about what was out there. The snow. The park where the snow covered the grass. The river which flowed from far up in Canada all the way down through New York State, all the way past their city to the Atlantic Ocean, all about the Atlantic Ocean, about the palisades across the river, the boats coming downriver, the garbage truck which came up their block so noisily, what was garbage, what was a day, what were eyes, what was a fire hydrant and a fire truck and fire, what was concrete what brick what stone, what was a building then what was a cave, what is an archway, what is light, what is air, what is cold and what is warm, winter, spring, what could be seen, what is a window, what is breath, what are animals, what are those animals' names, what is the sky above them, what water, what is earth, what is food, what are tastes, what are feelings sensual and emotional, what are words.

Then Dahvid would sleep. His first day would pass.

Toward midnight, Thomas opened a book.

—I'll read you a short story, Dahvid. It's very peculiar. It's like a poem perhaps more than a story. Soon you'll be too young to understand it. Well, perhaps I barely understand it myself.

But you might never grow up to understand it, so I want to read it to you now when you might just be able to absorb it. It's an old story, by an African writer who lives in Africa. In Tanzania.

—When I was born, Thomas read, —they put me right away into a burlap sack. Why, I didn't know, and I still don't know. Were they protecting me? Was I some precious, precocious being? Did I require some very unique treatment? And the sack? What was the sack? The oldest sack ever made? the earth's first sack? Is it a sack-womb? So that in some sense I have been born, but remain enwombed? I've grown up inside the sack. As I grow, the sack grows. I think I'm quite large by now, though I have nothing but my own apparent growth by which to gauge size at all. I might be quite small. How is it that I can know about the relational concepts of size or age to even speculate about how big I may be? I have no reference. I'll tell you later how I calculate these things. It was difficult; the sack grows as I grow. I can tell you a great deal about the sack—everything about the sack—about my thoughts, about the voices that I hear.

—I hear two kinds of voices, one lower, the other in a higher tone. There must be two kinds of people outside the sack. Or, if it's one person, that person has two modes of speech. If I were to speak I'm sure I would have only one kind of voice. I don't know which kind it would be. By listening, I have learned to understand their language somewhat — that's not so impossible for a child — still, I understand them a lot by the tone in their voices.

—This is what I understand. Often they want things of one another. Especially the two voices I hear most, one of each kind. They talk to each other all the time. It's not hard to tell when they like or they don't like what's happening because when they don't like it their voices sound like they have to squeeze through a small space to get out. They seem to be pushing their voices. But at other times, let me tell you, those voices come in bellows, in great and sometimes terrible sometimes ecstatic rushes, broad and deep voices filled with air. I have figured out that voices are made of air. How? I'll tell you some other time. It was shrewd. Then the words often seem to be very short, brief words. There must be something about the longer words which requires a different kind of mood, because they speak them more quietly. I too know about being calm and being agitated. What agitates me? Thinking that I want to get out of this sack. What calms me? Is there a sack? Am I the sack? Haven't I grown woven into the sack? Aren't I, in part, burlap?

—Some of the voices resemble each other. Some are very distinct, nothing like any others. Once you hear a voice, most likely you'll hear it again. The strangest voices — well, there's one that's almost of one tone. It comes at regular intervals just as it has gotten dark. You see, I know about dark and light. It speaks frequently of the same things because I hear the same sounds repeated. I think it tells the other voices something it knows or gives them something they require. Sometimes it says awful things in a calm voice. That contradiction lends to its credibility. I can tell they're awful things because something inherent in the words clings to them. Other voices may repeat the same sounds that voice has articulated. I want to figure out what that voice says. If I could, then I would understand a great deal. I listen for what it repeats. Some day I'm sure that instantaneously in one terrific moment it will be revealed to me what it says. I want to go to that voice, with that voice. It understands. I know about the possibility of faking. I think it understands. Once I fell into a long trance believing it was my voice. Perhaps you think my entire condition is a trance.

—After that voice, each time it comes, then the other most familiar two voices speak, while some other noise happens. The other noise seems to come from a similar source as the•voice•I•want•to•go•to. Strange. I like the other noise. I like it more than any of the voices even the one•I•want•to•go•to. I don't want to go to that noise. I want it to come to me.

If I go on growing some day they will take me out of the sack. Or I will outgrow the sack. I will absorb the sack into my body so that, in essence, there will be no sack. There will be only myself. I want to get out of the sack for my own reasons, just because I do. But do I want to be with all those voices? They are sometimes very confused. Sometimes I hear a voice — other than the•one•I•want•to•go•to — which comes in from time to time and I want to be with it. Then it goes off, not coming back for quite a while. Would I ever be able to find it? If I do come out, will it stop coming altogether? I would hunt for it. I would give up the•voice•I•want• to•go•to and the noise•I•want•to•come•to•me to hunt for that other voice that I know I want to be with. There is only one. I have heard it. I have heard it hum. Not often. Nothing would stop me.

—Then I would bring to it the•voice•I•want•to•go•to — because it's not confused —and the noise•I•want•to•come•to•me — although it sounds confused, limited, still it seems able to enjoy its confusion and even to play with its limits. I want to enjoy myself. Perhaps I can learn from that noise. Even here in this sack. Is that strange? Yes, it is very strange. Very very strange.

—That one voice I hear that I•want•to•be•with and would hunt for if I got out of the sack — the only thing that might stop me from hunting for it would be that I might exhaust myself and give up. Interesting that I should already know about that peril, isn't it? But, if I tired, if I despaired, I would recover. I could go on.

—The next time I talk to you, I will have understood more about voices and noises. I don't know who you are. I know that you're here, that you listen, that you seek me, that you want to know more. I promise you, because I keep learning. If I pay very careful attention — that is required — I can learn a great deal that will be helpful to both of us. Sometimes I think there is no sack. Then I feel it. I touch it. I move the sack. Why did they birth me and put me in a sack? I ask this my most important question. Asking the question, then listening, I seem sometimes to have an answer. As I can discern more of what their voices are saying, as I understand more of what their voices are, I see an answer flicker.

—I like talking like this, if this is talking. Does it mean that I too have a voice and that someday I will learn to talk with a voice? I'm not sure I want to do that. I think I prefer this. Talking like this, without a voice. I prefer it. I'm sure that the language we use now is superior to what they use there. It reminds me a little bit of the noise•that• comes•to•me.

—Who wrote that? Jebii asked.

—A writer from Tanzania named just Malkah.

—But Malkah is a woman's name.

—Yes. He wrote about that. He took that name Malkah from his Grandmother, whom he adored. He wrote an essay about her called —The Fictional Voice. His grandmother constantly told him stories, family stories, stories about strange scientists, philosophers, speculators, con-men, politicians she had known. He believed them all. Only after her death, he discovered that she had invented them all. He had lived vividly in a putative world of invented narratives, of potential reality. Initially, he wrote in his essay, he felt betrayed. He worked to expel not only the stories from his mind, but, to expel his lying, fabricating Grandmother as well. Unsuccessful in those attempts, he examined the strangest details of her stories, then rebuilt his image of her from the images of those details. She had given him the exact shape of reality.

—Do you think he invented her?

—Because of the title of his essay?

—Yes.

—You're so clever, Jebii. He may have made her up. But maybe not. He leaves it up to us to decide.

—What do you decide, Thomas?

—I'm the one who named our baby Dahvid, the King of Id-iocy. So, yes, I believe that his Grandmother was fictional. He describes her at great length, the way she stood, the way her arms would move as she spoke, he spent terrific energy on her mouth and eyes. And yet, of course, she never really lived.

—Don't be bitter, Thomas. We can't afford it. Here, take Dahvid again. Show him what's outside again now in the light of the streetlamps. I love when you do that. When you show him the world telling him about it.

—I don't know how much of it he'll ever know, Jebii. I want to get in as much as I can before whatever it is that he is or he has really sets in on him.

—Yes. Thank you for reading us the story by Mister Malkah. Strange, as you said. I like that about it. I'm so very tired. My eyes have already closed. I dream of living inside of a sack from where I hear voices speak. I am as empty as this sack is filled with myself. There is no sack and I am inside it. Funny, it's such a lovely dream. Will you watch Dahvid as I sleep?

Alphabet

—Jesus.

—I know. It's a mess.

—Don't apologize. It's extraordinary.

—An extraordinary mess.

—Strong, Thomas. No. Wrong word. Strange. Moving. Very moving.

—And none of that.

—It's unbelievable. I could say it scares me. It does. But then it elates me. Not a jubilant elation. A clear one. A clear ring of elation in a continuous present.

—It's all eluded me.

—It eludes me, too. Just.

—Just?

—You read it one line at a time, left to right, but it's like reading it all at once.

—Nacheinander—nebeneinander.

—Exactly. The beginning is the end the beginning's in the end.

Al takes up the 25 pages again, reading. —Shit! he declaims.

—It's a telescope looking into a telescope.

—Where?

—Everywhere. Each word.

—Non-word.

—And non-word. It does, Thomas. It really scares me. Takes me into a bright white solitude.

Thomas read through the whole 25 pages. —I worked all night. Never looked back. Read it over about 3:00. Had no idea. None. I'm an innocent man, here, Al.

—Innocent? You wrote it. You gave it to me.

—No, Al. I wrote. Fiction. New fiction. Words. a-b-c. Context. Syntax. The machine spewed out this total confusion. Not an English word in it.

—I don't believe this.

—I do. I know. Here we are.

—In a bright white solitude?

—I tried to decode it, Al. There are no patterns.

—But it reads…..

—Was I not the genius at this?

—You were.

—I couldn't get anywhere decoding it. I had to decode it. I'm talking to myself somewhere in here but I can't hear me. I was in tears. I'm telling you. Exhausted, hopeless, I went to bed. Could it be that only exhaustion prevented me from knowing the one thing I was trying to say to myself. With some rest, it would all later become obvious. I woke up at 4:30. Now, look, here it is, morning and past morning, and nothing in the way of a useful ordering of any alphabet. No sense at all.

—Can you calm down for a minute, Thomas? Just calm down?

—But what does it say, Al? What can you ever see there?

—I don't know, Thomas. Something. It's important.

—Gibberish. I spent a whole night working, in love with the work, happy to work, engaged, in the zone, seeing in my head all night exactly what I wrote. All alone in the house. Then, going back to edit. A typewriter with a mind of its own.

—You have to work on a computer! I keep telling you.

—That would have made any difference?

—Have you photocopied this?

—Why?

—Just do it.

—And then what?

—Send it off.

—To whom?

—To Noam.

—Gimme your coffee, Al. You need a drink. On the rocks, yes?

—Send it under a pseudonym, Thomas. Let Noam see it. I'll send it for you.

—It's random, Al, typewriter gone-mad random-generated letters. Nothing more.

—Make a photocopy, Thomas. Give me the copy. You keep the original. Then we'll go for a walk. Get breakfast.

Noam's on-line journal, *Ocean City Desert*, published —Interruptions/(error)ChaosOrigins. Readers wrote letters to the editor, selections of which Noam passed on to Thomas, via Alfred. They said almost ridiculous things:

No writing in our time has captured the arc of human history and the whole condition of our culture without being either sentimental or supercilious. This does it.

What other writing has encompassed our times with its obsessions, its expectations shattered, its pointless ironies, its wary glance ahead, as does this piece?

One comment was simple:

This writes the significance of myself and everyone I know or have read.

And one said:

This isn't the future; it's the end of an exhausted past. But when the future looks back it will see this among its beginnings.

The most exuberant letter read:

The language is beheaded. And you know what that means: not that it's not language. Not at all. It's language disillusioned of its attachment to repetitive reality, to initiate some more immediate yet abundant reality that it appropriates it and reincorporates it and reincorporates again. It makes us know so much that more accurate world which we would never have had. I keep coming back to the piece because every time I leave it I've left something behind in it which I need to retrieve. What I've left behind I can't tell, but it is structurally essential to my mind. My human mind. My conscious mind.

—Molly, this is a dream. Delirious.

—It's a delirious reality, Thomas. It's real.

—Come home.

—Listen: 'A species of cicada who burrow themselves into the earth and hatch only once every seventeen years in this cacophony of a guttural chirr, high pitched, rough, painful, that covers the whole midwestern plains.' I read that from a brochure. This is the year of their cycle. They don't stop day or night. Everyone hates it.

—So you leave it. You come home. Please.

—They rasp against your nerves, painful, Thomas. Raw. But they're so intriguing. Day and night and day. People go to movies, they play their TVs too loudly, roll up their car windows and turn on the air conditioning and the radio. They talk louder and louder to each other. They do whatever they can to not hear. But I want to hear, Thomas. I need to hear.

—Need to hear pain in your ears?

—They bring something with them from those years buried that I want to hear. I'll be in the library researching. I'll go to the university to talk to some ag people. All right?

—This is crazy, Molly. You're obsessed with them. It's just cicadas. You study the human brain.

—I study what draws me to itself to be studied.

—You're in another mad obsession.

—And you?

—I miss you.

—Every inch of me misses every inch of you. It's ok. I'm ok. I know. Don't worry. I'm ok. I kept the same room. Off the Conference rate, but I don't have to move.

—Do you miss me?

—Every inch of me misses every inch of who you are.

—Good.

—But every inch of my body wants to know about these little things. What can gestate for seventeen years? Can you imagine? Way underground. No light. Little air. What kind of birth is this? They're everywhere insisting on themselves. They're brutal.

—She's not ok. I fear for her.

—I fear for you.

—Sit here, just for a minute, Al. Do an experiment with me.

Alfred, sitting at Thomas's desk, typed in straight, ordinary prose. The keys behaved following their own lunatic inclinations. But Al's work couldn't hold a candle to —Interruptions/(error)ChaosOrigin. Nothing could. Nothing Al or Thomas composed on this typewriter or any other could.

—It's a one-off, Al said. —Never happen again.

—A giant step? Thomas asked.

—Yes, Al said. —A love supreme.

—That I'll never see again?

—Coltrane kept playing.

Thomas re-read his piece at different times of the day in different moods. He read it aloud to himself in the study, where his voice had the resonance of an echo that had originated no-where, and again in the more comfortable and ordinarily acous-tical den. He taped a reading he listened to alone. Alfred read it aloud to him, calling him a Moses who'd come to see the promised land that others would inherit—but Thomas himself would have to die without tasting the fruit of his own genius.

—If I could understand how I did this then I'd be a genius. As it is I feel like a stone, dumb. I'm behind all of you. I'm be-hind myself.

Al left, taking with him the typewriter in its case. —Peace, man, peace and love, Al said, flashing two fingers.

—Don't doubt it, Thomas said, —when the cicadas come home to roost, there'll maybe be peace.

wednesday the 28th

Can't work. why bother? write the mailaise? Write about how ground can liquefy, foundations shake, doors shut that won't open. ground liquefies, fails. I'll write a play with none of my-self in it with not even any characters with a few props on stage we'll see we'll have to see. good god how I doubt ordinary syntax, grammar, even words. unilluminating all of them. despair of any of that. Molly all right? the news all full of energies mov-ing frantically toward war. there are men whose lives are in-comelete without it and once again I fear they'll take us there.

At seven minutes to dawn on June the 25th, Thomas, after an insomniac revel of reading, called his father at the summer house on the lake, waking him up.

—What's it like up there? Look out the window. What do you see?

—I'm just opening my eyes. Wait. Good God, Thomas, it's

just dawn. You woke me up. I can't see a damn thing.

—Oh. Sorry, Dad.

—Now what is it?

—Sorry. I shouldn't have called.

—I'm up now. What is it?

—Well, it's silly. Look out the window. What do you see?

—I'm just opening my eyes. I'll tell you I don't see much. But I imagine I see everything. I see the boathouse down the slope…the lake…the steam off the water. I hear loons but I don't see any. I can see the pines that go down the hill to the lake. I think I can't really see a thing, Thomas. I'm just imagining all this. Or seeing what I know is there.

—Wait until it just begins to come clear.

—Yes. All right. It is now. I really can see the trees now. The edge of the roof of the boathouse, I can see that. Why are you asking me this?

—I want to know if you see what you expected to see?

—Pretty much. But I know this place very well.

—I know. Now tell me. Where do your perceptions and the real world meet?

His father didn't answer right away. Hearing the chirping of a bird over the phone, Thomas strained to identify it. Then after complaining about being awakened for a discourse on philosophical questions, his father said that his perception and the real world met somewhere between his own sleep and the objective world itself, in some other arena into which he had awakened, opening his eyes.

—By seeing it, you create it?

—I don't know.

—Then it doesn't exist while you sleep?

—Well, it's abandoned it while I sleep. I have to admit, you've got me somewhat interested. But these are old questions, Thomas, the oldest.

—And who abandons it? You do?

—Yes, his father answered, I do.

—And are you guilty for abandoning that awakened country to escape into sleep.

—No, I'm responsible, but not guilty.

—One more question.

—All right?

—Does that awakened territory contain language?

—Ahh. While I sleep or while I'm awake?

—Either. Or both.

—I don't know. Language maybe surrounds it on all sides infuses it from the inside.

—So language exists separately from your perception of an actual world?

—Well, I always thought it didn't, but maybe I'm wrong. It seems like this morning that I am wrong, that language certainly does exist separately from the actual world — as we're calling it — this morning but also of my perception of the actual world — as we're calling it — this morning. I wonder why I see it that way now?

—What will you do today?

—Wake up your mother, make breakfast, read, go fishing, write you a letter.

—Why write me a letter?

—To make sure you have some objective reality knocking on your sleepy head to wake you up.

—The words of your letter?

—The voice of your father.

—What are you reading?

—Paul Celan.

—But he killed himself. Why read a suicide?

—Why not?

—Because he had to completely abandon the territory between his dream and the objective world.

—Well, yes. But he's one of those few who had strong

enough reasons for suicide. Are you making moral demands of poetry now?

—Are there reasons really strong enough for suicide?

—Well, we probably all have just about the same reasons, don't we, but then for some of us the circumstances in which those reasons fester become unbearable. I always hoped I wouldn't have to face that.

Listen: —I've rediscovered them buried voiceless / solitary at the bottom of their looks of delicate cracks / in the cold shaft of a single word is to say / that doesn't find the power of the game.

—You really woke me up at this hour to listen to your new writing?

—Not mine, Tzara's. Where the Wolves Drink. 8: 12-15.

—Tzara's scripture now?

—Give mother my love.

—Can you hear the birds?

—You always ask me that.

—So? It's an exhausted question?

—No. Certainly not. Yes. I can hear the birds.

Thomas saw, out the window, a blond man walking along the sidewalk in faded Levi jeans, dirtied white tennis shoes, a green and white striped polo shirt. The man held a dog leash in his hand, and just before him, as he passed the large brown and green ash tree, his dog ran ahead eagerly, a golden terrier, about 30 or 35 pounds, Thomas guessed. The young man wasn't happy with the morning's task of walking the dog. Or maybe he had something on his mind, Thomas's imagination and automatic story telling raced on. Perhaps the man had some frightening problem to solve with his finances, his income wasn't matching his expenses, but he liked his work and he'd be damned if he'd give it up for some boring job just to make more money. Why did the culture reward less important work with more money: lawyers vs. teachers. football players vs. jazz musicians. Or maybe his life with his wife was troubling him. He was in love with her, but sometimes that love got threadbare in the work of daily routine into which he'd fall and he'd try to regain a spontaneity which was threatened in him by a tendency towards sluggishness. Or perhaps he felt grief about the sorrow of life itself, the passing of time, the quick growth of his children leaving childhood. Perhaps walking the dog was just a tedious reminder of the ashen repetitiveness of life, yet he loved the dog, he even loved walking with her, loved the light rising from the wet grass and the river. His walk quickened. He wanted to get home. Thomas made up all this about him and knew there was a distance between the imagination in which he thought and the fact of the man and the dog and even the tree. He read —Interruptions/ (error)ChaosOrigin again. He could feel the exact weight of the strange but disestranged language which seemed to hum and cavort. But he read it again and suddenly the language seemed restrained and formally constructed into syntactical units woven and interwoven into some logical pattern. Then Thomas read the piece and imagined that it was about the man and the dog and the ash tree. He could nearly imagine the Cicadae of Cleveland had been reciting his piece on interruptions and origins and chaos and order and orderlessness out across the wide fecund now-tamed and often-ruined plains of agricultural steel-mill America.

Thomas went back to the piece and added a dedication to his life-long friend, Roberto Alonzo Alfred Tapia y Contreras, who had emigrated to the United States after his father was killed in a Mexican Civil War battle between the troops of Huerta and Villa. Roberto was never able to find out from government records or any other source which side his father had fought for. A cousin once suggested that Roberto's father had actually died fighting as a recruit in the American Civil War, but Roberto calculated the dates, and decided that was clearly impossible unless his father was actually his grandfather, or even his great-grandfather, another impossibility. Roberto's cousin agreed that it was an impossibility that one man had been Roberto's grandfather or great-grandfather who died in one war, and then his father who died later in yet another war. So the question of his having died in the American Civil War seemed settled, but the question of which side he had died fighting for was not settled. Roberto had created imaginary versions of his father fighting for each side, although one of them must have been fairly close to the truth.

—If I don't eat, I won't die.

—Honey, only if you don't eat, will you die.

—My madness is not sexual.

—You are not mad. You are a genius. You are a great woman. You gave three papers at the Conference. You're on the verge of healing a thousand diseases at once.

—And look! Molly, yelling, raised herself up on tiptoes, swept a huge arm's-arc across the Midwestern fields of wheat, —I could not create one—not one grain of wheat.

—Come home, Molly. The cicadas are too much for you.

—They are our curative pain. That's my only genius I have to say.

—Yes. I know.

Molly, walking, sweated. So did Thomas. Sweat.

—Nebecheinander. Or nebeneinander?

—Do I see you?

—Do you know you?

—Do I know you?

—Can you lie in this field of wheat with me, Thomas, here, amid the pain of the noise of the 17-year cicadas and make love to me.

—Come home, Molly. We're all worried. We all miss you.

—Can you? In these fields of wheat? Here?

—I can.

—I can't.

Order Hemiptera. Two pair of membraneous wing. Compound eyes. Vibrating paired dorso-lateral timmbals. Folk medicines. Human food. Religious symbols. Cicadoidea. 600 rasping noises per hour. Per hour. I am swallowed up by this ugly sound. Its beauty. I. You become nameless.

They now and I go. homelessly? Hurts it but not them then. The absence of that pain hurts its heart for now but as a joy. unto itself. Also. I, who was Molly, promise you, Molly, herself I me that in seventeen years you will come be back again i. may. be. you, the wind that moves through here now lifting all the leaves dry it is to you I sing this hymn. You move me now through your field of wheat it is yours as am i.

On her way to meeting with an ag professor at the University of Cincinnati, Molly had missed her stop on the bus. She had to walk back, passing between the lush Burnett Woods on her left and the campus of Hebrew Union College on her right. The cicadae screeched. Might they sound like some ancient language? Hebrew? Aramaic? Some code? No. Screech.

Her meeting disappointed. The professor himself little interested in the cicada. Who could understand her? Dear Thomas? Could Molly begin to explain her obsession with the insect's buried gestation, the appeal of its awful cacophonous howl.

She sat on a concrete bench in the middle of the campus with photocopies of literature the professor had given her in her lap, watching the rounds of summer school students, a depression coming from below gripping her, a despair. It was an effort even to get up from the bench. Only a self-admonishing panic got her moving. No such panic moved her off her bed in the hotel. When the phone rang, Molly didn't answer it. For three more days she didn't eat. Perhaps her worst moments during that ordeal, which became timeless, happened when she tried, even most meekly, to cry. Her inability to cry at all convinced her of how far she had dropped and how suddenly; nothing had been there to stop her. Only one small mental activity stood between her and the immersion in her timeless depression: she pondered whether there was something emotionally dangerous in her contact with the cicada that made her so unbearably depressed; whether it was because she'd done something wrong in staying which finally revealed a secret she couldn't tolerate; whether it was that her experiments among the cicada had seemed to be grotesquely promising at first yet hadn't produced anything she might hold on to or understand. Once past those questions, though, fully unanswered, she watched them drift off and away from her, and that watching itself was a certain and remarkable change. Although she had left the Do Not Disturb sign on the door, day and night, someone from the hotel knocked on her door late in the afternoon of probably about the second day, asking after her. Without leaving the bed, Molly imitated as much of an ordinary professional voice as possible to tell the good gentleman that she was writing a post-conference paper which was due at the University of Ohio. Please not to be concerned. She would make up the room herself. After that encounter through the door, Molly nearly cried; from exhaustion, she thought. She lay in the bed and heard from her throat a thin sound repeat itself twice. She thought she heard the sounds she had spoken to the man as though they were the ghosts of the words she had spoken to him and they now floated in the room. Molly tried to think of food, imagining it might save her to eat. But she found the thought so dim that it was impossible to discern it clearly enough to cause action. The language of the thought bore no weight. She lay still. She thought of sucking on her thumb, but that, too, seemed a dim thought and not at all connected to the muscular truth of moving her hand up from where it lay between her knees. At times, Molly would slide her hands under the pillow, then later, move them back again. At times she would turn her body and lie on her back, staring up. But soon she'd return to her favored position: on her left side, staring toward the window-side of the room.

When Molly would close her eyes she would fall only a short distance across the plain that separated her from real sleep. There she would rest from the effort of despair. She dreamed in much the same way that she had visions while her eyes were open. She thought visually: in visualized feelings, and even making visual propositions of philosophy: the question, why would one lie here in a state like this? would become a visual image of herself, then someone not herself, lying on a bed in a room Molly had read a description of in a novel, or seen in a film: and in each scene herself or a woman much like herself — without displacing the characters from the novels or films — lay on the fictional bed limp and inert. The words she would ordinarily use to describe these things to herself, to think about them, were inaccessible, and so thinking itself was impossible, and so understanding or conclusion or resolution or motivation were impossible. Even in going to the bathroom she wouldn't think, —I have to go to the bathroom. She would see herself sitting on the toilet, and then she would be sitting on the toilet. But as she ate nothing, and even drank only little, she only had to go to the bathroom rarely during these days. She saw over again the walk she had taken in the Ohio woods, among the cicadae. She saw herself as she had first been on a lawn by the library reading about the insects, taking notes in a blue-lined notebook, listening, rapt; watching the people of Ohio walk around slightly grimacing from the pain which arrived every seventeen years to annoy them for a couple of weeks. Most of the people on the streets, she had noticed, weren't particularly marked by any happiness or any woe, any weakness or any vitality, but by a sense of bewildered isolation as though they were lost and their best response was to keep moving in the hope that eventually something would come clear about where they were or what they were supposed to be doing. She had begun to make up stories about certain passers-by which made her feel a bit more connected to them. Back in the hotel room, Molly envisioned the notebook she had written in that day at the library as huge, magnified hundreds of times so that only a few letters at a time were visible, then even that magnification increased so that only part of a letter filled her mind's eye. The curve of an f, the slope of g, the large line of b or l or i.

When her hunger came, Molly saw it too as something dim, which belonged to someone else. It occurred at such a distance within her that she could barely see it through the darkness. It came nowhere near enough to the surface to instigate action. She had no desire for taste. Her mouth was mostly dry and she wanted it dry. Her skin seemed pale, and she could tell it was drying out. But it was a great distance from her. It belonged to someone else, to someone named Molly who lay on a bed in one of those rooms in one of those novels or one of those films. She only smelled the mechanical hotel air. She heard the cicada dimly, but with a difference. Their dimness was not like her hunger — an impulse which arose from within — but a dimness from without, as if at a distance so far removed it existed in a place she would never go to, some universe only observed, only misunderstood. So during the even uncyclical days of her inert despair, only vision was acute, and it became increasingly elaborate, as if to compensate. Even her vision of actual, present reality became complex, as her perception of the window in which she saw, translucently, the very grains of sand from which it had been made, and the heat which had transformed them.

Molly found herself in the streets of Cincinnati at the corner of Lippincott and Vine. It was Wednesday afternoon, information she gained from the heavy black type of the Cincinnati Times-Herald. Judging from the light it was about 1:30 in the afternoon. She was aware of the cicadae now in the way she had been: they were ubiquitous, jarring, unintelligible, ineluctable, irreversible. She walked. It felt difficult but good in the muscles of her legs and hips to move with vigor. At times she would seem to be talking to the cicada, asking them why she had stayed, for what had she pursued them. But she hadn't actually spoken yet. Her first words were to a vendor at a shop open to the street: How much are these? she asked. The shopkeeper told her: 98 cents a pound, 50 cents apiece. Then the shopkeeper offered her a small sampler clump of grapes to take with her. She asked the time: 1:09. She ate as she walked, the afternoon still in the wide heat of its damp zenith. She wandered, walking around the Federal Building, then turning east, then north. She could smell the strange river. She kept walking northeastward, walked into Eden Park, entered the Museum of Natural History, left without seeing anything but the lobby, passed between the columns and went into the Art Museum where she spent an hour. Then Molly walked again, north, now passing through neighborhoods of the near suburbs, with houses that were rather small, wooden, with square front lawns undivided by fences or bush but running along one after another undefined and indistinct and apparently unnamed. The neighborhood children watched her pass. Mothers chasing babies noticed her. The only person she knew in all of Ohio, in all the Midwest, which she remembered was vast, was Elaine. The only person whose name she even knew was Elaine. She settled into this neighborhood as she had days before into the woods. The song of cicadae absorbed houses, lawns, children, mothers. She turned left, walked one block and turned right. She walked four blocks and turned left again. She hadn't noticed when the children and the mothers had disappeared, but there were none here. The silence belonged to the cicadae to fill. What have I done? I'm lost. I have no idea where I am. I keep walking. Why should I keep walking? Now the cicadae, which had sounded like many things and suggested many things, which had triggered memories and a retreat, which had drawn her to investigate them, had the sound of a kind of primeval insect laughter, not joyous, not funny, not cynical.

-Write in any language that you know, French, Spanish, even hobble along in your old Greek if you want to.

-But there's something to be *said* in this other language that's in the nature of something to be *done* with it, or by it, or with it but not through it.

-Don't let yourself wallow here. Molly's coming back. Call this whole time — these weeks — an interruption and get back to possible work. I think that — Interruptions is without trope. No metaphor. No allegory. No synecdoche. Lots of color to each now-word, I mean neo-word. Resonance. Lots of opposition and contradiction.

-But if it's not an actual language what's the use of it?

-What's an actual language?

Thomas's father died at 4:44 a.m., in the house in the mountains, by the lake. The doctor wrote that Thomas's father had said *I am no more. My eyes are closing now.*

What is entropy?

What is the energy of a word?

Why are Latin, Mangbetu, Doric, Ugaritic, Gaelic, Gallic, Chinese, French, Romanian, Chibcha, Paez, Bulgarian, Tagolog, Serbo-Croat, Hottentot, Bulgarian, Cree, Hindustani, Dano-Norwegian, Persian, Marathi, Lettish, Dutch, Lithuanian, Icelandic, Frisian, Thai, Magyar, Chinook, Aeolic, Cornic, Mixtecan, Baluchi, Italian, Bella Coola, Old Iranian, Triestino, Slovenian, Gothic, Osco-Umbrian, Otomi, Ionic, Breton, Welsh, Czech, Huilliche, Wendish, Polish, Apache, Algonquin, Nahuatlato, Jemez, Kiowa, Narragansett, Friulano, Uzbec, Buryat, Mongol, Estonian, Telugu, Punic, Manx, Kashmiri, Rajasthani, Amharic, Berber, Phoenician, Rif, Songhai, Afrikaans, Maji, Kuseri, and others. Compared to what the typewriter had produced?

A couple of weeks.

Punctures the cells of the host plants to suck the protein-rich....

I wish it would stop now but though fighting it with music.

It's time for them. I want only two things from life now. You, and some story so that I go on talking. That's my religious conviction, that it will go on talking after I die. I hold that firmly. It, talking as we live here.

A Doubt

WISPY, his thin, brown hair, if hit by a softened, golden light at a certain angle at a certain time of day, looked more red than brown. His beard, wispy also, bore the same tones. Although his face was not attractive, actually ugly in the coarsest way, the definitive strength of its individual features combined to make of it a fact one did not ignore. His nose, bumped and then flattened against his face, flared too much at the base; his cheekbones protruded roughly into the concave curvature of his features; his ears stuck out from the sides of his head. Nonetheless, within all this an enigmatic, undeniable, compelling, mysterious handsomeness resided.

His face was a fact of life and of life itself that one did not ignore.

People had always noticed him, since childhood. They would stare, as if to figure out exactly how an alluring handsomeness, a calm virility, a life force could radiate through such an ugly visage. They stared: if they could penetrate that mystery, they would answer some fundamental question of living, find some key to existence, discover some way into a region of knowing and being which ordinarily refused them.

Thomas hated his face. He hated the way people stared at him. He had no secrets. He knew nothing in particular. Truly, for Thomas, neither he nor his enigmatic face embodied any region of knowing or soul or self or spirit. For Thomas, this somehow peculiar this tumultuous extraordinary face had always been a disaster. How could he ever be a simple person interacting normally with people whose gaze he felt as a search, an investigation, a reproach, a quest. This response to his face, which had begun in childhood, kept Thomas forever isolated. Even an immaculate infant would look at Thomas with the same questing gaze. It was inevitable, then. Thomas became a loner.

That no one noticed his dissatisfaction didn't diminish it. Discontent ran with his blood, demanding recompense. He worked. He ate with little pleasure. He slept each night with even less. His life grew smaller, each routine or ritual he had designed to help himself withstand his circumstance drained slowly of coherence.

Each morning, Thomas would meticulously make his bed, tucking the plain cotton sheets carefully under the mattress, smoothing the whole, fluffing the pillow, arranging the simple brown comforter. All this was to give order, to make him feel he lent his own hand to the making of his day and night, and to give him a rewarding bed to look forward to in the evening, the prize of even uneasy sleep won from the rigors of his existence.

A man in Thomas's condition has to take action. After years he's driven not just further into retreat but further into that corner out of which he will have to finally fight his way. His limbs will become not paralyzed, but poised; his eyes will be covered not with the thick glaze of resigned cataracts, but pained, stinging.

For years, Thomas had studied the texts of ancient Greek, Chinese, Indian, Arabic, and Christian alchemists, and modern chemistry; nonetheless, one morning, the earthly elements that Thomas had mixed and recombined in test tubes, distilled, examined under microscopes, heated and cooled in beakers to discover a formula that, either ingested or applied topically, would transform his face—silver, copper, lead, iron, tin, mercury, sulfur, the corrosive salts, the vitriols, alums, chlorides—one morning, as Thomas worked with them they actually performed transmutations that he had only hoped for - they exploded. What a stupid thing to do! To push this ancient wisdom and this modern science beyond its boundaries! What an idiot! Now his spoiled life was a ruin. The explosion horribly scorched and further disfigured his face.

Yet, Thomas had done something more drastic than anyone around him — his landlord, his co-workers at the Post Office, the cop on the street, the kids playing on the street corner — none of them would ever do anything so incredible as to search in the very materials of life for the powers to alter reality.

It hurt less than anyone might suspect. You'd think he'd go into shock. The pain would be intolerable. You'd faint! My God, you'd die! No. Thomas stood amid the glory of it reveling. These mad revels brought the neighbors who saved his life. Bursting down the door when he wouldn't answer, they found him with his hands flaying the air: —I've done it! I've done it!

Thomas came out of the hospital more strange looking than ever. He wore a bandage apparatus which provided a passageway for air through his nasal passage and a defense against bacteria. Returning to work at the Post Office was out of the question. How could a man who had taken radical action against entrenched suffering work again in the back of a blank grey building. He had had no public contact on his job. He sorted letters the machines rejected. The machine was the extension of man's capacity; Thomas had become the residue of the machine's incapacity. He walked past the Post Office building. It was yet Fall. The small branch Post Office sat on a narrow street. Autumnal wind swept the air. He'd starve first. That was another noble act he'd learned: starvation. All acts against supreme frustration were as creative as they were destructive if done right. He was perhaps the only man alive who knew that, or the one man alive who knew it most. To be a drug addict or an alcoholic were simpering forms of protest. Only few methods carried the seeds of victory, elation, ecstasy. Thomas was now cleansed of his destructive—his self-destructive—urges, and content.

When Thomas walked into the foyer of his apartment building, doors opened ever so slightly. The entire first floor peered:

the Harrises, the Pattersons, the Gonzales family, the Super and his wife. They had no idea that Thomas might know their names; now they wouldn't give them out easily to him. He was, to them, a terrible and awful man. In talking about him they referred to him as that terrible and awful man. Hearing their whispers, Thomas now referred to himself, in his thoughts, as the terrible and awful man. The phrase pleased him so much.

On the third floor, Thomas walked through the gauntlet of doors cracked open to his own door, went in, raised the window which fronted on the street. He brushed layers of dirt off the outside sill. He scrubbed that ledge clean with soap and a brush. In the bedroom, his bed was made. That satisfied him. He had enormous plans. How could he possibly know what they were, except that they were monumental, and that they had to be formulated in a chair sitting by this front window in the Fall breeze.

Contemplating not only his ugliness, but also the life-long baffling riddle his face had posed, Thomas decided for the first time in his life that he wouldn't have traded it for anything. He rested his feet on the windowsill, sipped cup after cup of tea.

Mrs. Mariani brought him his first food. She brought a hot chicken cacciatore to his door. He sat in the chair by the window when she knocked. He couldn't imagine who it might be, other than perhaps a social worker from the hospital. He thought they would leave him alone.

Thomas crossed the dim rug of the living room to the foyer. When he opened the door, he kept the chain on its latch.

—Mr....?

—Yes?

—I'm Mrs. Mariani. Down the hall. 307. I've made something for you....you being in the hospital...

—I have conquered hunger, he said.

—But...eat... you've got to eat, Mrs. Mariani persisted. — You've been sick. If you don't eat you won't get well.

—I haven't been sick, he said.

She pushed, but lightly, at the door, —you've had a...trauma. You've been in the hospital. You need nourishment.

He had spent the last two days sitting by the window in the Fall breezes, pleased with the pain the slightly sharp air caused his wound. The doctors had warned him against cold air, but he triumphed in the sharp feeling of it passing through the still raw, stitched nasal opening.

—If I'm not hungry why should I eat, Mrs....

—Mariani.

He closed the door. She knocked again, freeing a hand to knock with by clutching the pot of chicken against her thin, aproned stomach. He thought to ignore it, intending to return to the solitude of his ongoing victory celebration silently in progress by the open window. When he opened the door she spoke immediately.

—Why don't you let me in? Do you mistrust me? Don't. You need someone to take care of you a little bit. It's a wonderful chicken. Cacciatore. Mushrooms, peppers, a delicious sauce. Still warm. Feel it.

Thomas's hand came through the chained opening. Touching the white crockery dish, he found it was as Mrs. Mariani had declared it: warm, hot even. He withdrew his hand.

—Mr....?

—You don't want to see me, he said. —I'm not a pretty sight.

—You never were.

Silence.

—I'm closing the door, unlatching the chain, unlocking the handle. Then I'm going back inside to sit by the window. The world itself in all its wonder is open to me as I sit there. You may not believe that, Mrs....

—Mariani.

—You may not believe that, Mrs. Mariani, but it's true. I don't imagine it's something you would understand. It's not something I would ask anyone to understand. I, too, am a wonder open to myself as I sit there. This may sound insane to you. You may want to leave. Go home. That's fine. But, if you like, when I go back to my window, you can open the door. You can bring the food into the kitchen. I didn't ask for it and I don't owe you anything but to say thank you. Thank you, Mrs. Mariani.

The door closed. Mrs. Mariani heard the clack of metal move, then stop. She waited a moment, turned the handle, the door opened. The hallway before her was empty. There were two white arches, one of which probably led to the living room, the other to the dining room. A cool breeze blew from one direction. She went the other way. The dining room had no table, no chairs, no sideboard. It was an empty, unused cubicle. She pushed at the white wooden door which swung on hinges, then entered the kitchen. The kitchen wasn't dirty so much as it was encrusted. Little had gone on to dirty it, but even that little had not been cleaned up after.

Mrs. Mariani lit the oven to put the cacciatore in to keep warm. She felt the presence of her neighbor through the kitchen door, imagined him sitting at his window. What could he mean, the world in all its wonder was open to him? What could he mean that the wonder of himself was open to him? Was he mad? He must be, at least somewhat mad, to have done what he did. What might his face look like now, noseless. How could someone live without a nose? How would they breathe? Could he smell the cacciatore? He was right not to let her see him. She would have to hide her repulsion and he would see her hiding it. Why do such a thing? Mrs. Mariani was afraid to be in his kitchen with a fear unlike she had ever felt before. A fear which was inescapable by movement or thought. Her shallow breath. Her confused thoughts. She couldn't find a thought to hang on to as a way out of this fear. Looking around her, she couldn't be sure the world was real. Was really there. The cabinets. The stove. Even the lovely smell of the cacciatore, was it an hallucination simply? A memory? A reality? How could she know? She didn't even know his name; there was none on the mailbox. What kind of man would do such a thing? What was wrong with her that she had to come over here? Was she a hopeless sucker for the weak? But a man so extreme wasn't weak. Was he?

Finally, to at least assuage if not to conquer her fear, Mrs. Mariani took up a sponge to clean. She should have left, but now she was even afraid to leave the kitchen. He might catch her on her way to the door and...do what? Good Lord. She washed the dishes, cleaned the sink, counters, stove, cupboards. She opened the refrigerator: a nearly empty quart of milk, almost gone, an old head of romaine lettuce shriveled on the bottom shelf, a can of walnuts open with a few left over, an open jar of mustard so old a cottony layer of mold had formed around the edges. She threw it in the trash.

What more could she do? She wiped down the refrigerator, inside and out, and then pulled all the courage which she seemed to have had at one time when she was much younger, even before Victor, gathered it in her stomach by the force of memory, took the garbage bag to dump it, but also as protection: she could hurl the bag at her nameless invalid neighbor if he attacked her. She pushed against the door and in one affirmative movement walked through the ghostly dining room, turned abruptly under the archway into the foyer, opened the door, stepped into the hallway and breathed out as she pulled the door shut. Just before closing it she called, but finding her voice meek, —The food is in the oven, and left with no response, without being sure her neighbor had heard her.

When Mrs. Mariani got into her own apartment she was sweating. She threw open the living room window. She fussed at the mirror, fixing her hair, imagining her face without a nose. How could anyone do that to themselves? A beast. She almost regretted taking him the food, but she remembered the sight of his clean kitchen with pleasure. The vision of it just as she had made her move through his swinging kitchen door lingered in her mind: neat, arranged, clean. A pleasant place now to make a cup of tea at least. Mrs. Mariani spoke to the photograph of her husband. —Victor, she said, —life is very strange without you. But it was strange with you, it was strange what we were together, wasn't it? We just hadn't seen it so clearly. We were happy, Victor. That's what we had. We had our happiness.

Trying to find her neighbor's name, terrified now of asking him, Mrs. Mariani called the hospital. She claimed to have been a patient who had by mistake taken a book of his home with her. The receptionist switched her to the duty nurse who refused her request. Mrs. Mariani called the building's Super, who was now afraid to give out the man's name. Mrs. Mariani wanted the name to call, because she wasn't sure he had heard her about the cacciatore. For the sake of the chicken she delved into the trash bag with the molding mustard and found the name on the discarded half of a utility bill: Thomas Merisi. He, too, must be of Italian descent, like herself. But his two names didn't seem to belong together.

Mrs. Mariani hadn't yet called the telephone information service when the knock on the door shocked her because she knew it was him and said right off, —Coming, Thomas. Thomas started and put his hand to his missing nose. He touched it a slight bit too hard. It throbbed. When Mrs. Mariani opened the door Mr. Merisi kept his hand to his nose, but even so she saw his odd, ugly/fascinating face as she had sometimes seen it coming down the hallway, or in the elevator, on the stairs, on the street in the neighborhood. It was a long face. His lips, thin, well defined, looked as if they held a thousand words he had wanted to speak, but had withheld because they belonged more to thought than to speech, and perhaps more to feeling than to thought. And perhaps more to consciousness than to feeling. He was tall and too thin. He had eyes you searched for, but, once you found them, you could look straight at them easily. They were no redoubt. Unlike his lips which withheld ineffable words, his eyes absorbed all that they saw. Overall, his face held a prehistoric sort of presence for Mrs. Mariani, or, perhaps, she might say, a universal presence, an inescapable presence, certainly she, Mrs. Mariani, could not escape him, could not turn away, could only stay looking at him.

—You shouldn't have cleaned my kitchen, he said.

—It was filthy.

—I owe you nothing.

Mrs. Mariani held herself up. —I expect nothing, Mr. Merisi, she pronounced the name roundly, but even so her self-possession was a shadow of his: he could barely discern it in the dim hallway though he did perceive it as a gesture of acknowledgement.

—Don't do it again. He turned to leave. He walked down the uncarpeted hallway. His soft-soled shoes made no noise. What occasion might there be for her to clean his kitchen again? None. But she couldn't take her eyes off his back until he had gone into his own apartment and shut the door. He didn't glance back at her, and she was angry at herself for wanting him to. —I certainly won't do it again, she said.

Thomas Merisi sat again by the open window in crisp air. He set his legs on the windowsill, pushed the straight-backed chair up on its two hind legs. The empty cacciatore pot sat on the floor beside him. He'd eaten as a victory feast. All afternoon he gazed out at the buildings across the street, at the small slice of sky he saw between those buildings. He'd gone to the bathroom a couple of times and each time stopped to look in the mirror. The white bandages stood out against his skin, and seeing that, he smiled. They were held to his face by strips of brown tape. Although they bulged slightly because of the shape of his face and the protrusion of cartilage, they looked nothing at all like a nose. And good. He never wanted a nose again. He went back to his chair and stayed there until long after sunset when the streets, the buildings and sky had darkened, and then he enjoyed the nameless darkness.

Mrs. Mariani hardly slept. She muttered to her husband about Thomas Meresi, distressed by his rudeness, yet it wasn't ordinary rudeness so much as it was a certain self-possession, attracted by what she confessed to be a magnetic power his very rudeness contained. True, she had tried to imitate him that afternoon in her curt reply, but she knew it had been a transparently bogus attempt. What attraction can a man like that really have? Her husband, speaking to her as he always did, or as she always heard him, warned her not to get involved. This Merisi character was dangerous. Each time she heard Victor say that she felt more pulled down the hall. So went her night, trying to sleep, pacing the living room, reading the paper, tidying up, talking to her husband's portrait on the television. In the morning she went to the store and bought the ingredients for a hearty chicken soup.

When she knocked, Mr. Merisi opened the door with the chain still latched and she held up the soup like an offering.

—Mrs.....

—Mariani.

—Yes. You shouldn't keep doing this.

—It's a wonderful soup. I've never made better. You inspired...you must be in such pain. I knew you'd need something to give you strength.

—Pain is strength.

—Oh. Yes.

—Leave it in the kitchen. The door closed on Mrs. Mariani, the latch unhooked, and then silence. The apartment looked the same. When she turned toward the kitchen she glanced quickly through the other archway, hoping to see Mr. Merisi, but saw only as far as a tattered grey rug. She set the soup pot on the stove and lit a small fire under it. The kitchen was as clean as she'd left it. She had expected to find the cacciatore pot from yesterday in the sink perhaps filled with water, with a fork in it leaning against the edge. She had imagined herself cleaning it there in Mr. Merisi's kitchen and so challenging his prohibition. But it wasn't there. Steeling herself against his recriminations, she stepped out of the kitchen door, walked through the bare dining room to the very edge of the archway leading into the living room. Without peering in she dared: —Mr. Merisi.

Just as she called, Mr. Merisi was rising on a memory of the explosion itself, recalling the threat he sensed in the percolating test tubes, the terror mixed with the determination that propelled him beyond himself into the experiment, past Thomas Merisi, past the borders of old realities. That next moment — when Thomas knew his concoctions were growing extremely dangerous, and yet he also knew he would keep pursuing them — engulfed everything else, fear, hesitation, reason, every restraining gravity engorged by a swift and certain knowledge of impossible accomplishment made potential motivated forward by absolute need and a vitality which arrived in the flow of his blood, his muscles relaxed and alert. He knew in that moment that whatever the outcome of his dangerous alchemy it would be right, would not be stupid, would be true and worthy of a man of his extreme state, that it would be altogether forgiven and received. It would be graceful; it would be grace. It would open the portal of contradiction that everyone, peering into his face, had sought. The pain would be stupefied, sent flying. And he knew that when he felt the pain later he'd welcome it because it would remind him that when he had needed the pain to be silent — like every other element of his being — his pain conformed itself to the gathering momentum. Just then he heard her call: —Mr. Merisi.

—What?

His voice pulled her from the shield of the archway and she stumbled over herself into the living room and nearly pulled him over backwards as she touched his chair for support. Like the dining room, the living room was bare. He pulled himself forward and braced against the windowsill while she stood beside him.

—I was just...

—You were just what...?

—Just....

—Yes? He had sat the chair on its four legs again and looked up at her. The late afternoon light from the window, no longer excited but now diffuse and calm and simple and clear fell over him, carried the city's actual noises in distantly from the streets and the avenues. It pulled Mr. Merisi's face out of all shadow, giving Mrs. Mariani a clearer look than she had yet seen of Mr. Merisi and his noseless, bandaged face. It looked like he couldn't breathe at all, though his mouth was shut and yet he seemed to take in air. His long body was as relaxed as the afternoon light. He watched her with his ever receptive eyes. She wanted to touch it. Wanted to rub her hand around it, feel its edges. Ferma Mariani had such an urge come over her at her age. She moved her right hand up to caress the rough edges of the violently inflicted wound of a man who was obviously in less than full control of himself. The muscles in her forearm felt constricted, her fingers stiff. A brown tape held the bandage to his face, but the gauze itself was a secret part of the man turned inside out for the world — for Mrs. Mariani — to see. He knew exactly what she was looking at and exactly how it was that she looked. She stood before him, thin, straight, horrified. Her grey hair fell from her temples around her face. Her greenish eyes sat fully flush with her face and exposed to the world as though life had not ever presented her with anything more than what she could look straight into. Thomas Merisi took Mrs. Mariani's right hand by the palm, lifted it, watching all the while carefully, and set the small fingers to the edge of his bandage, where it met with the thin strip of brown tape. Mrs. Mariani, hardly breathing, caressed the bandage. Her eyebrows raised to the full extent of their human musculature, her brow severely ridged and furrowed, her eyes wide, wide, her skin flush with an earthy reddish hue, her mouth pursed in concentration conveyed to Thomas an incredulous astonishment, a confrontation, a shock of the new, a voiceless unquestioning seizure of the imagination.

Mrs. Mariani felt everywhere on the cloth bandage with the tips of her fingers and the palm of her hand, along the rises and folds of a simple woven cotton cloth. Then her hand, coming off the bandage, stroked the bare unsmooth flesh of Thomas Merisi's face. He tipped back his head. As the chill breeze came in the window raising the pain in what had been his nose, Mrs. Mariani's now intrepid hand stroked over his forehead.

No sleep. Pacing. Tidying. The New York Times. Apologies to her husband. —I know you told me not to get involved. It was too late. —Why didn't you stop earlier? Why did you take him food? she heard him answer. And she answered him: —No. Too late in my life. What might she sacrifice? Victor's photograph? It held her soul together through many years now. But to sacrifice it would be a gesture, not an action, not taken from desperation and so not fully consummate as Mr. Merisi's action. All her life an undesperate woman, Mrs. Mariani wanted desperately to know Thomas Merisi, and she did know him as if he were the first thing in actual life that she actually knew, had no doubt that she actually knew. Her head pounded. She took aspirin. She gazed. She tried to sleep. She tried to dream a retreat but only frustrating images repeated themselves. She awoke sweating. She showered and powdered her body and changed her nightgown and splashed an eau de toilette on her neck and straightened the bed before returning to it. She lay for a long time before she heard a soft knock at the door, though it wasn't her front door, it was her bedroom door. She'd had such a night that the knock didn't frighten her. The sound coming from one of her dreams, a knock on one of the closed doors she had dreamt of. She knew it was still night not from any internal sense of how much time had passed, but because she still lay in the dark.

—Mr. Merisi? she called.

He stood in the opened door.

Mrs. Mariani sat up in bed against the old headboard carried over from Italy which she had shared with her husband, against which they had leaned many nights discussing the progress of their happy, worthy lives. Each secret, large or small, that they had kept from each other was embedded in the polished grain of the reddish darkness of that headboard.

—Anything I might say sounds absurd to me, she trembled as she spoke.

—Anything you might say you would have to say with words, Mrs. Mariani, —and now you can trust your words.

—But I mean ridiculous. I mean inane. I mean unworthy. Small. But I don't feel small at all, Mr. Merisi. I don't feel dishonest. I don't feel any despair. Or fear. I feel all the opposites of those things. But I cannot name that feeling.

—Are you glad, Mrs. Mariani, that you brought me food. An offering? That you touched the edges of my wound. Or are you sorry?

—Does it matter whether I'm sorry or not. It's happened, hasn't it? There's no end to it now. Is there?

—No. Mrs. Mariani. There is no end to it now. It goes on now forever.

—Mr. Merisi, do you think that you might one day come to love me?

—Do you think that matters?

—How did you do this alone? What you've done to yourself?

—Who says I did it alone, Mrs. Mariani?

—Who helped you? Who was with you?

—Everything was with me, Thomas said, —everything that

was ever born was with me. Why don't you come over tomorrow. We'll sit in the window together.

—Mr. Merisi.....?

—Yes?

—Are you leaving? It's very dark in here. I can't see you.

Mr. Merisi turned on the light at the switch on the wall. She sat in the bed. Her arms lay above the covers, the palm of each hand open, facing upwards.

Mrs. Mariani began to laugh, lightly at first, then more, then fully, she laughed fully. She didn't bring her hands up to her face. She felt as though she would never stop this laughing, never stop smiling and giggling.

In the doorway, Mr. Merisi, in response to her, also smiled. Then his smile subsided into the eternity of his face.

Awful Evil

5 May '85

Dear Uncle Thomas, Dear Uncle, Dear Thomas,

I quote from President Reagan yesterday as he spoke from the platform on a cold day at Bergen-Belsen: —The awful evil started by one man—an evil that victimized all the world with its destruction... I read that this morning as I rode the subway to work and all day it's echoed in my mind. Why? —....the awful evil started by one man. —Awful evil. By this afternoon I had fantasies of what evil I might start. Mightn't I start an evil as large as Hitler's? I thought, Yes, and why not? I'm not afraid to tell you these things, Uncle Thomas. I would never talk to my mother or father like this. Of course. I wouldn't talk to anyone like this. But I tell you because you're so accepting and I know that you won't judge me or condemn me or call me—or even think me—crazy. It frightens me and I wondered where do they come from, such strange feelings? Can I find them out by writing you?

OK. The most common interpretation of the Holocaust is that it was a unique event in history, not just different in quantity or method or bizarre degree of prolific organized success, but utterly different in quality, intention, origin. Origin's the word here. I know you subscribe to that interpretation. We talked about it last year at Thanksgiving. Do you remember? In my parents' den. We were both escaping everyone else. But I wonder, good Uncle Thomas, if I sit in my office at the bookstore with my fine-for-now job and I'm taking a class and I have studio space to work in and I do work and I have a fairly chaotic and fairly difficult and fairly confusing but reasonably I suppose decent life and feel that I might start an evil as large and devastating as Hitler's, and conceive I could do that and would do that, where does that come from?

I know, my affectionate Uncle Thomas. You tell me: —Mary-Ellen, you have your personal demons to work out. Do it, Mary-Ellen, you say to me, —for you own sake. But for mine as well. I know, my fine U.T., I have my father the out-of-touch idealist my big sister the angry one the violent one who gave me every day my daily dose...I know tender U.T., I know. But let's move on from there.

Am I the only one who thinks like this? Who feels this? (NO. This letter I can't send even to you. But I can write it to you, can't I, forgiving U.T.? Then I'll rip it up. I promise.) Am I a fascist because I feel these things? Is the Holocaust unique because the fascists carried out what others think? Not the anti-Semitism, the evil underlying it. That's not war, it seems to me, but art. That's not the awful evil started by one man but a common evil dreamt of by all. Is that the human condition, or is that the social condition, the streets and the century into which I'm born? Oh, perhaps I'm not being unique in my honesty, but then I dare say, our President is a naïf to talk about the —awful evil of one man, n'est pas? Neglecting his own very considerable, very destructive evil of the past few years resulting in poverty starvation death plenty of destruction, homelessness, despair. He's no Hitler, no, of course not, I'm not saying he is who now could be that evil, but he's caused suffering and one who causes suffering is....evil? Why does everyone want to put evil somewhere outside themselves? Is the second great evil of Hitler in this century going to be that he becomes the repository of evil for all other evil people and acts as the scapegoat of evil, the big cauldron of evil into which everyone else can throw their own evil and be rid of it by some ritual incantation of the name —Hitler Hitler Hitler? Reagan was even afraid to say his name, just said —one man, —the awful evil started by one man What about all the other Germans who enthusiastically went along? What about the Italians or British or Americans who thought it was all a good idea? Henry Ford was one of them! You know, magnanimous U.T., that I couldn't commit that kind of evil, don't you, and it's even strange of me to think it. Maybe I was just over-hungry today, didn't eat much. Oh, I know. Her personal demons, you say, my idealist distant father my cruel bigger sister. Sister Cruel, we used to call her, do you remember? But what group would I destroy? Jews? Of course not. So who? Blacks? Never. Latinos? Ridiculous. But someone. I could destroy someone, I think, and that sticks in my throat so I want to gurgle and choke and scream and spit it out. It bothered me all afternoon, pleasant U.T., all the way home on the subway. I thought of Richard Goetz. I could have shot those little bastards too. In the back. Couldn't I? But that's not it, not just self protection, something much more frightening. And anyway, no, I couldn't, could I, anyway, have shot anyone in the back?

In my Shakespeare class last year Prof. Truax said that Iago was a great character precisely because Shakepeare threw himself full evil full force of all his own evil into the creation of Iago's pure evil. But that's a far cry from Hitler. Shakespeare turned his own probably very small even amusing impulse of evil into a large evil impulse of art and gave us a chance to turn our own evil or see the delights of evil or exorcise our evil or whatever it was Prof. Truax said we do watching Iago, and so Shakespeare's creation is, in the end, good. But if Iago is great—follow me—by virtue of the sensation of his unbridled hatred, wasn't Hitler also great by virtue of his utterly unbridled madness. He hated Jews and Catholics and Gypsies and homosexuals like Iago hated Othello, wrongly and fully. So he is a complete evil, Hitler is, at least, and, after all, to achieve completeness in life, that's something. Oh, my caring U.T., don't hate me for this. I'm just in a mood. A weird mood. Scaring myself. I'm just asking crazy questions. I know your memories of it. You were there. You know I've seen the pictures. You looking weary. You looking young and snappy and stunned. But I'm a new generation from you. I have to explore my world. What has my world got to do with Hitler? With Ronald Reagan even? I sit here on a cold night overheated in a very, very little apartment, closed in, alone as is much too usual these days, frightened by worries and the terrors of my own life (do I want to be alone? If yes, then, please, why?), by my own progress in my own little world. (Do I have far too many terrors? A cruel older sister violent in extremis. Oh, get on with it, MaryEllen, MaryEllen tells herself. Who got her daily dose. You weren't beaten down you were beaten strong and supple and compassionate. Yes? No? What do you do about loneliness? About terrors? My respectable, even my noble U.T. I know you've learned how to deal with them, because I know there were times in your life you've been very lonely, even desolate. Is it rude of me to say that to you? To speak so boldly to my elders? You know that I love you. Have you ever been desolate? Have you ever felt, my excellent U.T., that the territory you covered each day was some kind of sandy arena, dry and circumscribed only by painful thoughts, by confusions. And you know that tomorrow will be no better though you hope it will be and then sometimes it is and you wonder even more. What happened? What revenge do I ever get? Oh, come on, don't smile at me like I know that you do. Tell me the truth. I'm a young woman too much alone in New York City who needs advice from her uncle who understands her, maybe even just a little comfort.

My friend Suzanne got mugged in her apartment hallway three days ago. I'll never get used to it. She's so remarkably strong! She hasn't broken down over it like I know I would. But what if that guy had wanted to rape her? What if he'd killed her? Isn't that like unto the evil of one man imposing himself on the world? The world is wherever you are, whoever you are, isn't it? Or, do you remember, I told you about that lawyer I went out with last year. He kept making obscene calls to me trying to disguise his voice, but I knew right away who he was. He was another evil man who victimized the whole world. For you yourself are the whole world, are you not? You are everything. He didn't mean to harm me, just to do what he wanted? Maybe that's exactly the point, not to think about the harm to the other is the evil. Or—God! Maybe that lawyer did want to harm me. That sends shivers down me. I'm too alone tonight to think about things like that. It's such a vacant, anxious, cold, difficult night. To think that someone really wanted to harm me badly. Why? The way I thought today I could do that much evil. It just flashed so fast through my mind, my knowing U.T., I couldn't stop it. Do you think I could do that much evil? Do you think I could torture someone? Of course not. Never. Never ever ever. But I want to think about it. I want to pursue that thought to its fullest end. Put someone on a rack and turn while they scream. Yes damn it. I could do that. My heart almost races with the thought. My blood becomes light and thin with it. I feel so safe in telling you this as if you'll catch me, you'll save me from myself if I go too far. You will, won't you, safe U.T.? Save me. Not go too far. I can count on you, I can, so don't ever die. I think I've gone too far now, right now. I think I could scream. I think I could torture someone while they moan and scream, but they couldn't scream because they wouldn't have the strength left to do even that. I'm flying. I'm exalted by evil. Why? What's wrong with me. A very much violent older sister. A father... No. It's just me. She was here last week she had some meeting I had dinner with her one night then when we parted on the street I walked away thinking I heard myself thinking clearly, —OK, Cruel One, you go your way and I go mine even if yours be up and mine be down or whatever, and I heard her walking away she was laughing. Enough of cheap psychologies. Let's us really ask ourselves honestly, why? And why am I writing this to you? I want you to help me, that's why. I want you to love me so hard I will have the strength to become someone else. Do you think that Hitler felt desperately lonely and that's why he did what he did, because of an unbreakable loneliness? Did someone torture Hitler and so Hitler started the awful evil started by one man who tortured everyone? That's so very very awfully simplistic and there are dozens of psychoanalyses of Hitler and I haven't read a one of them but what do the psycyhoanalysts know? Their own loneliness? Their own desperation? Their own frustration? Their own fear of themselves? Or are they free of such fears? Are you free, my boundless U.T.? Does even the blameless U.T. have his own personal demons? Or is it just MaryEllen? We're put on our little planet, a beautiful place, truth be to tell, or we arrive here somehow, and we're scared or scarred and alone and so often lonely, and we get frightened and we sit in our room at midnight on snowless evenings in winter and we feel alone and desperate and want to strike out at someone. (Am I striking out—writing out—at you, receptive U.T.? Please no. I hope not.) I have gone too far. No, I haven't gone far enough because I'm going to confess everything to you now. I'll tell you one secret with our always very always agreement that you won't tell anyone, which means mom and dad. Or, of course, Helene, but you never talk to Helene or you do I guess once in a while you have to but you don't tell her anything I mean I know that for sure I know you've been the most honest possible person in the world with me all along of course you have you're the indefatigable U.T. you're the one who knows all about it with me. How are you the brother of the whirlwind of hysteria they call my mother, you, oh к & г Uncle Thomas. That's what I call you sometimes to myself when I think of you: kind and gentle Uncle Thomas—where is your refuge or don't you have such storms? OK. Now. My confession that I promised you: When I was in college a math professor cornered me in her office. She was so very very sad. Pathetic. She pawed me. Why didn't I tell you this before? Because I was ashamed, that's why. That stupid shit of a woman (I know—stretch for more expressive language, MaryEllen) made me ashamed of myself. Maybe not, maybe I just am ashamed. Why? Ever think of that? Have you ever been totally ashamed of yourself, of your body, of your sex? Am I rude again? Of course you never have been. You're a man. You're proud of your conquests. Anyway, I didn't go to the University, to the Art Department people, to my advisor, or anybody. I went to the professor's husband. Yes. She was married. Can you imagine? I hit her where she lived, and her husband left her about a year later. He must have been disgusted by her. I sent him a letter and he actually wrote me back demanding that I make such an accusation in person. So I met him and I told him. Your wife, I said, pawed me. Slobbered over me. Cornered me. Trapped me. She made me feel awful, my poor U.T., so I made her feel awful. You see? But I think, well…she just felt so lonely. She felt desperately alone. She had a husband and two children and still she felt desperately lonely among all her numbers and figures and theories on the mathematical harmony of the mathematical frigging universe. So I squeezed her. I made her husband leave her. He was plain, ugly even, but somewhere in him he had an untapped and incipient and very, very fragile dignity, so transparent a composure. He wore it like he'd bought it somewhere and wanted to dress himself up. It was easy. I am exhausted. Suddenly I am exhausted. I had to draw a line somewhere didn't I? and say, this is me, this you cannot defile without consequence. So her husband left her and I'm exhausted and probably I too started some awful evil and victimized someone's world. I was wrong. Yes, my wise U.T. I want to repent. I don't know quite how. Who is it I am afraid of? I'm lost and suddenly I can't find your hand to pull me out. Where are you?

Do you remember once when we went hiking? I was twelve. We went out and climbed all the way to the top of a great slope in the mountains. It probably wasn't all that high after all. Mother was afraid, but you kept turning back and pulling me up after you. When we got to the top you kept quoting some one of the Romantic poets or someone   you were laughing and you kept laughing. You were a god to me, my divine U.T., and you still are, even now when I want no more gods in my life, no one telling me what to do or who I am or what I am or where I am or how I got here or what I should be. Was I evil? Am I just an alienated latecomer reciting to you the litany of the dregs of her adolescent guilt so that she can be free of it? Am I evil? That's my question. No, I am just your niece in her little apartment playing a big girl in the big city, run away from home and writing her uncle for comfort for solace. Or, yes, I am as evil as the next person, as imbued with it, as riddled with it. You are the very real world to me—and I need you. See? I can admit that. I need you. Dear Uncle Thomas—Dear Uncle Thomas—I depend so very much on you. That must mean I'm not too far gone, doesn't it?

Am I indulging myself? my stable Uncle Thomas? You have told me before: discover, but don't indulge yourself, MaryEllen. I remember everything you tell me. But Blake says that the road of excess leads to the Palace of Wisdom. Will I ever walk in the Palace of Wisdom, my regal U.T.?

I must tell you something strange. The night grows now superbly late. Almost safe. Almost without fear or threat. Everything is unreal and heightened and unusually clear. I went, just now, into the kitchen for another cup of tea. There was a spider on the stove. For a moment I stood looking at it. The light in the kitchen is harsh, but limited. There's only a bare bulb. And there, where the light glinted off the porcelain white surface of the stove, stood a spider. It was all surrounded by the dark night at the window and the darkness from the living room. He stood perfectly still. I thought I should just kill him, of course. No big deal. A simple hygienic reaction. But I'm slow, my reactions glance off the hour and the mood and the barrier within me before they become action; my thoughts fill the air around me before they cohere into movement. Why kill him? A silly question, a sort of child's obsession. Staring at some strange living thing, wanting to see it move. I touched it and it fled off away from me for a dash across the white stove top, then stopped. Static. I stood there pondering that but more dreaming it than thinking it as though I were dreaming on the edge of my own evil. Then I turned out the light. I came back in here with my tea. Drinking tea in this apartment. It's so small but it is within my means it's what I can afford. But over the desk in the living room, there's a window. The window's left open the heat's on. I'm losing touch with one reality but I'm very much in touch with another. I'm sailing over myself. I bring tea here to commune with civilization's elixir.

What if I'm a horrible coward afraid of all life? What if I'm mad? And you're mad, too, my sane U.T. But if you were mad, you couldn't reassure me at all that I'm not mad. Hold me, comforting U.T. Once long ago I told you that I needed you and you told me that someday I would need you a very great deal. Do you remember? That day is come, my patient U.T. Will you never hold me again like you used to? You haven't in a long time. Now we talk, you and I. We discuss. We laugh. We forget those very things which bound me to you at one time: the way you held me, the way I climbed all over you. The way you promised me that someday I would become who I wanted to be and I believed you. I don't mean to be sentimental, not at all. But you have known isolation and aloneness and fear. I know you have and you can't tell me otherwise. Sometimes your eyes will dart suddenly away from me and I know that's your loneliness trying to hide. Or I think it is. Aha! You see? Your niece is growing clever, isn't she? I declare the poseur dead. It is the next death after God's. Then loyalty based on real affection and a real bond of very, very much openness. Not just reflecting mirrors of self-substantiating self images. N'est pas? I am your strange niece. I know you think so. And I am, I admit it. But someday, my enduring Uncle Thomas, I won't seem strange to myself. In the meantime, I am going out into the night to shatter it with some violence, some evil as great as Hitler's. Do I just want to be noticed? To be taken seriously? I have my human self and where's the bottom line of that? And what of it is actual evil? And what of it is perversion I never asked for? I know I have you. If Reagan had you to talk to the world might be safe from his self-unacknowledged evil. God-damn it Uncle Thomas he's destroying America. And I'm destroying only myself, aren't I? Isn't that enough? Isn't that a whole world? Is it a world worth saving? I *will* send you this letter just as it is. If I threw it away I'd drift after it searching for it to send it to you. Don't let me go. Hold me. I won't shatter and I will not break I promise. I won't go out into the night. Of course not. What would that purge? Nothing.

In my artwork, my dear perceptive U.T., I don't indulge myself. There I submit myself to art. I promise you, I do. Well, you can see for yourself. You can look at the work and see. Someday I too will catch up with the work and I will become unindulged and all engaged. My Palace of Wisdom.

Please don't let the night end. Please don't let me get so tired as I'm getting, so wired and so tired together. This small place—I could almost fall from my desk right to my bed in the other room. When will you come see me here? In New York. Maybe if I'd felt you'd been in this apartment it wouldn't feel so infused with absence. Walk up the stairs four flights with me. Slide your soft hand along the wood banister. See the marble steps worn to slippery curves. Open the two locks and come in with me over the bare floor. I've done a good job on a little place. Everyone who comes tells me I have. My isolation is a large spacious palace, and my apartment a little real place. What will happen if I stop writing/talking to you? Will I be safe from my own evil all night? Won't I finally be exhausted? And is that all the truth we get, my honest U.T? No. That's too easy. I think you would tell me that we do get more but for now it must do.

I fear your reply actually as I crave it. Please write back to me soon. I won't shatter and I will not break because I promised you I wouldn't.

Very much love
MaryEllen

Thomas laid the pages down on the desk. Picking up the telephone, he made a flight reservation for New York. He all but told the reservation agent that his name was —Kind and Gentle Uncle Thomas, he just gave his last name and his first name simply: Thomas. Then he called his friend, Janice, in New York, asking her to look in on his niece, MaryEllen. Then he called MaryEllen. They talked for over an hour. MaryEllen agreed it would be a good thing if Thomas came to New York just now to visit. It was a good time for her to have him.

As a physically weakened man in his 90s, when he sat by the port watching the grey ships come and go, with their names in unreadable languages, he often remembered the one night she had given herself to him, as she promised she would, as she threatened she would. What amazed him wasn't merely that he'd tasted her pleasures one night, or that her ways of lovemaking were so sweet, so seductive and stimulating, dragging out his lust, but that she had been telling the truth when she said, before they were married, that on their wedding night she would make love to him twice, draining his desire into a languishing and contented revel of his flesh and his mind in a dual harmony of ecstasy. More, he'd never make love to her again. More, he'd never want another woman. He'd laughed when she said it. Either she was wrong, and she would end up giving herself to him over and over, or he'd find other women. He'd have to. He wanted her for his wife.

A tanker, coming in long and deep-hulled with a belly full of oil, plainly grey and grumbling, would remind him of a night he had come in drunk, his own belly swollen and his voice grumbling in his throat. Continuous. Gruff. His eyes sunk into the recesses of his sockets, his fingers thick and his feet were rubber. She was in bed. He sat next to her, ran his hand across her arm, listened to her voice in that repetitive vow which rolled automatically out of her: —No, Thomas. Never. That night he rolled over beside her on the bed clothed and exhausted and, in a way, very content. Her denial by then had become an intimacy they shared. He relied on it. He heard it like some men hear, during the day as they work or talk or eat or think, they hear the love-moans of their wives, or they remember that embrace by the front door as they went, late because of their morning frolics, into the world of self-reliance.

She couldn't have possibly meant it when she'd first said it, but reaffirmed her oath on the second night of their marriage in the sunscarred white Spanish hotel by the sea. The words had their own momentum they embodied the independent force of convenance. Maybe she didn't want to know where they came from either. She was beautiful when he married her, supple and sensuous. She had wide round eyes that looked gamey, laughing with a little dreaminess. Her dark hair fell straight around her full face, her eyes that he wanted to search out and make contact with. On their wedding night she proved everything he suspected of her, hints he garnered from their courtship: she was both restrained and abandoned, she made love instinctively, moving level by level past seduction and teasing to suggestive touching and then caresses and then to stronger impulses, urges, and her eyes all the time working on his body like they were some kind of oil she rubbed over him. An oil that penetrated his skin, seeped into his muscles relaxing them wholly until they released a combination of joy and terror neither one overwhelming the other. What he hadn't imagined before the wedding was the array of personae he found in himself that responded to her. He laughed and moaned, waited and delighted and was timid, and was himself demure and then passive, and begging and urging her and answering and going towards her and opening himself as he opened her as he saw many selves emerge from a storehold he hadn't ever suspected he'd held, full selves, identities. That's what astonished him. Himself.

Other women couldn't interest him anymore.

Some longshoremen thought him romantic, imagined him not unhappy, and in a way fulfilled with his meditations, an old man contemplating change, death, and the eternal. But Thomas thought mostly about his wife, the only person he'd known who'd ever kept such an entangled promise. What had it meant? He'd weaken with frustration and then ask her: What does it mean? Is it punishment? No. Are we supposed to achieve some spiritual heights by denial? No. Am I married to a madwoman? Saint? Perverse whore? Silence. Am I married only to myself?

No, she'd answer. You're married to me, the woman who gave birth to your twin sons.

Huge cargo ships from Japan Hong Kong Malaysia sailed daily into the port. Coming from a long distance, they filled out a distinguishable shape against the horizon. Their markings becoming reciognizable for a few days they sailed slowly in, grey ships settled into and maneuvering the bluish, thick waters. At night he'd see them again as he lay in bed before sleep.

His twin sons would stop by in the evening for a few minutes, sometimes with their families. Vlatko (Vladie) the eldest by 2 minutes 18 seconds, took care of Thomas's cactus garden. Thomas took notice of the garden each morning on his walk to the docks.

Vladie was deft with the cactuses. He grew rare breeds that curled and twisted or else shot straight and lean into the air topped with bright yellow flowers. Yellow against green. Green against blue.

Once, Thomas had come home early in the afternoon. The boys were gone. He'd had it. He'd waited through patient years and he deserved her. He remembered every moment of their wedding night. He'd coax her into it. Because they had a long-standing secret about stolen roses, he'd stolen five fully opened roses from a neighborhood garden. Two hundred petals. With his penknife he'd scored off the thorns and held the stems in a bouquet. He rang the doorbell. Dinara, who had been working, was quieted. She came to the door. When she saw Thomas with the red, red flowers she gasped. —Oh, she said, —you sweet man. He kissed her, pressed the roses against her chest. He bent over to kiss the round curve of the top of her breasts. Her white blouse draped away from her slightly. His erection had grown so naturally beside his thigh. Holding the flowers between them by the closeness of their bodies he placed her hand on his erection.

—How beautiful, she said.

—Does it feel nice?

—Yes, she answered, —it does. She took the flowers into the kitchen, then came back with them in a vase. —You're such a wonderful man, such a strange mixture of colors yourself.

—I'm an artist, a painter, that's all. And I'm your husband. I married you because ...

—Because you wanted me. she finished. —You've got me. I'm your wife; you're my husband. I'm satisfied.

—I'm not. I live in this house. I share food with you. I share a bed. But we don't share our bodies. That's a disaster, not a marriage. I won't put up with it anymore.

—Who do you share your body with? she asked.

—No one else.

—Then you do share it with me.

—What is it? Are you frigid?

—You answer, she said.

—No. He said —You're very. . .

—Finish.

—...very passionate. Do you love me? he asked.

—You answer.

—You're even desperate for me, he argued. —You love me more than you love anything. He walked out the front door, back to his studio. He painted all afternoon. For dinner he scrounged into the studio refrigerator. He worked and ate. He kept working dim colors on a large canvas, working them into the cloth, drinking vodka and changing the mixtures: plain vodka, vodka and orange juice, vodka and tomato juice. By midnight he was watching the moon on the water, still working to bleed color into cloth so that it would come back out the right way. He went around the studio cleaning everything but himself, leaving his jeans and t-shirt and tennis shoes paint-splattered. He walked six blocks climbing narrow streets. In the garage he loaded his shotgun.

—This is it. Pull down the covers.

—Don't talk like that, Dinara said, —it sounds so ugly.

—Ugly? he fired a shot through their window. —Is that ugly enough? Will you take me now?

—No, Thomas.

He'd heard that so many times. In honor of it he let go another shot upwards into the lamp and through the ceiling. He reloaded.

—No, Thomas.

He let a shot rip above her head through the wall. —You love me. Don't deny it.

—I don't, Thomas. I swear I don't deny it.

—And you want to fuck so bad your heart can't bear it. Your body won't stand still.

—You're absolutely right.

—And you've never slept with another man since me.

—That's true, Thomas. I never have and never will.

—Are you crazy?

—No.

Thomas shot again through the empty doorway away from the bed. He ran outside. Shot once in the air. Laid waste a sapling. He shot out the front windshield of the Ford truck. He put a shot through the barn. Shot at a nighthawk and missed. Missed! He threw the gun across the yard. It hit the basketball pole with a ting. Dinara came from behind, put her arms around him. They swayed. He watched the shotgun.

—Have I betrayed you? she asked.

—No.

—Have I lied to you?

—No.

—Do you understand it?

—No.

—Do you think I understand it? she asked.

Her hand rubbed across his belly. —I don't think you do understand it, Thomas answered.

He'd left twice, once while his sons were still small. He'd abandoned them.

He went to New York for an opening of his work at the Richard Hubbard gallery, then disappeared into New York City. He neither called nor wrote. Though the idea had been brewing for some time, he only realized it on his way to New York, 37,000 feet above the earth, crossing Iowa, staring down through thin clouds onto the cleanly squared-off greens and browns. He didn't believe it was happening, but, the night after the opening he found himself in a railroad apartment in Brooklyn with a woman whose name he couldn't remember, who likely didn't remember his.

They were drunk on wine and marijuana. He hadn't had a night like this in years. They came out of a party in Soho and wandered the lower east side, walking to Yonah Shimmel's to get knishes, then walked back towards Broadway, eating and drinking sodas. They wandered in the Village, stared through a storefront at a dinner party of transvestites where the men, seated at tables, were dressed to kill in evening gowns. Women, wearing tuxedos, serving as waiters.

It was a dream of a heightened and perfect world that appeared as if in relief against its truest idea. They staggered around the clubs. They watched a Black street comedian who told hysterical racial jokes, then tumbled through the subways back to Brooklyn. There they smoked more and drank more. By the time Thomas walked across the Brooklyn Bridge it was cold and sharp dawn. The water a hard surface. Watching it as he walked Thomas grew confident of his hazed memory: he had not made love to the woman. Amazing. —No, Thomas, he heard. He was so hungry and so cold. He wanted to get warm and watch Wall Street, watch busy human bodies fill these silent stone buildings.

He took an apartment on 3rd Street between Avenues B and C, next to an empty lot where winos slept where junkies did business. Quickly Thomas got to know them, feel comfortable. He had friends, he met women easily. He'd go out with them, go to their apartments, bring them to his apartment. He talked with them, got to like and admire them. He liked going around the city with some of these women, loved eating in restaurants with them, going to museums and galleries, theaters. He'd set up a corner of his apartment with paints and canvas and worked. There was a lonely brashness to the paintings which he liked, a boldness which lacked the richness of his typically more subtle work. He was painting a bizarre form of cityscape. That he didn't hear at all from Dinara might have bothered him at first, but after a couple of weeks it seemed her nature that she wouldn't hunt him down. He felt her with him often, and heard her often at night when he went to bed. He missed being next to her. He knew he must seem strange to other women, not sleeping with them even when they got to know each other well. He never told them about Dinara. He didn't know how to explain her. He was just a painter from California, doing well in New York, and maybe kind of shy.

In a rented car Thomas drove through Connecticut, Massachusetts, Vermont, and Maine. A lost man who felt fine as long as he kept travelling. He only feared stopping.

He crossed into Canada, taking hundreds of pictures. It snowed and grew colder. On a ferry down the St. Lawrence River to Montreal, Thomas met Michelle. She was small, quick, and kept talking a lot, filling the conversation with ideas and observations. They spent four days in Montreal, in her apartment which looked like a cave. Because, she said, it made her feel more primitive, closer to her guts. She was a jazz pianist, very good. They'd sleep til noon, eat, talk, walk around until finally it was late enough to go club hopping, picking up one or two friends on the way.

On their third night together, Michelle lay beside Thomas in bed, her hand rubbing quickly but lightly over his pubis.

She talked about the last musician they'd seen that night, a tenor sax from New York. He played some synthesizer pieces which were disparate, dissipated and meaningless. But on sax he was one of the good true sons of Coletrane cutting some singular path through Coletrane's complex woods. She remembered riffs. Hummed them. Patted Thomas on his lower belly. They could be in a cave, he thought, the ritual and the consciousness and the act of human sexuality going far back into primitive time, giving rise to much else that is human. Thomas turned, kissed Michelle. His erect penis slid between her thin legs. She squeezed herself around it. Her kisses, like her talk, were quick, flickering things. Her face was so tiny. On top, just about to enter her, Thomas hovered.

—What's the matter?

—Something I ... I can't go through with this.

—Don't you want me? She offered her body.

—Yes. But it wouldn't be right.

—What? All of a sudden it's...

—No. Certainly not all of a sudden. I'm sorry.

Michelle wiggled out from beneath Thomas. —Are you crazy, or... ?

—No, I'm not crazy.

—Well, I didn't mean are you actually crazy. I mean ...

—I know. I'm sorry.

The next morning, making coffee, Michelle asked Thomas was there something wrong with him, or was it her, didn't she appeal to him? That was all right, she said, it's all chemistry, you can't make it happen. The couple crashing on the floor in the living room groaned. Thomas, wrapped in a sheet, stood barefoot on the linoleum kitchen floor. Michelle threw a towel for him to stand on. He shuffled to the table, sat, drank coffee.

—There's two worlds, Michelle said, —the visible and the invisible. Sound, she hesitated, then repeated it, leaving a silence after the word as accent, —sound ... is the invisible become visible. Sex...is the invisible... — she searched for a moment, —...become...tactile. Hey, she smiled, —pretty good.

Thomas agreed. —Become Tactile might be a useful name for a recent painting.

—And if there's no visible,

Michelle continued her discourse, —there's no invisible. See? You can't make it up. You don't have to leave. I'm just trying to set us straight.

—No, Thomas said. —If there's no visible perhaps the invisible...

—What? Michelle asked.

—Belongs...

—Yes?

—I don't know, Thomas said. —Something. But I just don't know what that something is. If there's no actual, perhaps the potential...

—Yes?

I don't know anymore than that.

Thomas drove back through New York State, down the Taconic Parkway from Albany. That was a trip to behold. At one stop he took a panorama of twenty photos to show Dinara because he knew she could imagine the perspective he saw, the sloped, undisturbed, snow-covered hills

In New York Thomas still saw friends, but he didn't go out with women anymore, and that had been the purpose of staying: to outlast the memory of Dinara's hold on him to move into a more fulfilling life. No life he could imagine with any woman he had met seemed fulfilling. Interesting, yes. Fun. Intimate. But that was the limit. He could go home. Or he could pursue himself on one more axis: decadence. He had enough money. He could do drugs. Hang out. Meet different women, crazier, the strata of frenetic hysterical New York. He could do it. He could bend and exhaust himself on that line until he gave in and gave up or Dinara gave up her—No, Thomas. Her eyes.

All 12 paintings he had made in New York sold. They changed his work, too, in that they brought it more to the surface. His intention was still to go into the canvas and then try to bring out what he had taken in with him, changed as it was. The difference now was that at the end the surface was more active. Something had been gained.

—Do you love me? He was playful.

—Do you think?

Thomas became quiet, lying on the bed. —How much do you love me?

—How much do you think? Thomas watched Dinara's face.

—If you don't insist that I make love to you, I can't tell you 'No', and then you'll miss hearing that.

—And you'll miss saying it.

—Oh, I would, she answered.

—Do you mean it? You would miss it? He ran his finger around her lips as she spoke.

—I'd miss it like crazy.

—Really? What was her serious meaningful tone, jarred by a pungent longing?

—Oh God, yes. While you were gone don't you think I missed that?

—Did you miss me? Thomas said.

Dinara said nothing, touched Thomas's face.

—Make love to me now, Thomas said.

She answered him with a grave sadness, —No. No, Thomas. Embracing, they slept. Deeply. Relaxed into each other's arms, each other's bodies.

Thomas nearly forgot about sex. His life filled with work, with his sons, with other connections. His painting presented enormous problems now, and those problems absorbed him. There are times when either you make risky leaps in your work or you fall back to never recover.

Thomas's life with Dinara was active. They went hiking

often in the hills. They ate late, as they always had, after the boys, and talked over dinner. Not infrequently Thomas would go back to his studio and work until 2 or 3 in the morning, then walk home nearly dazed in a pleasant exhaustion. Sometimes as he crawled into bed beside Dinara, he'd ask, —Make love to me? and she'd answer him. It was more habit than actually expectant desire. One day Thomas came home to find Dinara asleep on the hammock in the back. He sat on the steps of the back porch overlooking the yard and the sea and watched her, beer in hand. She breathed like any ordinary woman. Her dreams he sensed were the ordinary dreams of anyone. Of all the attachments in his life this was central. The yard, the sea, the very hammock depended on it. That's why Thomas decided, right then watching her, watching the sea, decided he would leave. This time it would be no joke. He would plan and execute it as though it were real. Then it would be real, and not some momentarily inspired but realistically impossible escape to New York. It didn't have to be far. The boys were old enough. The calm depth of his decision made it true. It had no emotional edges. Asleep on her back, Dinara's body gave itself to the hammock which swayed minutely under the influence of her movements. As she turned, Dinara moved her arm to keep the sun from her eyes. She grumbled. Was she suddenly troubled and serious? After several days of winter storms the small waves came in well defined, thin lines. It was emerald. It was not hard to do this. It would get chilly soon, and that would wake Dinara. The endropes of the hammock were taut from each tree. The thick salt air cut right through Thomas's words.

—This time I may not come back.

—That's our risk, isn't it?

—No, it doesn't have to be. Sleep with me and we won't go through this. Wouldn't it be great after all this time? Think of how happy I could make you.

—No, Thomas.

—This is your fault, not mine, he said.

—There's no fault. The last time you came back, from New York, I could hardly stand to be near you or see you.

—What you're doing is demonic, Dinara. It's from some other world, not this one. You're a ghost. A shadow. I'm not coming back.

—Only make promises you can keep, Dinara said. Thomas looked stunned, so she added, —Please. Please?

He thought it was because he stopped painting that he went back. The house he had found was excellent. The small town was perfect. Its closeness to the city was especially opportune. He didn't chase women. Life settled out, as he'd hoped that it would, but at the end of that settling there was no painting. Books were dry. Ideas died in him. Idea itself died. Nothing was particularly wrong, but the death of idea, conception, context of thought or perception, that was intolerable. He waited many months, faithful to his intention to stay away. He wrote letters to Dinara telling her everything he did and saw and felt. He asked her questions about herself, the house, the family. She opened every envelope, apparently read the letters, put them in a new envelope and sent them back to him. He read them as though she had written them to him. His next letter to her would contain answers to issues he'd raised in the letters he'd received back from her. The questions about her, the boys, her parents, and other family and local news, all seemed like answers, instead of questions. He kept the letters in a wooden box.

He'd thought of them as letters she'd written to him. He didn't know if the death of idea had been the end of his painting, or the end of his painting had been the death of idea. He posed that question many times in his letters, but when they came back they read only as questions. He tried to conceive of the world as idea. He'd look at the trees in his yard and think about them: trees, growth, color, reproduction, change, dialogue, slow, wrenching and small destructions, death even, politics, mistakes, errors of nature, incomprehensibility. Flat language which refused the organic life of living idea. Even the hellishness and terror which would sometimes fall on him seemed inaccurate. So it suited him to think that it was because he stopped painting that he went back, because to think of the death of idea was to chase the tail of your own lack of existence, and that was to court too much despair.

—You're going to make love to me now because you have to.

—I do, don't I? she said.

—Where do you want it to be, he asked her, —indoors or out?

—Indoors, she said, then changed her mind. —No, out.

—In the back?

—By the rocks. Where that patch of ground . .

—I know where you mean.

They walked side-by-side around the house, through the yard, across the rocks until they came to the level, grassy spot she'd mentioned.

—You're lying, he said to her.

—No, I'm not lying, Thomas. I just ... made a mistake. I was confused. I wasn't expecting you back.

—It's OK, Thomas said. —I didn't really expect that we would.

—But we always have been, she said. —Look, Thomas, do you love me?

—What do you think?

—No, Thomas. That's my answer. Give me your answer.

—OK, I'd do anything for you. I'd build a house for you and hang it from these cliffs. But good God, sleep with me.

Thomas would think about that as he watched the ships. Dumb, hard facts of metal set in motion by men out to a great wide sea.

Thomas knew that the longshoremen thought him romantic. He chuckled at the idea. There is no romance in change or death. They're violent activities we come to endure fairly well, sometimes to awe, often to awe. When he heard her voice say, —No, Thomas, a welter of longing would take him away. He'd have to wait a while to come back to earth. He'd hear that and nothing would seem worthwhile. Then her voice would come to him again: —No, Thomas, and this time it would enter his blood and make him at one with everything around him, the sky, clumsy ships and rickety dock shacks. That whole riot of the many selves he felt on his first night with her would surface, blossom.

In the winter Thomas would normally pick up food at the market for dinner and come home near dusk. He would watch the news, prepare dinner, talk on the phone for a while, and read. This particular evening though he went in the front door sensing that something would be different. The house had taken a chill, which would get worse, so as he passed the thermostat in the hall he turned the heat on, and heard the gas flame whoosh up. He walked through the hall, passed the living room on his left, thinking to shut the drapes when he came back from changing into his evening jacket and slippers. He turned on the kitchen light, set the filet of sea bass on the counter, checked the refrigerator to see if he remembered correctly that there was asparagus, and saw that there was. Darkness came at the windows already. This was a time for him, all his life, of a little emptiness, and he felt it now. It would pass by the time he started cooking.

But the bedroom door was closed.

When he opened it he found Dinara sitting on their bed. He couldn't speak, but his legs held firm. Dinara almost immediately began to explain. —I had to come back.

—Why, you... ?

—I don't know a thing more than I ever knew about us. About what happened with us.

—I still want to sleep with you. Even now, even right now.

—And I still have to say the same thing. I have to say no.

—I want to sleep with you even as you are. But I'll tell you something I know now. It was a kind of truth, Dinara, a kind of Great Truth. I've come to that sitting by the water everyday.

—It was suffering, Thomas. I must have been mad. I must still be mad.

—It's all suffering, one way or the other.

—But there's a joy in lovemaking that would have renewed us, sustained us.

—You think there wasn't joy in what we had? He stood back. Dinara's face was so strikingly unchanged. Only there was a little different look in her eye. There was a pall to her demeanor. Her hair, abundant as ever, fell as always around her face, though it had lost the height of its sheen. Thomas lost the ordinary dimensions of time and space. Had their life been some continuous hell, or some difficult to perceive but gifted fulfillment in a strange kind of paradise? Even the outline definitions of his own body became vague. He stared at Dinara until it was clear his words had been scattered for years and had just now caught up with his breath. —Lay back he said to her, —I'm going to make love to you, even though you're ...

—Dead? Say it. It doesn't please me, but it doesn't sound so god-awful hollow as it used to. Are you afraid of me?

—Yes.

—Very much?

Thomas came to the bed, and he kissed her neck. It was awful to touch a long-dead woman. It violated essential laws. Yet, so had their life violated some basic human premise, even though Thomas had come to believe that only by that violation had they affirmed it so strongly. So little held him anymore to the living. His old body responded slowly to her smokey, grey touch. Unlike their wedding night, Thomas felt not a joyous presence, but a terrible absence.

—Touch me, she said, —with forgiveness.

He protested. —I had what I wanted, Dinara. Whatever it was. I had your love. You loved me.

—Not well enough I didn't. I held to that insane vision. He kissed her again and again.

—But there was something true about it.

—Don't talk like that. I know there is some strange truth there, but I can't fathom it, even now. Touch me. Just forgive me.

—There's nothing to forgive.

Putting his hand on her face, he caressed her. She felt her flesh as though it were coming alive. —Let me make love to you, Thomas said, —grotesque as it is, as we may be now.

—No. No, Thomas. You know that I can't. Not because I'm dead. That has nothing to do with it. It's for the same reasons as always.

—Please, Dinara. For God's sake, there's so little time left. What could it hurt us now?

—No, Thomas. I must say no.

—I can do it. I have so much power left, so much energy. I could make you hum with pleasure, but who knows what you feel now?

—I feel the same, Thomas. And I have to say the same thing. I have to say no.

—Then you've come back to torture me. To torment me.

—Of course not. I love you.

—You've come back to tell me that even in my old age, even in my dreams, I can't imagine that it had ever been other than what it was. Even if I've come in some way to understand it as having been in some inexplicable way so very deeply right.

—No, Thomas. I've just come back to see you.

Thomas's meditations by the sea changed. He still went every day. Old as he was, he was vulnerable, and each time Dinara arrived to sit together with him, Thomas absorbed death little by little from her. It was tolerable. It was a vaccination: when the real thing came he'd be infected, he'd eventually be absorbed, but with some understanding of what was happening to him.

Afigitis

AFIGITIS

built.
Afigitis
built
walls.

That wasn't his profession. By profession, Afigitis, a contractor, built houses. But in his own mind, he was a wall builder. In his own mind, his imagination conceived of walls. The other parts of the houses that he built, the floors, ceilings, cabinets, driveways, windows, skylights were appendages to what occupied Afigitis's thought.

Afigitis built freestanding walls. He built a wall around his wife's garden; walls around their house, their yard, a curving wall that followed the line of their driveway along the side of their hillside home in the Southern California. No one could understand Afigitis's passion; Afigitis didn't try to understand it; it wove itself through his life.

As a child, Afigitis built a sandcastle wall at the beach. Everyone watched as Afigitis, but eight years old, built an exquisite sturdy sand wall over 40 yards long and 3 feet high. The days' sunbathers stayed well into the late summer sunset to watch the little craftsman singly at work. Two days later, a freak summer coastal storm raised waves far onto the beach changing the shoreline. As the water retreated, Afigitis's wall stood, intact. In testament to the remarkable young craftsman's talents, the local residents named it "Afigitis's Wall." To this day, as you read, it stands.

Afigitis's activity as a wall builder extended from the near at hand to the remote, exotic. He built walls of classical simplicity; he also built walls that embodied and displayed and celebrated elaborate, intricate, decorative complexity.

Afigitis had built walls around his house, but even inside the house, Afigitis had built several walls. Two walls divide the living room into thirds. One, a red brick wall reaches east to west, coming short of the western wall of the house by 4 feet. The other wall, stucco, stretches from the southern living room wall to Afigitis's brick wall, coming short of it by 3 feet. They partition the living room into a maze. These, the first of Afigitis's interior walls, ordinary in scope of design, conception, location, execution, took eighteen days each to complete, working evenings. Yet, Afigitis never dwelt on descriptions or measurements of his achievements. Afigitis built walls. He wasn't a scorekeeper. His family and friends began to call him Afigitis Wallbuilder, a name they teased him with, especially at times when he would become more than ever lost in the design or construction of a wall, a name which, over time, came and went. For Afigitis Wallbuilder, the building of walls expressed an unqualified, absolute, unrestrictable, natural freedom.

Once, Afigitis built a wall inside a motel room in the Central California wine country. Outside the motel where he and his wife, Kalyôpé, stayed, construction workers were expanding the motel's driveway. At night, Kalyôpé asleep, Afigitis went out. After all-too-easily befriending the worksite's all-too-lonely guard dog, Afigitis gathered tools, mixed cement, came back into the room and, with wire for armature, he built a wall through the night without waking Kalyôpé.

In the morning, Kalyôpé awoke inside a wall which curved several times within the room, forming a narrow channel she had to negotiate to reach the bathroom. When she found the end of the wall, Kalyôpé found Afigitis. Slumped on the floor, he leaned, asleep, against the wall. Was this worn-out, ragged, stubble-bearded, wall-obsessed, materials-thief man the man she had once been so honored to marry? His forearms, his fingers, his shirt, his face plaster-smeared. They'd be arrested. They'd have to pay for the damage to the room. Afigitis could be jailed for the theft of material from the construction site. Jesus! Kalyôpé shook Afigitis, who woke, lazily, with a smile on his face. —Do you like this one?

—Afigitis, she pleaded.

While Kalyôpé dressed, Afigitis packed. He took her from the motel, leaving his wall behind. The motel owners had their name, their license plate, Afigitis's driver's license number. Kalyôpé waited every day to hear from the motel, from the motel's lawyer, from the police. She heard nothing. Ever. It was the first thing which she never understood.

Two years later, five years into their marriage, Afigitis and Kalyôpé went through a period of bitter argument, separation, alienation. Reconciliation seemed hopeless. Kalyôpé seemed empty to Afigitis; Afigitis seemed cruel and cold to Kalyôpé. Every word between them, every gesture one towards the other was ice. The distance between them threatened to shatter the delicate crystalline psychic organisms each had evolved to flourish in life.

Afigitis pulled apart the two single beds he had once merged with metal couplings, wired in a second light switch, then built a wall in the middle of the bedroom, separating everything: the two closets, two dressers, two dressing tables, the two people. For a time, Afigitis and Kalyôpé lived within this estrangement. It threatened to become comfortable. In a different couple, life could have crept on like this, each going their own way, ignoring the other, speaking vague common phrases between them, enduring, accepting, resigning themselves to then coming to believe in a certain disappointment with life.

But for Kalyôpé, as for Afigitis, the estrangement caused a pain sharp enough to insist on change. One afternoon, standing on his side of the bedroom, Afigitis watched out the window as Kalyôpé worked in her herb garden. The midsummer air, still, had a heavy, full, round quality. Through the screened window, the herbal aromas filled the bedroom, each one distinct. Afigitis closed his eyes, breathed in the smells, separated each one out, saw the specific shape and the individual color of each herb in his mind's eye, named each one aloud: —rosemary, he said, then he said —mint, then —sage, then —thyme,

—basil, —lemon verbena.

That night, Afigitis went to Kalyôpé's side of the bedroom wall. —Sit here with me, Kalyôpé invited.

The next evening, Kalyôpé, a pan-Mediterranean cook, made a Greek-style cacciatore. Afigitis ate with his old pleasure again, holding his fork and knife as though he were a craftsman of the dining table, tasting each mouthful as though it were a rite to be performed with grace and with gratitude, as though the dining itself, every bit as the previous evening's love-making, was re-humanizing him from an alienating exile.

After dinner, Afigitis tore down the wall. It was the only wall Afigitis ever destroyed. It was also the only wall about which he made any public announcement. He said that the wall had not been a mistake, that he tore it down because its time had come. There is a time, Afigitis said, for all walls to come down. For most walls, that time is in the unforeseeable distance, often the work of the next generation, or the one after that, or for time itself. Yet, anyone who examined the bedroom wall would have seen Afigitis hadn't built it for permanence. It was a slight affair of cheap wire and thin plaster. After Afigitis tore that wall down some of his friends called it —Afigitis's Hope, and —Afigitis's anti-Wall. But the wall, Afigitis also said, left an unresolved edge in his mind. —That I built it for impermanence, and that I tore it down, he wrote in a long, epic, 18-page letter to a friend, —makes me feel uneasy, inauthentic or irresolute. If I had intended to tear it down, why build it in the first place? The building of that wall violates a sense of commitment I have about walls. I can't shake that feeling of violation. And yet… he questioned his correspondent, —and yet, was I wrong to build that wall? Never. Not wrong. Simply not wise enough as I did it. Never wise enough? Ever never. And yet, wise enough. Ever. Time and change and flux and difference are not wise enough. We are wise enough. Our genius is always wise enough to act in our knowledge. But time and flux and difference have no knowing and need no knowing. Do we always act as part of a world which separates us from it? If my first wall, the one on the beach, I might have called 'One,' this wall I would call 'Zero'.

When Kalyôpé's and Afigitis's only child, their daughter, Diihima, grew up, she said that her father built walls to keep her and her mother metaphorically out — at a distance. She had, after all, to zigzag past three walls to get from her bedroom to her parents' bedroom. But she also said there was a larger, less explicable truth. Her father built walls because he was Afigitis Wallbuilder. What could one do with a man like that?

When a wealthy family near where Diihima went to college on the California coast hired Afigitis to build an ornate wall around their large estate, Diihima went to watch her father work.

Day by day, Afigitis, with his best supervisor, a man with exceptionally sensitive hands for the feel of materials, selected stones from the truckloads that arrived, placing them in piles arranged around the grounds of the estate. They accomplished this activity with the grace of a pace mesmerizing in its regularity. Sitting inside their trailer, Diihima would study. On her desk, she had placed a few vases of her collections from the nearby woods, odiferous wild herbs and her favorite, what they called locally the 'mountain honeyflower.' Often, she would walk around the worksite, watching her father who kept his eyes attuned to the process of preparing for the actual building of the wall. A backhoe dug a hole several feet deep, leveled and angled by men with shovels; supervisors admonished truckers to proceed carefully with their loads; the workers, by their own choice, worked quietly. Finches and sparrows chirped isolated sounds from the surrounding live oak, cedar, and underbrush. If she listened carefully, Diihima heard the sea, or thought she did. It was far to the shore. Did she only imagine that she heard the sea? Am I dreaming, she would ask herself. Wake up, she would tell herself, wake up. But still, she would smell the distant sea. She was in her last year of college, studying classical languages.

Three times a week, on Mondays, Wednesdays, and Fridays, Diihima drove down the narrow road between farms and vineyards back to the main highway, and just twenty minutes on the highway and she was at the university. Oftentimes that semester Diihima stayed late in the library, then would make the trip back to her father's worksite by dark.

Coming back one night, walking from her car to the trailer, a soft, resonant singing not of words but of rhythmic sounds came from the ditch where the wall would someday stand. It was dark, moonless. Diihima, walking towards the ditch, called out, —Who's there? Are you all right? Diihima walked closer, finding her way with difficulty through piles of heaped up stone, stumbling in turned over and dug up earth. She was quite sure she still heard the singing, a low, guttural, absent-minded but physically robust sound of repetitive strings of non-word sounds.

When she got to the ditch, Diihima followed it along a few steps. There she found, spread out on his back inside the ditch, her father, Afigitis, singing so that his body shook. She knelt in the dirt, not caring for her good clothes — the dress she had worn to classes. —Papa, she said, —Tell me. What is it? Papa?

Afigitis rolled over to her, his body covered in dirt, even his face dirt-smeared. He wore the coveralls he wore all day. —Diihima, my angel, how can I tell you what it is? You're a child. How could I explain it to you?

—Try, Papa. She pulled Afigitis up by an arm, but his heavy body wouldn't come. The weight of it fell back into the ditch. She stroked his arm folded over his chest. His hands covered his face.

—Try, Papa. Tell me. What is it? Are you drunk?

—Useless, Diihima. How difficult these walls are! Sometimes so beautiful, but with something so beyond me, too. What do I want? Even I don't understand them. Hopeless, inexplicable, beautiful, mysterious walls! They are me, and they are not me! They are you, Diihima, I have built them all for you. No. All for all of us. For us all. All for your mother. I don't know, Diihima. All for nothing. But a great nothing. No. Nonsense. I'll tell you something, Diihima. Afigitis sat up. —Every wall I build wants to be built. I build them to fulfill their desire! Afigitis laughed. —Now I can only sing, Diihima. I can only go on singing wordless song.

Taking a cloth from a pocket in Afigitis's coveralls, Diihima wiped his face. Bending, she pushed aside little bits and clods of dirt. —How can you be so disconsolate? It's your gift to build walls. I came to watch because I want to know what makes you so good at it, so dedicated, so single-minded in your attention to one thing. Oh, Papa, don't despair. I love you.

Several days passed before Afigitis spoke to Diihima about his night in the ditch. He told Diihima he was sorry that she had found him that night. —But I am glad, too, he said. —If you hadn't found me I might have lain all night long in the dirt, singing like a madman. I don't understand what happened. I wandered around the wall that night. It's a fine wall, splendid. The unmortared laid stone sections; sections plastered, with marble inlay, one section with a tile scene of the Madonna and child. I walked up on the wall that night and gazed into the moonless sky. Rather than the satisfaction I might have felt, something possessed me, the demon from some star. I walked out by the edge of construction near where you found me. I lay down and sang as if I wanted to dissolve into the earth, to plant myself, to grow out of the earth as I imagined my walls did. Perhaps, he confessed to Diihima, I am growing old, perhaps even going a little mad. I've built so many walls. The first one, the one on the beach. As we left the beach that day, I saw a man at the window of his beach house with an infant in his arms, pointing to the wall, showing it to his newborn child as though it were one of the wonders of the world. My walls, it's as if sometimes they are too much even for me. Perhaps you can understand what possessed me to lie in the ditch, madly singing my fate. Maybe in school you read about such failings in those philosophers you read.

—You seem, Diihima said, —sitting here on this plain wooden chair reciting your lyrical confession, like some king in his kingdom become suddenly a peasant mystified, suddenly at the mercy of gods whose propitiation you had left all your life to the expertise of priests. Zeus and Poseidon and Hera and Hades and Jehovah and Christ bound together, forming a new name in the New World. Your peasantness now, she said, —your humility is altogether both innocent and painful to me.

—I have always been a peasant, Afigitis said. —I have always been humble. Do you see? You're so much wiser than I am. He smiled at his daughter.

—Do you want to stop building walls? Diihima asked. — You can stop whenever you like.

—No, Afigitis insisted. —I don't dare to stop. I see a vision in my mind of a wall. I see it whole and complete and perfect. Until I build that wall, until the vision becomes a wall in the world exactly as I see it in my mind, I cannot rest. Something has changed, though. All along everyone was right. The walls are strange. You see? Who can understand them? But I won't stop. If you ever come to understand what happened to me that night in the ditch when I lay and moaned and sang, don't explain it to me. I'm too old now.

Seven days later, Diihima again came home late from college, bearing books. She heard the same sounds again. She followed the ditch along a few steps. There, she found her father, spread out on his back, singing. His hips lifted and swelled and fell as another paroxysm of song gripped him.

Afigitis crept through the dirt towards the end of the wall

where the workmen had left it incomplete. Reaching the dark stones protruding from the wall's edge, he crawled up to them, pulled himself toward them, into them. Afigitis stood, supported by the wall, embracing it trying to enter the wall, trying to become his wall. Diihima watched her father's agon. His body dissolved into the wall.

Diihima ran to the trailer for a flashlight. By that white, white light against the wall, Diihima saw the figure of her father now an ornament built into his wall, a figure carved excellently and dimly by some workman. She scratched at the figure; it became only dimmer. It disappeared. Afigitis had dissolved into his wall.

Beside this wall, as it was beautiful, sensuous and expressive, colorful, imaginative, intelligent, Diihima's legs gave way. Staring at the wall, she fell to her knees. There, she kneeled for some time in silence. Then, tears came, she let them come. She wept. —Am I dreaming? she asked herself. Distant seasound becalmed her; the weeping subsided. No sound intruded. No animal rustled in the underbrush. No bird sang. Diihima stood as if to run, but forced herself not to leave. —This is insane, she said. —Come to your senses. But did she speak to Afigitis, or to herself? She touched the wall, she ran the palm of her hand over its surface. —You are you, Papa, a wall is a wall. She turned off the flashlight. —This is not insane, she spoke to herself now, —it's ridiculous, she said. She laughed, and, while laughing, called out to her father. —Papa! she called. —This is ridiculous. And insane! Diihima sat in the ditch. —Oh, Papa! she cried aloud. —Afigitis Wallbuilder.

At first, Kalyôpé wept. Then howled. Then, she smiled at her daughter. —Now, she told Diihima, —people will talk about him forever. You will have to hear it all your life, Diihima. They'll use the name we used to tease him with, 'Afigitis Wallbuilder'. They'll make up all kinds of things about him. They'll give him exotic, mythical origins, they'll say it all came from those origins. But this is the beginning of the next story, Diihima. It's page one. It contains in it the old one. All of the old ones.

—The old one, Diihima complained, —is a story of the abject and the sacred.

—No, no, Kalyôpé said. —More. Much more.

When the police will question Diihima, as the one eyewitness, and, for a while, their only suspect, Diihima will offer what explanation she could. —Yes, she will tell them, —I was there. I put my hand to the wall. It was real. Solid. But it was a wound, the wound of my father. And my wound? An open wound an opening nonetheless. You can disbelieve me. But you can't prove anything. You can believe me. And you can't prove anything. If there is a God, she will tell Chief Detective Captain Beshem Thomas, —then God has his ways. Life is a wild an extraordinary mystery, which immense mystery of sight and sound we can choose to disbelieve in—but to our own immense peril. Had my father gone mad? Maybe. He had a story to tell us. His walls were the only way for him to speak. Was he, in the end, selfish. Self-indulgent? A coward? Was it an act of radical communion? And what of me now? I, who have with her own hand touched the wound that is my legacy from Afigitis. Beautiful Afigitis. Beautiful wound. Will I go mad, now, from this knowledge, an awareness of this radical communion?

Captain Beshem Thomas put his arm around Diihima. He found her body trembling. He told her a story of the life of his desires. He told her that, if she needed him, he would never leave her. As she stepped, ever so lightly, and barefoot, into the littoral of cool, refreshing water, he was not there.

MARTIN NAKELL is the author of 18 books—fiction & poetry; the winner of numerous grants & awards (NEA, Gertrude Stein, Fine Arts Work Center, et alia.); he has read from his work and presented his multi-media productions nationally and internationally; he is on the National Board of &NOW. Nakell earned a Doctor of Arts degree at SUNY Albany, and now teaches at Chapman University in Orange, California and is Affiliate Professor at Haifa University, Haifa, Israel. He has developed and written about two theories of literary (& art) composition: Chaos Theory and Radical Communion, both of which envision the creative act as a special form of communication of the whole. He lives in the village of Orange [the Democratic 46th Congressional District of the finally liberalizing and growingly aware Orange County] with his wife, the novelist Rebecca Goodman.

Made in the USA
Las Vegas, NV
29 March 2023

69837050R00187